THE BODY IN THE SNOWDRIFT

THE
BODY
IN THE
SNOWDRIFT

A Faith Fairchild Mystery

KATHERINE HALL PAGE

WILLIAM MORROW
AN IMPRINT OF *HARPERCOLLINS*PUBLISHERS

HarperCollins books may be purchased for educational, business, or sales promotional use. For infor-mation please write: Special Markets Department, HarperCollins Publishers Inc., 10 East 53rd Street, New York, NY 10022.

FIRST EDITION

Designed by Jennifer Ann Daddio

Printed on acid-free paper

Library of Congress Cataloging-in-Publication Data

Page, Katherine Hall.
    The body in the snowdrift : a Faith Fairchild mystery / Katherine Hall Page.—1st ed.
        p. cm.
    ISBN 0-06-052530-4 (hc : alk. paper)
    1. Fairchild, Faith Sibley (Fictitious character)—Fiction. 2. Women in the food industry—Fiction. 3. Caterers and catering—Fiction. 4. Ski resorts—Fiction. 5. Cookery—Fiction. 6. Vermont—Fiction. I. Title.

PS3566.A334B675 2005

2004059673

05 06 07 08 09   WBC/RRD   10 9 8 7 6 5 4 3 2 1

In memory of

WILLIAM F. DEECK

My dear friend and learned partner in crime

*Accidents will occur in the
best-regulated families.*

—CHARLES DICKENS, *DAVID COPPERFIELD*

ACKNOWLEDGMENTS

My thanks to the Margaret Clapp Library at Wellesley College for providing solace, space, and expertise. Also thanks to Dr. Robert DeMartino for medical details; Jeanne Bracken, reference librarian at the Lincoln Public Library, for all the rest; Carol Edwards, my copyeditor; Sarah Durand, my editor; and always, Faith Hamlin, my agent. And to Dick Aylward of Waterbury, Vermont, thanks for the information—and for keeping "Pine Slopes" going all these years.

THE BODY IN THE SNOWDRIFT

ONE

The curtains at the window didn't quite meet in the middle, and a sliver of gray winter dawn cut across the bedclothes like a dull kitchen knife. Boyd crept out of bed, groping for his slippers as his feet touched the cold floor. At the door, he stopped and fondly looked back at the motionless figure under the bedclothes, aware that he was alone in his belief that the early hours of each day were the most precious. He closed the door to the adjoining bath noiselessly, turned on the ceiling heat lamps to take the chill off, and dressed quickly. He'd laid his clothes out the night before, even his parka. Holding his boots in one hand, he went back into the bedroom and then out into the hallway. The bedclothes hadn't stirred, but the shaft piercing them was brighter. It was time to go.

In the kitchen, he put on his boots, fed the cats, and stuffed some Clif Bars, an apple, and a bottle of water into his fanny pack. He'd eat breakfast on the trail. His skis and poles were in the mudroom, where he'd left them the previous day. Reaching for the rest of his gear from one of the shelves, he noticed a pair of boots that had been kicked off and left sprawled next to a heap of outerwear. The untidy mess was crowned by one of those Polartec court-jester hats in Day-Glo orange and blue. So, the guest room was occupied. He was tempted to pitch the stuff into the snow.

Instead, he grabbed his things, pulled the door open, and stepped outside. The cold air almost took his breath away. His annoyance vanished into the clouds of vapor from his breath. Hastily, he pulled his neck gaiter up, knowing that as soon as he got moving, he'd be peeling it off.

It was quiet. Too cold for birds. No sound except the steady schuss of his skis as he made his way through the woods, heading toward the resort. He moved effortlessly, rhythmically poling, side to side, a graceful Nordic dance. He passed the base lodge. The lifts didn't open until 9:00 A.M., and not even the ski patrol was up at this hour. He glanced toward the employee parking lot. Pete, the head of maintenance, was pulling in. It was a toss-up as to whether his truck outdated him or the other way around. He'd managed to keep the ski resort going since the1960s with, as he put it, "mostly baling wire and duct tape, plus the odd piece of chewing gum." Boyd was tempted to stop for a chat, but the mountain beckoned, so he continued on his way, climbing high up into the backcountry.

They'd had about ten inches of much-needed new snow overnight, and he soon paused for some water, stripping off his gaiter. He'd reach the groomed Nordic trails soon. This shortcut was his secret, and even though it meant striking a trail through the powder, he wouldn't skip it for the world. The sun was rising higher in the sky. Soon it would be one of those picture-perfect Vermont snow-scene days—the sky so blue that it looked dyed like an Easter egg and, beneath it, Christmas trees dusted with frosting. No holiday could compete with the everyday sights on the mountain as far as Boyd was concerned. He'd been skiing here all his life, even before it was a resort. He and his father would ski up the mountain, pushing themselves to the limit; then there would be that long, mad, glorious run down. In some museum in Norway, he'd heard, there was a pair of skis over four thousand years old. What he and Dad had used seemed just as ancient, Boyd realized, looking down at the new Fischers he'd treated himself to in December. But what held true for those early Norsemen, and their descendants everywhere, was their addiction to the sport. Speed, endurance. It was a kick. Endorphins, adrenaline, call it what you will.

Boyd liked to ski fast, straight up or straight down. It didn't matter. That was the beauty of it. All you needed was snow. No chairlifts. No technology, unless you counted the skis, Salomon boots, carbon-fiber poles, Swix waxes, even clothing. He laughed to himself. He was wearing Craft underwear—the self-proclaimed "Apple computer of underwear"— made of some kind of miracle fiber.

Global warming was shrinking winter, and these last few years, he'd hungered for skiing to the point of taking summer vacations in New Zealand and Australia, trying to sustain the feeling, sustain the pace.

Last March, he'd gone to Norway to ski in the Birkebeiner, a fifty-eight-kilometer race from Rena to Lillehammer. He'd wanted to do it for years, attracted as much by the story behind it as the event itself. During a period of civil unrest in Norway in the thirteenth century, the Birkebeiners, the "birch leggers," were the underdogs and so poorly equipped that they used the bark from birch trees for boots. To keep Haakon Haakonsson, the tiny heir of the dying king, safe from the rival faction, the Baglers, two Birkebeiners took him far across the mountains to safety. It was a perilous journey to make in the winter, freezing cold, but the skiers, with the boy strapped to one of their backs, made it. He grew up to become King Haakon and defeated the Baglers, bringing the country to new heights of glory. During the annual race to commemorate the event, each skier carryied an eight-pound pack to simulate the little prince. Boyd had thought he would be the oldest, but he found many far older—and in better shape—among the nine thousand entrants. It had been one of the happiest days of his life. The route was lined with cheering crowds; the skiers constituted a community unlike any other he had experienced. In Norway, skiing was as natural as breathing—and started almost at the same time. He'd go back next year.

Thinking of the Birkebeiner, he pushed himself to ski faster up the wooded trail, enjoying the ease with which his body moved, and anticipating the descent—the way the wind, his own creation, would cool his face and clear his mind. He always did his best thinking while he was skiing. He didn't need a psychologist to tell him why. He knew the woods were where he felt the freest—and the safest. His refuge.

He thought back to the days after his parents' deaths, which had been years ago. Both had died from cancer, and only a week apart. He'd barely come inside to sleep afterward, skiing with a headlamp, determined to make sense of it all, to make amends. Should he have pressed for more chemo? Should he have moved them from this cruel climate to someplace warm, where they could have spent their last months in the sun? He tried to picture the two of them reclining next to a pool in Florida, but the only image that kept occurring was his father stubbornly chopping wood for the stove until he couldn't lift the ax anymore and his mother putting up more preserves. Boyd had eaten them for over a year afterward, her legacy: clear glass jars of brightly colored fruits and vegetables.

Rudderless. A friend had given shape to the feeling when she'd observed, "You must feel as if you've lost your rudder." He'd found it again, but it had taken awhile. Odd to think he was now older than both of them had been when they died.

At last, he was at the top of the highest ridge, and the view was spectacular. The resort would be teeming with activity soon: lines to buy lift tickets, lines for the lifts. But up here, he was alone, although tiny tracks in the snow showed that some creature had been this way recently. He ate his apple, buried the core in the snow, drank some more water, and considered a Clif Bar. They were a bit sweet for his taste, but convenient, a staple for Nordic skiers. Inside the wrapper, there was everything you needed in the way of vitamins, minerals, and carbs to be an Olympian. An Olympian. Like Vermont's own Bill Koch, with his silver at Innsbruck back in 1976. An Olympian. His parents would have liked that. He'd been good enough to make the team. Medals from races when he was a young boy and then a college student were shoved in a box in the attic. But he had never really liked competing—funny, since he'd ended up a lawyer. Maybe it wasn't competition, he realized, the air, as usual, crystallizing his thoughts. It was that the races didn't have anything to do with his kind of skiing. Skiing solo. Just ol' Boyd and his mountain. The experience in Norway had been an exception. Something to do once in awhile. He smiled to himself.

Emerging from the backcountry, he crossed swiftly over to the trails. One of them was named for him: Boyd's Lane. A black diamond. He'd have accepted no less.

He stood poised at the top of the trail, the curving vertical descent beckoning as seductively as a woman. He took a long drink of water and pushed off. He'd barrel down the mountain—the hell with form.

He was sixteen again; sixty—and soon seventy—was some other Boyd Harrison, not the one flying down the mountain. Not the one who couldn't resist letting out a whoop of pure joy into the sun-filled stillness of the day.

A second cry filled his throat, blocked the air, and sent him hurling into an ungainly halt by the side of the trail. The pain was as overwhelming as it was sudden. He closed his eyes, and the blackness behind his lids threatened to take control of his entire body. This was the worst one yet. Worse than the first one—the one that had led straight to a triple bypass without passing Go. He felt as if a forklift had lowered an entire yard of bricks onto his chest.

Don't panic, he told himself, opening his eyes. The light was so glaring, he thought his head would explode. Don't panic. Get the pills. Take your nitro and you can make it down the mountain.

He reached inside his parka to the zippered pocket where he kept a small vial. He was never without it. He began to breathe more easily as he unscrewed the top and placed the small white pill under his tongue. He held another between two fingers, waiting for the first to dissolve and do its magic.

But it wasn't dissolving. He closed his mouth and breathed through his nose.

It wasn't a nitroglycerin pill; it was a mint.

Frantically, he emptied the container into the palm of his hand. All the tablets were the same—and they weren't his pills. He flung them to the ground, dropping the useless vial. Someone had switched the contents.

The pain was excruciating. He could hardly stand up. Sweat ran down his face and an uncontrollable nausea racked his body.

"Breathe, damn it!" he screamed. "You have to keep breathing!" Fear was feeding the attack; he struggled to calm down.

"You are *not* going to die," he whispered into the stillness. No screaming. No more screaming. He'd have to get down without the pills. He'd make it. He *had* to make it. He leaned over the skis and crouched down into a tuck position. The skis would take him. The skis would save him. They always had. It was a sure thing, like an old dog knowing the way home.

Boyd was moving, dimly aware of passing trees, boulders jutting out of the snow, trolls turned to stone at first light. There were only two thoughts in his mind: making it to the bottom, and that he knew who had done this.

TWO

Faith Fairchild and her sister, Hope, were lingering over coffee at the restaurant Jean Georges at Columbus Circle. They'd had a spectacular prixe fixe luncheon—$20.04, the price having increased a penny each year since the millennium. The meal had started with lobster salad on a crisp buttery rectangle of puff pastry, moved on to poached chicken in a sauce redolent of wine and winter fruits, truffled potatoes, and tiny brussels sprouts, then ended with a warm ginger chocolate concoction. And those had just been Faith's choices.

"This must be the greatest bargain in New York, and you don't even have to wait until restaurant week," Hope said, popping one of the truffles that had come with the coffee into her mouth. During restaurant week, the city's establishments offered inexpensive prixe fixe lunch and dinner menus. The moment the list was posted, there was a frenzy to snag reservations at the top places—you might not be able to afford Daniel Boulud's twenty-nine-dollar hamburger (it contained foie gras), but you could get your foot in his door and taste some of his other mouthwatering concoctions.

Faith nodded in agreement. The menu was a bargain, but there had been no stinting, no dubious cut of steak and mound of greasy pomme frites or tired, dried-out salmon, the staples of so many prixe fixe menus.

She was feeling almost too relaxed to talk. It was freezing outside, but sun was streaming in through the windows of the pretty, unpretentious dining room, which faced away from the newest addition to the neighborhood: the Time Warner Center, the $1.7 billion towering plate-glass behemoth that had replaced the old Coliseum. Yes, the Coliseum was a building that had seen its day, but it had had a quirky presence, projecting the spirits of auto shows, food fairs, toy expos, and international forums of years past into Columbus Circle, where they mingled with the exhaust fumes from vehicles playing Russian roulette at this intersection of Broadway, Eighth Avenue, Central Park West, and Central Park South. Horns honked and middle digits were extended, all under the benevolent eye of Gaetano Russo's Christopher Columbus, standing proudly atop the seven-hundred-ton, seventy-seven-foot-tall monument erected in 1892 to mark the four hundredth anniversary of his famous voyage, a voyage considerably easier than crossing the intersection now, should a pedestrian be foolhardy enough to try. But the Coliseum. Its footprint had not so much been obliterated as stamped out. Am I getting to be an old fogy, Faith wondered. Opposed to change simply because it's change? Yet she couldn't help thinking that the new structure was the ultimate monument to excess of the "Too Much Is Never Enough" school—already well represented in the city. It cast a figurative and literal shadow on the streets below. One of the restaurants was offering tasting menus at three hundred and five hundred dollars. And the retail stores in the center—don't you dare call it a "mall"—featured $24,000 French stoves and $258,000 diamond-studded Swiss watches. She tried to ignore the fact that she was sitting in the ground floor of another of these twenty-first-century temples. Jean Georges was located in the quite hideous Trump International Hotel and Tower. Resolutely, she concentrated on the view of Central Park out the window and an instant replay of the meal she'd just consumed.

"So what are you going to do?" Hope asked, breaking into her sister's rather random thoughts. She reached for another truffle, then stopped herself and straightened one of the purple anemones in the vase on the table instead. She'd had a baby in July, and while she'd lost the weight she'd gained during the pregnancy, she found she had to resist temptation as never before. She seemed to be hungry all the time—exactly like her son, little Quentin Forbes Elliott III. Unlike her sister, Hope loved the Time Warner Center. With its upscale shops, and an enormous Whole Foods market below the ground floor, it offered one-stop shopping for an upscale working mother. Not that she actually cooked, but her house-keeper did. And the restaurants, which offered such a range of extrava-gant choices, charmed clients weary of the same old, same old.

"Go shopping when we finish our coffee. Maybe see the Rosenquist show at the Guggenheim if you haven't and can spare the time. It's clos-ing soon. Then—"

"I mean about Vermont. Are you sure you really have to go?"

Faith knew what her sister had meant. They'd touched on the subject at the beginning of the meal; then she'd steered the conversation to the baby. She had wanted to put the Green Mountain State out of her mind for a while.

"Yes, I really do have to go. It's Vermont or witness protection. Dick is very serious about the whole thing." She motioned to the waiter for more coffee.

A year ago, her father-in-law, Dick Fairchild, had announced that he was celebrating his seventieth birthday by taking the entire Fairchild clan for a week of winter fun at Pine Slopes, a ski resort in Vermont. "Don't give me a party, especially a surprise party. I hate surprise parties. Faith can bake me a cake, the kids can make cards, and I'll take care of every-thing else," he'd said. Dick had already done his homework and had arranged things for the February vacation week, so his grandchildren would be free to join them. Announcing it a year ahead meant that caterer Faith couldn't use bookings as an excuse, and her husband, Tom—the Reverend Thomas Fairchild—had plenty of time to allocate parish duties to others. Not that Tom had wanted to opt out. He'd thought the whole idea was terrific the moment it was proposed—or rather, proclaimed—as had his sister and brothers, who also would have plenty of time to re-arrange their schedules.

Faith sighed and drank some of the fresh coffee. It was delicious. With his attention to detail, Jean-Georges Vongerichten was probably cultivating the beans himself.

"It's not that I don't like Tom's family, but in smaller and shorter doses. And I like to ski, but . . ."

"In smaller and shorter doses," said Hope, finishing the sentence for her.

The two sisters had grown up in Manhattan, Hope arriving almost a year to the day after Faith. Their mother, Jane, was a real estate lawyer, and having her two children so close together was typical of her organiza-tional skills. Plus, in this case, it had eliminated sibling rivalry. Neither had really known what it was to be the sole focus of her parents' atten-tion. They were more like a small litter than sisters a year apart. The two girls grew up as good friends—and as different as night from day. Both were striking. Faith was a blue-eyed blond, while Hope's green eyes, vivid as cabochon emeralds, offset her dark brown hair. Faith had drifted through school, giving scant thought to the future until a stint at the French Culinary Institute had reaffirmed her earlier leanings toward the kitchen—the recipe for dense, chewy brownies (see recipe on page 237), that she'd come up with at age eight was still one of her staples. Besides walnuts, her eight-year-old self had decided to add dried cherries and semisweet chocolate chips to the already chocolaty batter. After her train-ing and an apprenticeship with one of the city's top caterers, Faith had started her own firm, Have Faith, in the late eighties. Soon her food was a must at the Big Apple's glitziest parties, just as she had been as a guest ear-lier. New York loved the new twofer: Faith Sibley *and* fantastic food.

Hope, in contrast, had asked for a briefcase instead of a knapsack in elementary school, and her determined Jimmy Choo–clad feet had never strayed from the path where success is measured not merely in dollars and cents but in options and bonuses. The path where your own initials are enough and most words are acronyms.

The two sisters were also bound together as PKs, preacher's kids. The Reverend Lawrence Sibley ministered to a Manhattan flock, the only venue his wife, Jane, would consider. She'd grown up in the city, as had her ancestors before her. They went back to the original Dutch merchants, who had known a good thing when they saw it. After all, what were a few beads and blankets compared to the future of bright lights, big city they must have envisioned in their dreams after a few meerschaum pipes? Faith and Hope had vowed to avoid the fishbowl existence even a parsonage in the form of a duplex on the Upper East Side afforded. There was no way either was going to marry a man of the cloth, no matter how high the thread count. Hope had kept her vow, tying a firm knot with Quentin Forbes Elliot, Jr., who, like she, made money the old-fashioned way—a lot of money, which kept on making even more. Faith, however, had failed. She'd fallen for Tom at a wedding reception she was catering, unaware that he had traded his collar and robe for mufti. By the time she realized that the deal also meant leaving the city for Aleford, Massachusetts, a small town west of Boston—dooming her to a lifetime of bad haircuts, boiled dinners, and below-zero temperatures as late as April— she couldn't imagine herself without Tom and didn't want to. The years had passed with alarming swiftness. She'd started up Have Faith again and continued the product line of sauces, jams, jellies, and chutneys she'd launched in New York. Their son, Ben, was almost ten, and his sister, Amy, was six and a half (woe to he or she who left the half off). It wasn't the life Faith had foreseen for herself, but it was the life she had, and mostly she was very happy with it—except at the moment.

She drained her cup and set it down on the saucer firmly. Her consolation prize for agreeing to the week in Vermont had been a weekend in the city, a transfusion. Tom was looking after the kids—and receiving the kind of support that only men get when they're on their own: babysitting offers, casseroles, invitations to dinner. Women, when their husbands are away, have merely an easier bed to make and, if the kids go to sleep on time, *Sex and the City* reruns.

"I need to get some of that French Thermolactyl underwear. You know, the *'Moi froid, jamais!'* people. It's the only stuff that really keeps me warm. I've found a place that carries it. It's incredibly hard to find, even here. I was beginning to feel as if I were trying to score drugs. I'd call one place and they'd whisper the name of another. Come with me and I can whine while we shop. It won't take long. Then we can go wherever you want. Need anything?"

Hope never needed anything, but want was another matter. "I wouldn't mind getting some warm undies myself. We're going to Gstaad for a long weekend. Did I tell you?"

This *was* news. Both Hope and Quentin considered *workaholic* a high compliment. They seldom took vacations, lest someone oil the next rung on the ladder while they were away. The baby had made very little difference in their schedule so far. A nanny and a housekeeper will suffice for a few years, Faith thought, but wait until later: the science-fair project due the next day, the depths of despair produced by not being invited to your "best" friend's birthday party, and those phone calls from school, "Mrs. Elliott, could you . . ."

"No, you didn't tell me. What's up?" Faith asked.

Hope blushed. For a corporate shark, she blushed easily. "I think Quentin is the teensiest bit jealous of Terry." To avoid the confusion of two Quentins in the house, the baby had been nicknamed "Terry," from the Latin, *tertius,* as "the third." It was, on no account, to continue once the little scion was in school. Quentin he was born and Quentin he would be.

"That happens," Faith said. There were days when she felt as if she were being stretched to fit Procrustes' mythological iron bed, except it was a three-way pull. She reached for the check. Hope pushed her hand away.

"My treat. You can get it next time." She slipped her platinum AmEx card in with the bill. "Anyway, it's going to be great. The place is sort of Heidi meets Donald Trump. We hit the slopes, then dinner in our suite, snifters of brandy, and, I suppose, me on a bearskin rug or whatever in front of the fire. At least that's the picture Quentin has, and I'm not objecting. Between work and Terry, we haven't had much nooky time lately. What's your place like?"

"Aside from being in a condo complex with Tom's entire family, plus Ben and Amy, I don't think Pine Slopes runs to much privacy or bearskin rugs—or snifters, for that matter. It's pretty stripped-down. Say Heidi meets Tom Bodett. Rustic."

They got up and retrieved their coats. Outside, Hope hailed a cab.

"Good rustic or rustic rustic?" she asked as they got in and told the driver their destination.

"It's a small place, family-owned and geared toward families. The Fairchilds have had the condo since the place opened in the sixties, and they all learned to ski there as soon as they could walk—maybe sooner. There's a cute picture of Tom and his father coming down a slope. Tom doesn't look a day over six months, and his father's holding him on top of the skis."

"Sounds sweet. And you've been there before, right?"

Faith shook her head. "The kids have been there a few times with their grandparents and once with Tom's sister, Betsey, and her crew. Tom's gone up with his brother Robert, but I've always managed to avoid this treat. My idea of a vacation is not doing all the cooking—much as I love it—for a large number of people, plus housework. Although Dick is paying for the hotel housekeeping staff to clean for the week, I think. This is why Marian takes trips. Between the condo and the house on the Cape, family vacations have been anything but for her."

Faith's mother-in-law, Marian Fairchild, had caused a stir several years ago by booking herself onto a tour to the Galápagos. She informed Dick that he was welcome to go along, then added that if she waited for him to have the inclination to travel anywhere but the Cape and Vermont, she'd have to die to see someplace new. Since then, she'd covered a great deal of the globe—much of Europe, Machu Picchu, the Serengeti, and Beijing.

When they arrived at the store, they paid the driver and got out. It had been a rare cab drive: the driver hadn't yelled at them for wanting to go such a short distance, he hadn't endangered any pedestrians, other vehicles, or his passengers, and he had known where he was going.

Inside, the two sisters concentrated on the task before them.

"Trust the French to combine practicality with frivolity," Hope commented, holding up a lacy camisole that was as filmy as milkweed and the same color. "Are you sure this can keep you warm?"

"Absolutely," Faith assured her. "Almost too warm." Having Hope along was making the errand, which she'd been dreading, fun. She'd been dreading it because it meant she was really going. She wasn't sure she wanted to go into the whole thing with Hope. Not that she wouldn't be sympathetic, but it felt like a betrayal of Tom to dissect his family. Eminently dissectible though they were.

At Barneys, the next stop, Faith found a great Marc Jacobs cashmere turtleneck, which she would definitely not take to Pine Slopes. But merely contemplating how warm, cozy—and chic—it was made her feel better. A week wasn't *that* long. Hope bought two of the sweaters for Switzerland. Then they went up to the Guggenheim.

"I've never been able to decide whether I always like the shows here because I like the space or whether it's that they mount great shows," Hope commented.

"I know what you mean," Faith agreed as they slowly wound their way up Frank Lloyd Wright's ramps to the top of the exhibition. "But these really look marvelous here, especially when you look across at one, or down." She gestured toward *Welcome to the Water Planet,* a huge canvas filled with exploding images of celestial and aquatic images, dominated by a sensual water lily.

"I'm so glad I came. I almost didn't. Arranging to get away, even packing, seemed like such a big deal." Faith gave her sister an impulsive hug. "Now that I'm here, I feel as if I've been gone for weeks. The city does that. Something about being anonymous. Nobody I've passed today cares that my daughter's teacher has suggested extra time tying bows on the practice shoe or that my fourth-grade son is a teen wanna-be."

"And that would be a bad thing because . . ." It sounded to Hope like what she had wanted at that age—a time-saving device.

"Because he's still a little boy and kids are pressed to grow up too fast." Reading her sister's expression correctly, Faith added, "It's not like what you did. Yes, you followed the market, but you used your crayons to take notes and make those charts."

"I loved those crayons. Remember, Aunt Chat gave me a huge box? Fifty, a hundred? How many were there? And all those names—burnt sienna, goldenrod, spring green, maize. When the company celebrated their hundredth anniversary in 2003, for some bizarre reason they let people vote four colors out and new ones in. Teal blue, my favorite, is apparently wild blue yonder now. So much for preserving our past. I should pick up a box for Terry before carnation pink disappears. I know, I know," she added. "Finger paints first."

"With chocolate pudding," Faith said, noting that her sister didn't spend all her time on financial Web sites. Obviously, the Binney and Smith one was bookmarked.

"Chocolate pudding, what an idea! Ooooh, I get it." Hope dissolved into laughter and the Sibley girls half-ran, half-walked down the spiraling museum and spilled onto the sidewalk, where they each consumed a Sabrett's hot dog with everything before going their separate ways. Faith was having dinner with their parents, and Hope was going to clock in a few more hours at work.

But, darling, we can easily eat here. I have a nice piece of fish and some salad. I'm sorry your father was called away. Poor Mrs. Hammond. I'm afraid she really is dying this time."

Mrs. Hammond had teetered on the brink, only to claw her way back so many times in the last few years that it had become a private joke between Hope and Faith. And the deathbed calls always seemed to come just when the Reverend Sibley was about to go out to dinner or the opera, his only indulgence, so far as his daughters could determine. Mrs. Hammond had second sight—or the Met's schedule close at hand.

"I've already booked a table for us at Vivolo. You know how much you like their veal, and we can get them to pack something up for Dad."

Jane Sibley's idea of dinner, especially since her daughters had left home, was a nice piece of fish and a salad or a nice piece of chicken and a salad. She regarded her eldest's career with astonishment, finding it as exotic—and difficult—as, say, mapping the genome.

In the end, they left the nice piece of fish for another meal and had nice pieces of veal at Vivolo, essentially her parents' Upper East Side nabe. Faith found herself face-to-face over coffee with another nearest and dearest for the second time that day. It was mother and espresso instead of sister and espresso, but it was the same relaxed feeling. She nibbled a biscotti and realized that she hadn't thought of those other nearests and dearests up in Massachusetts for several hours. Then Jane spoke.

"You know when you marry, you don't simply marry an individual, but a family."

Hope had been blabbing, obviously.

"Oh Mother, I know that. This is about the Vermont trip, right? Well, I'm going with a smile on my face and a heart full of goodwill toward all Fairchilds. Don't worry."

"I'm not worried," her mother said serenely. "I just know how it is."

"But you adored Gran and Granfa—and what about Chat!" Faith's aunt Chat was her father's youngest sister and the only one who had ever been around much. His two older sisters were Faith and Hope. It was a long-standing Sibley custom to name the girls in each generation Faith, Hope, and Charity. Faith had a sneaking suspicion that Jane had stopped having children when she did to avoid the possibility of the appellation. Aunt Faith had died of breast cancer before Faith was born, and Aunt Hope lived near Seattle, a childless widow. Chat, who had never married, had been and was a major presence in her nieces' lives. She now lived just outside the city, in New Jersey, after retiring from the very successful ad agency she'd started. Most of her friends assumed the flight into Jersey was a temporary aberration, but it had been several years now, and they were forced to cross the Hudson when they wanted to visit her—an undertaking more daunting to a New Yorker than crossing the Atlantic. Gran and Granfa (Hope had invented the latter name at age two) had lived long enough for both Sibley granddaughters to know and love them. These three very important relatives and a bunch of second cousins once and more removed made up the Sibley side.

Since Jane was an only child, Faith hadn't grown up in the kind of clan Tom had. The Fairchilds numbered Dick, Marian, and their four: Tom, his older sister, Betsey, along with her husband, Dennis, and their sons, Scott and Andy, and Tom's younger brothers, Robert and Craig, plus Craig's new wife, Glenda. Marian and Dick came from large families, and the aunts, uncles, and cousins were as numerous as Winnie-the-Pooh's friend Rabbit's relations. Tom had been surprised at Faith's paucity of kin. Although he denied it vigorously, Faith knew he associated it with the city. When they'd first met and engaged in those heady conversations typical of couples falling madly in love—the desire to know everything about one's beloved: favorite color, favorite song—Tom kept coming up with queries about her childhood. "But where did you play?" he would ask. He'd regaled her with tales of lazy summer days spent building rafts on the North River and winters filled with sledding, skating, and ice fishing. She'd countered with Central Park and the rink at Rockefeller Center, followed by hot chocolate at Rumpelmayer's, but he had remained skeptical.

"Of course I'm very close to Chat," Jane Sibley said. "I've been lucky to have three wonderful sisters-in-law—and Gran and Granfa were very special to me. But I wasn't used to *en famille* gatherings so en masse. Forty assorted Sibleys at my first family Thanksgiving almost caused me to cancel our wedding plans and elope. There were . . . well, so *many* of them and they were so bumptious—you know what I mean."

Faith did. Jane was not a hugger. Faith had married into a family of huggers and had been converted, but she understood her mother's early dismay. For all her high-powered wheeling and dealing in the business world, the confidence that exuded from every pore as she strode into a boardroom, Jane Sibley was actually quite shy.

Faith tried to explain her reluctance about the birthday bash. She'd successfully avoided the topic with Hope. "It's a little of that—the 'so many of them' part—but it's more the kinds of interactions that take place when they're all together. It's as if they are all still living at home and relating to one another the way they did when they were children. Somewhere along the line, roles were assigned, learned—and no changes in the script, please. Not Tom, of course." Or not so much, she said silently to herself. "But the others—and we'll be together for a whole week!"

Jane gave her daughter's hand a gentle pat—a gesture tantamount to a Gallic kiss, Eskimo nose rub, and Bavarian bear hug rolled into one. "You'll survive, darling."

That night in bed—the bed she'd slept in all her life postcrib and prenuptials—Jane's words reverberated in the familiar room that still contained a bookcase filled with childhood favorites and the Brunschwig & Fils wallpaper she'd picked at thirteen and still loved. It had been a lovely day, a great escape. Her eyes fluttered closed, then opened wide as she recalled her mother's words. She'd survive, but would they?

Pete Reynolds, the head of maintenance at the Pine Slopes ski resort, stood with his thumbs looped on his belt, surveying the damage with the resort's owners, Fred and Naomi Stafford. Naomi's face was flushed, and there were angry tears in her eyes; Fred was biting his lower lip. Pete was just looking.

"Animals! And the chaperones swore that this was a good group!" Naomi cried.

A high school ski club from the New York State side of Lake Champlain had rented a block of rooms over the weekend. Judging from the number of empty kegs, the kids had packed more than their ski equipment. Towels had been stuffed into toilets. There was vomit on the rugs, the drapes had been torn, and two trashed microwaves sat there, aluminum containers melted onto the interior walls. And this didn't include the sheer mess—food ground into the floor, broken plates, trash everywhere, and dirt that had been tracked in from outside, since apparently no one had thought to remove boots at the door.

"Well, we've got a damage deposit, but it won't go far," Fred said. "I'll call the school and talk to the principal, but . . ."

"But it's a helluva long way from here and they're not going to do anything about it. Add 'em to the list and I'll get Candy up here," Pete said. Candy Laverdiere was the head of housekeeping. "When are these rooms booked for next?"

"Tonight," Fred said glumly. The list of schools not welcome at the resort was growing. The room rentals, lift tickets, and often the equipment rentals, plus the revenue the kids generated at the cafeteria and the Sports Center, were an important part of the resort's income, but in the past few years, the cost in damages was seriously cutting into their profits. He'd talk to Boyd and see if they couldn't draw up some kind of ironclad contract that would make the school groups responsible for any and all costs incurred. He'd thought of it before. The big resorts all had them, but he had wanted the business. For the snowboarders, they'd added a terrain park with a half pipe, jumps, and a rail slide, which had been a blessing and a curse. It had brought the families with teenagers back, but it had also attracted school groups and clubs.

"I'll get Ophelia and we can help," Naomi offered.

Well out of Naomi's sight, Pete raised an eyebrow at Fred. The day Naomi's sixteen-year-old daughter, Joanie, who now insisted on being called "Ophelia," pitched in to help would be one for the record books.

"It would have to be one of the new units, of course," Fred said. Last year, they'd renovated the existing hotel units and added some new ones. "I'll go over and tell Mom and Dad; then I'll get back here."

It was good to get away from the stench of way too much beer and cigarette smoke, which was going to be a problem, too. These were smoke-free rooms. Fred took a deep breath when he got outside and instantly felt better.

His parents had started the resort in 1969 and he'd grown up here, attending the small local school down at the bottom of the mountain and then driving to Burlington for high school and college. He'd never wanted to do anything but work at the resort. It was his mother, Mary, who'd insisted he go to UVM in order to have something to fall back on. He'd been a business major. But, he realized as he walked quickly past the main lodge, with the economy the way it was, degree or no degree, if Pine Slopes failed, the only thing he'd be falling back on was his own keister.

Fred had hoped that once he took over for his parents, they would be able to settle back and enjoy a stress-free retirement. Maybe travel a little. The first season had been fantastic. Plenty of snow and plenty of people. No problem finding help, either. But in the last five years, things had been a little iffy. Thank God for Boyd. Without the capital he'd pumped in, Pine Slopes would have joined the long list of defunct family resorts. It was amazing to think that in 1966 there had been eighty-one ski areas in Vermont, more than any other state. The small rope tow and T-bar areas began to disappear rapidly in the seventies. Now conglomerates owned the resorts, and there were only seventeen commercial areas left.

He hated to be the bearer of bad tidings, but his father and mother probably already knew by now about the rooms being trashed. The grapevine was an especially efficient one at Pine Slopes.

He'd intended to inspect the rooms before the group left at six o'clock that morning, but the chaperones had spirited the kids away before then, knowing full well what had happened. He was surprised Simon Tanner, Pine Slopes' manager, hadn't heard the buses—or what must have been at least some commotion the night before. During the season, he moved from his cabin up in the backcountry into a unit in the hotel and kept a close eye on things. Chaperones! They'd probably been partying right along with the kids. He shook his head. It was a beautiful clear day. A good crowd for a Monday, and it was supposed to snow some more that night. They were so high—2,100-foot base elevation—that any precipitation at this time of year would be snow. They'd had to use their snow-making equipment occasionally, but for the most part Mother Nature was cooperating—and she was the one who could make them or break them. He wished he could invest in some new equipment. Pete was keeping the old stuff going, but only just. It wouldn't be this year, though. Not with what they'd had to put out to update the Sports Center and fine-tune the terrain park.

Animals! Naomi was right! He'd liked to have a good time when he was their age, hanging around with his friends and enjoying a few pops, but they'd never destroyed property this way, or drunk the way these kids did—not only the boys but girls, too. What was it all about? Were they simply spoiled brats who never had to face the consequences of their actions, or was it something else? Copping an attitude toward an adult world that they didn't regard as particularly worthwhile? Ophelia flashed into his mind and, just as quickly, he forced himself to think of something else.

He was almost at the small A-frame his parents had built as their retirement home. It was tucked away behind the Sports Center, where they could see the entire resort but were hidden from view themselves. It was also near the snowshoe trails. They'd picked up the sport after his mother decided her skiing days were over. His dad at seventy-eight, was still consistently placing first in all the races for those over sixty-five, both here at Pine Slopes and at Stowe, Killington, and the other area resorts—the major resorts. Pine Slopes could have been a contender, just as Harold Stafford could have been an Olympic champion, but he liked his life the way it was, he'd told his son once. He didn't need anything more.

Fred would have liked to give him something more, though. Something—or someone—for both his parents. His first marriage had been a brief one, ending in divorce. They hadn't had children. He and Naomi hadn't been able to have any children together. Her daughter was from her first marriage. Fred had always wanted a whole bunch of kids. He'd imagined them growing up at Pine Slopes, loving the mountain the way he did, skiing with their grandfather and snowshoeing with their grandmother, hiking with them both in the spring and summer. As beautiful as it was in the winter, late spring—just after mud season—was Fred's favorite time. Wildflowers covered the slopes, and streams as clear as fine crystal cascaded down into the meadows, where the deer gathered at twilight.

The Fairchilds would arrive next week. He couldn't wait to see them all. They were like family, especially Craig. Craig Fairchild—he smiled to himself—the little brother he'd always wanted. Grown up and even married now.

He reached the house, climbed the stairs, and knocked on the door.

"Mom? Dad? Are you there? It's Freddy."

Scott? Andy? Where are you, boys? I'm home." Betsey Fairchild Parker had been showing a house. Normally, she arranged her schedule so that she was there when her boys came home from school or from practice during soccer and baseball seasons. She'd told them that morning that she would be late, but she said that she'd leave a snack, and then they should get right to their homework. The chart of their assignments for the week was hanging in the kitchen. She'd told them she expected to see some of today's tasks checked off by the time she returned.

Betsey was in a good mood. She was virtually certain the young couple was going to make an offer on the house. She hadn't even needed to dangle the specter of "other interested parties" before them. It was a great house—well maintained, terrific location, tastefully decorated—no chartreuse walls or outdated wallpaper. Not even officially on the market yet. Sure it would be a Fairchild Realty listing, she had called the sellers directly, telling them it would be a propitious time to take the dogs for a walk. Daddy would be proud of her.

"Boys? Where are you?" She took off her good coat and hung it up on a padded hanger in the front hall closet, then went into the kitchen. From the granite countertops to the gleaming unused copper pots hanging from faux exposed beams, it was her dream kitchen opening into the Great

Room, with its cathedral ceiling and imposing stone fireplace (she'd insisted on gas—wood was so messy). "What's supposed to be so great about it?" Dennis, her husband, had asked the first time he saw the room. One of his typical attempts at humor.

Normally, her two sons would have been doing their homework at the long table under the Palladian window overlooking the backyard. She could get dinner ready and make sure that what they were doing on their laptops was work and not surfing the Net or sending instant messages. But the two heads weren't bent over computers or books. She thought of fifteen-year-old Scott's brown curls, too long again—she made a mental note to get him a haircut before next week—and thirteen-year-old Andy's, the same color but straight as a pin. The healthy snack of fruit and sugar-free Jell-O (in the winter, they could pork up if she wasn't careful) remained on the counter, untouched.

She went upstairs. They weren't in their rooms. She checked the answering machine, thinking she should have done that as soon as she came in. It was blinking. She was relieved. Probably a meeting of one of the after-school clubs they were in, although she kept track of the times by going on-line to check their schools' daily announcements.

The first message was from the young couple. They wanted to make an offer. Would she call them back? they asked. Would she! The next one was from Daddy. He wanted to make sure the boys remembered to bring their cross-country skis. Last time, they'd forgotten them, and he was looking forward to some backcountry trips with them.

The skis were in place in the garage, along with all the other equipment for the trip. And this time, she'd make sure they weren't "forgotten." The week in Vermont wasn't about them and their snowboards, she'd told Scott and Andy. It was about Grandpa. It was all about him.

Robert Fairchild got into his car and popped a Dan Fogelberg CD into the slot. It was *Full Circle,* Robert's favorite. A great day. His personal best. He'd only sold this much a few times before. He sang along with

Fogelberg: "Funny how the circle turns around." It had been a terrific fall, and now the winter was proving even better. He'd been promoted to regional sales rep. And all those commissions and bonuses were adding up to a very tidy sum. He was hot. He was golden. And he had to go away for a week.

It really sucked.

Like it?" Glenda Fairchild twirled around slowly in front of her husband, showing off a new ski outfit she'd bought. Turquoise to match her eyes—or rather, the turquoise contacts that camouflaged her pale gray irises, so not in keeping with her platinum blond hair, she'd decided years ago.

"It's stunning, honey. You're stunning," Craig said. He hoped it wasn't too expensive. It wouldn't matter in the future. They'd be sitting pretty in a few months, maybe weeks. It was just now.

"Let me show you the next one. It's exactly like one Paris Hilton wore at Aspen." She flashed him a big smile.

"Another one?" he said weakly.

"Another two. You're not mad are you, Craigie?"

She walked over to where he was sitting on the edge of their bed and leaned over, unzipping the outfit and shrugging it off. She was naked.

"Mad? How could I be mad at you, sugar?" he mumbled, burying his face in her absolutely perfect breasts.

Marian, are you awake?"

"I am now, dear. What's the matter?"

Dick Fairchild sat up and switched on the lamp on the nightstand by his side of the bed.

"Nothing's the matter. Just think, next week we'll all be together at Pine Slopes. I don't think I've overlooked anything. Craig's been a big help—his idea to start with, you know—and if I have forgotten anything, the Staffords will take care of it."

"I'm sure you haven't. You've done a marvelous job organizing it all. I'm proud of you." Marian gave him a kiss and rolled back over. She was almost asleep before she realized her husband was still talking to her and expected some sort of reply. She reached a hand to her forehead, the better to keep her eyelids from closing.

"Hmm," she said.

It served.

"I'll tell you one thing," Dick said.

"Okay." She was almost awake now.

"It's not every family that gets along the way we do. Not by a long shot. They're all just tickled pink to be going. Hey, that's a good one, considering we'll be there on Valentine's Day. Got to remember that. 'We're all tickled pink to be here'—I'll use that for the toast Saturday night."

"Hmm," Marian said again.

Faith was up in time to have breakfast with her father and mother before church. After the service, she'd head down to Penn Station and get a train north. She'd left her car at the Route 128 stop so that Tom wouldn't have to pick her up. As she ate her oatmeal, traditional Sunday-morning fare in the Sibley household, she realized how much she missed Tom and the kids—although not the Sunday routine that went something like, "Are you sure I don't have a clean collar?" "No, you can't wear your tutu to Sunday School," and "Mom, I was supposed to write a poem about loving your neighbor. Where's a pen?"

The Reverend Lawrence Sibley was subdued. Mrs. Hammond had actually died this time, and recalling the more than slight irritation he'd felt last night on being called out yet again, he resolved in the future to answer each cry of wolf with total and absolute dedication, no matter from whence the utterance came.

Jane, who, unlike some long-married couples, had not grown to look like her tall, distinguished white-haired husband, had remained a medium height with an unvarying honey blond coif. Instead she had grown quite astute at reading her husband's mind. At the moment, she'd had enough of his unspoken guilt. Slathering an English muffin with Dundee thick-cut marmalade, she said, "Really, Lawrence, let it go. She lived to be a good age, had a husband and children who loved her, plus an extremely attentive pastor. And just think, we'll be able to go to the opera again."

Faith couldn't help laughing.

"Is this what Tom and I will be like in heaven only knows how many years?"

"If you're lucky." Her father winked at her and got up to get ready. There were always plenty of clean collars in his drawer—and pressed shirts, robes, and dark socks without holes in them.

"It's been a lovely visit," Jane said.

"For me, too," Faith replied.

They started to clear the breakfast dishes.

"Send us a postcard from Vermont," her mother said as they went into the kitchen. "When is it you're going?"

"Dick was born on Valentine's Day. We're all due at Pine Slopes on Friday the thirteenth."

THREE

At first, Faith thought someone had dropped a glove. It protruded from a snowdrift, a jaunty red-and-blue flag against the crusty white surface. But the angle was wrong. And the fingers too stiff. What could be holding it in place? A branch?

It wasn't a branch; it was a hand.

It was a body.

She struggled to keep her balance, teetering on her narrow cross-country skis, although the trail was flat. If she took her skis off, she'd sink into the powder. Buried in snow. The trees whirled crazily about her and the achingly blue ski seemed to be pressing down on her. She was having trouble breathing and gulped for air.

There had been a good snowfall the night before, and it had covered most of the body—except his hand and part of his head. It was a man, an older man. His hat had fallen off, revealing gray hair and a face—Faith could hardly bear to look at his face. It was too late to get help, but not too late to see the pain and anguish of his last moments.

Shaking, she started to retrace her path. The ski patrol's command post was next to the main lodge. She'd go there. They would come and take the body away. The dead body. The corpse.

What had happened to him?

When she reached the ski patrol, she had trouble getting the words out at first, but as she did, someone put a mug of hot sweet tea in her hand, urging her to drink it, while another threw a blanket around her shoulders. The third person on duty was making a call. Calling the Staffords, Faith thought. She wished they could call Tom. Tom! She wanted Tom, but he would be skiing by now—out of reach.

"Do you think you could come and show us where he is?"

She knew she had to, and after a few more sips, she went outside, got onto the snowmobile, and shouted directions into the driver's ear.

The body was where she had left it. She had had an unreasonable hope that it had all been a dream, a hallucination induced by the high altitude.

She stayed where she was. Two other snowmobiles pulled up, one with a stretcher.

"Oh shit, it's Boyd!" she heard the young man who had driven her out to this spot, this beautiful, dreadful spot, say once softly, then louder, turning to the others. "It's Boyd! Boyd Harrison!"

He got back on the vehicle, leaving the others to their task. He'd told her he would take her right back. She knew he wanted to stay. To help place this man, Boyd Harrison, on the stretcher. She knew this because he was crying, had started crying as soon as he saw the face. She felt very sorry for him and sorry to be the cause of his having to abandon his friend lying so stiffly in the snow. But not sorry enough to say she would stay and wait. The face had a name. A person, not an inanimate object in the snow. Somewhere there were people who cared for him—family, friends—who didn't know what she knew. She could feel the presence of their grief waiting— what, a half hour, an hour from now? The reality of Boyd Harrison's death hit her, and she couldn't wait to get as far away from his snow-covered body as possible.

He was a very, very sick man. Everyone, most of all Boyd himself, has been expecting this for a long time. And he died doing what he loved most in the place where he was happiest. This mountain was his best friend—that's what he always said. A good death, Faith."

There was that oxymoron again, Faith thought sleepily. She was in bed, lying under a pile of eiderdowns, and Marian was holding her hand, stroking it gently. A good death. Faith knew what it meant, but she wasn't old enough and hadn't been close enough to someone near the end to believe in it.

Marian had been waiting with the Staffords at the ski patrol's hut when she'd returned. They were looking for Tom. Ben and Amy wouldn't be finished with their ski programs until the late afternoon. She couldn't imagine why she was so tired. Marian had taken her back to the condo and made her drink some more tea—chamomile this time. Maybe she'd slipped a Mickey in it. Faith could barely keep her eyes open. The blankets were so warm, so soft and light, fluffy—like new-fallen snow.

"Close your eyes, dear. You've had quite a shock, but everything's going to be all right. When you wake up, Tom will be here, and I'll still be here, too. . . . No, don't try to talk, just let your mind drift off."

Marian had such a soothing voice. Faith could imagine how the little Fairchilds must have felt when they were home from school, sick with the flu or a cold, Marian putting a cold washcloth on a hot forehead, reading stories and bringing ginger ale, saltines, and weak tea as they recuperated.

Drift. Not snowdrifts. She forced her mind away from the image. Let it drift. Drift to last night, she thought as she fell asleep.

For once, they'd left the house on time. Knowing how little would be accomplished on a Friday afternoon before a vacation week, Faith had asked that the kids be dismissed at noon. The car was packed and Tom had miraculously not been faced with an ecclesiastical crisis, not even the "We don't have anyone to do coffee hour this week!" kind. They'd picked the kids up and popped Jim Dale reading Harry Potter into the CD player. In what seemed like no time, they were pulling up to the condo; the three-hour trip had flown by under Harry's spell. Plus, eager to see his older cousins and get to Pine Slopes, Ben had neither whined—"Are we there yet?"—nor encroached on his sister's space, crossing the invisible line in the middle of the rear seat to annoy her.

To Ben's and Amy's delight, they were the first to arrive. Their grandfather handed them each a goody bag he'd filled with things like Chapstick on a string to go around the necks of their parkas, a tiny Skigee to keep their goggles clear, Turtle Fur neck gaiters with the Pine Slopes logo, and Gummy Bears. He'd immediately whisked them away to sign them up for their ski programs—the Seedlings for Amy, the Saplings for Ben. The ski school for kids and teens was consistently rated one of the best in New England. There were goody bags for Tom and Faith, too—sans the Gummy Bears, and with ski passes for the week.

"Dad, this is crazy. Please let us pay for ourselves," Tom protested.

"No way, youngster. This is my birthday and I can do anything I want."

"Humor him," Marian said. "It's easier in the long run."

"Speaking of which, we have time for a few runs before dinner. What do you say?" Dick proposed.

The Fairchilds were bodies in motion that tended to stay in motion, Faith had noted early in her relationship with Tom. She begged off to get dinner ready, and Marian stayed behind to welcome the others.

There wasn't much to do to get the meal on the table, but Faith thought she'd get it organized and then sneak down to the Sports Center for a quick swim and some time in the sauna. She'd insisted on supplying dinner the first night. The birthday dinner tomorrow night would be at Le Sapin, the resort's well-known restaurant. Its chef, John Forest, rechristened Jean Forestier many years ago, when he realized a French *nom de cuisine* added to his credibility, had built the restaurant from a small ski lodge bistro into one of the area's top dinning spots, winning rave reviews year after year.

For tonight, Faith had brought her vacation chili, which she'd developed to please a crowd that might span a broad age range, like this one. Chili aficionados would turn their noses up at it. It was a far cry from the real thing, the kind dished up at places like M & J's Sanitary Tortilla Factory in Albuquerque, arguably the best *carne adovada*—red chile with marinated slow-baked pork—in the Southwest, but her vacation chili was an invariable palate pleaser. She used light and dark kidney beans, ground beef, onions, garlic, and catsup spiked with some barbecue sauce for a slightly smoky flavor. Ground pepper, a little salt, and a few flakes of red pepper were all the seasonings she added. But she'd brought along more pepper flakes, several kinds of hot sauce, and chili powder for anyone who wanted to spice it up. She also had sour cream, shredded iceberg lettuce, taco shells, and both yellow and blue tortilla chips to put out. Her sister-in-law Betsey was always on some sort of diet and tended to snatch anything resembling a carbohydrate from her sons' mouths, so Faith had a platter of crudités for hors d'oeuvres especially for them and another of cheese and crackers, plus some stuffed mushrooms she'd heat up for everyone else. Marian had made some of her famous coleslaw—famous in the Fairchild family. Faith had yet to figure out what, if any, secrets it contained other than cabbage, shredded carrots, and Hellmann's—never a bad combination, but not unknown to the general public. For dessert, Faith had brought apple crisp. Pine Slopes had a small general store that sold Ben & Jerry's ice cream, whose headquarters were in nearby Waterbury. The store was also convenient for other things, from juice boxes to Duraflame logs.

When Marian saw Faith take out the apple crisp, she said, "Oh dear. Did I forget to tell you I was bringing one of Aunt Susie's cakes?"

Aunt Susie was not related by blood to the Fairchilds, but by very strong ties of friendship. Marian had met Susan Houston, a warmhearted southern lady, when both were young and the two families had visited back and forth over the years. Besides, being the type of person who looks out for everybody before thinking of herself, Susie was a wonderful cook. Aunt Susie's cake, a delectable concoction that included mandarin oranges and pineapple, was a rare treat (see recipe on page 237).

"You did, but we can save the crisp for another time," Faith said.

Dick had laid a fire in the fireplace. Faith was tempted to skip the

Sports Center, light the fire, and curl up with a book instead. She'd keep Marian company while she waited for the rest of her offspring. Craig, thirty-two, was the youngest, and had recently married. The couple had tied the knot last fall in Hawaii, going straight to the honeymoon, although after meeting her new sister-in-law, Glenda, at Christmas, Faith thought the honeymoon had probably started a whole lot earlier. The woman was a knockout, and her mother-in-law's floor had never been so clean, what with every man's tongue dragging on it. Every man, including Tom, who had literally taken a step back when Craig had introduced his bride. It had been left to young Ben to give voice to the testosterone-laced thoughts filling the room: "Wow, Aunt Glenda! Are you a model or a TV star or something?" Aunt Glenda—and contrary to Faith's first cynical thought, Glenda *was* her real name: "After my Daddy, Glen"—gave Ben a hug and said, "Well, I have done a little modeling, but I'm a housewife now." When Faith had described the scene to her assistant, Niki Constantine, Niki had commented—after she'd stopped laughing— "Save your Saran Wrap coupons for her, although she doesn't sound as if she needs any tricks to keep the sparks flying in her marriage."

The official Fairchild line was that Craig had done very well for himself, marrying a nice girl, taking that final step into adulthood, an event they'd been waiting for since he graduated from UMass, dropped out of law and med school, and then left two other graduate programs and five jobs. At present, he'd returned to his boyhood home, renting a place in Norwell, not far from his parents, and working with a local property developer. It wasn't clear where or when he'd met Glenda, but she'd quit whatever job she had as soon as the ring was on her finger, then spent most of her days at her health club or shopping. Craig had been adamant that he didn't want his wife to work, the unspoken message being: not like my brother's wife and my sister.

Glenda had never learned to ski. Faith had the idea that she was from the South, or maybe New Jersey. Someplace like that anyway. Jersey girls were tough, and under all that carefully applied soft makeup, Glenda,

Faith suspected, was pretty tough indeed. Of course, this went for southern women, as well. Craig was looking forward to taking his wife down the bunny slope, and Dick had booked her a full week of private lessons.

Just as Faith had decided to head to the Sports Center, urged on by her mother-in-law, the Parkers arrived—Betsey and the boys. Betsey's husband, Dennis, a periodontist, would be coming later.

"Hello! Where is everybody?" Betsey called out.

Well, two of us are here, Faith thought to herself, but she knew that at least she wasn't on her sister-in-law's A list, and maybe Marian wasn't, either.

"Dad and Tom are skiing, Ben and Amy are watching a movie at the lodge in the Kids' Club, and the others aren't here yet. Come give me a kiss, you two," Marian said, holding her arms out toward her grandsons. Scott and Andy had been hanging back, sports bags hugged to their chests like armor. Faith had watched in dismay as the two outgoing youngsters she'd teased and tickled as little ones had turned into mute adolescent strangers. Ben worshiped them, and since he repeated their jokes ad nauseam, they obviously behaved differently around him. Faith wished she knew them better. Maybe this week. She'd organize a trip to Stowe or wherever they wanted to go, prying them away from Betsey, if possible. Her sister-in-law gave new meaning to the expression, "control freak." Faith had seen the lists posted in their house on the South Shore—they lived in Hingham, one town over from Norwell. You could open any drawer and not even a pencil would be out of line.

"Don't just stand there. Give Grandma a kiss—and Aunt Faith. Then take the bags upstairs to our rooms."

"Oh Bets, you know we've rented the Collins's condo for the week. There isn't enough room in ours for everyone. I've put you there with Tom and Faith," Marian said.

Faith knew she and her family were going to be staying next door in a smaller unit with a galley kitchen. The idea was that everyone would gather at the family unit for dinners, getting their own breakfasts and picking up lunch at the cafeteria or general store. She hadn't thought to ask who would be with them. She'd only thought as far ahead as getting to Vermont, not much further. Obviously, Betsey had.

The room went very still. "But we always stay here with you and Daddy." Each word was uttered with the precision of a speech teacher.

Marian, who never looked flustered, looked flustered.

"I know, dear, but we've never all been here at the same time, and there simply isn't space. Robert will be in the other bedroom upstairs and Craig and Glenda will be in the one down here, so they can have their own bath. Besides, I knew the cousins would want to be together. Why don't you go over now with Faith and sort it all out. I'm sure you two"—she went over and put an arm around each of her grandsons, who had remained rooted to the floor, waiting for instructions—"want to go see the movie or get out on the slopes right away."

That did it, and they dashed for the door.

"Stop," Betsey ordered. "There's a car to unpack."

"I can help you with that," Faith said. "Ben and Amy are dying to see you guys," she added, turning to the boys.

"Thank you, Faith, but this is Scott and Andy's job. And the sooner they get to it, the sooner it will be done." She followed her sons out the door. If she'd been standing any straighter, the brick on her shoulder would have ripped through her parka.

"Oh dear." Marian sighed.

"Don't worry," Faith said. "You planned everything perfectly. It will all be fine."

But after the car was unloaded and the boys had grabbed their snowboards, rushing out the door as Betsey admonished them not to be late for dinner, it was clear that everything wasn't fine.

"I don't know why Mother didn't speak to me about this. It makes much more sense to have us in with them. Scott and Andy will keep Ben and Amy up late, for one thing. And I don't see why we all have to share a bath," Betsey said, looking around at the luggage hastily piled in the living room by her sons.

"We don't. This is a custom unit, and there are two master bedroom suites with baths upstairs and a half bath down here. The bedroom on this floor is big. It has two sets of bunk beds, which will be fine for the kids. Once Ben and Amy are asleep, nothing wakes them. Besides, it's vacation. Ben will be staying up later than usual, maybe even Amy, too, although she usually conks out early, despite her most valiant efforts."

"Don't you find if you veer from the regular routine, even during vacations, that children get off schedule and it can take weeks for them to get back?"

Faith had never thought about it this way. Vacation was vacation. When she'd been a teenager, not exactly in the Dark Ages, she'd gone to bed and gotten up when she'd wanted during vacation, none the worse for wear.

"I know you think I interfere in my boys' lives too much," Betsey continued, "but wait until Ben is their age, which won't be long. You have to know what's going on all the time. And deep down, Scott and Andy are grateful for the guidance and support."

How deep down? Faith was tempted to ask, but she kept her mouth shut. Betsey's words had struck a sore spot. Faith *was* worried about Ben, who suddenly couldn't seem to wait for his voice to change and his hair to grow in all sorts of new places. My God, he'll be using deodorant soon! Faith thought but what was upsetting her the most was that Betsey's words weren't all that different from those of Pix Miller, Faith's best friend and next-door neighbor in Aleford, whose own children were in high school, college, and beyond. Pix Miller, the Dante of child rearing. What Pix said repeatedly was, "Your children need you more in adolescence than they do in early childhood. Pretty much anyone can child-proof a kitchen, see to a nap, or read *Caps for Sale* three thousand times. But it needs to be a parent who's home when, say, the police call (Danny in the car when a friend hit a pole, fortunately no injuries, no alcohol) or your daughter arrives home from school in hysterics (Samantha, the last girl in her class to get her period).

Faith reached out to pat her sister-in-law on the shoulder, hoping to dislodge the brick. "I think you're a wonderful mother, and of course your boys appreciate everything you do for them."

Betsey brightened. "Did I tell you that Scott is going to do the Johns Hopkins program this summer? It's *very* selective, and we're all just thrilled. And Andy's going back to music camp. He has real talent. Fortunately, a flute is portable, so he won't have to miss practicing this week."

So much for vacations. There would be no veering.

Tom and the kids returned, followed shortly afterward by Dennis's arrival. Suddenly, the condo was filled with activity. Except for Dennis. Dennis had the affect of one of the large philodendra that typically grace a dental practice's waiting room. He and Betsey had been college sweethearts, marrying the day after graduation. She'd done office work while he got his D.D.S. degree, studying for her real estate license at night. Both tasks accomplished, Dennis joined a practice in Plymouth and Betsey joined Fairchild Realty. Having colonized the South Shore early in the twentieth century, arriving from Ireland by way of Boston's West End, various Fairchild branches had established Fairchild's Market, Fairchild's Realty, and, later, Fairchild's Ford. Dick had all but retired from the real estate business now, and Betsey was the only Fairchild in the office. Dick hoped to take Craig on, but he hadn't gotten his license yet. What Faith hoped was that the issue wouldn't come up this week, hot potato that it was. The last time it was discussed, Betsey had exploded at her brother—out of her parents' hearing—and informed him in no uncertain terms that she wouldn't let him destroy the family business, which she was carrying to new heights. He'd told her it wasn't her decision and he'd do what he wanted. Faith had left at that point, conveniently hearing Amy call.

Robert, three years younger than Tom, was Faith's favorite. He was the quintessential uncle, sending postcards often and surprising his nephew and niece with gifts. He was a sales rep for a sporting goods manufacturer and looked the part. All the Fairchilds were attractive, but Robert was handsome. He'd been a star high school and college baseball player, "the

Sox's loss," in family lore. He still played in, as he put it, "an old folks' league" and carried himself with the muscular grace certain athletes have. Robert loved sports—any and all sports. He'd watch grass grow just to see which blade came up first. He'd never married. Faith supposed it was a combination of life on the road and not having met anyone who would surf past any nonsports channels. He seemed happy to turn up for family gatherings—it had to have been difficult for him to take this week off, Faith realized—and happy also to quietly vanish from the room at said gatherings at the first indication of a "discussion."

Leaving the kids to Tom, Faith went next door to get dinner on the table. Robert had arrived and had already set places for the grown-ups at the big round table by the fireplace, and ones for the kids at the breakfast bar.

"Are Craig and Glenda here yet?" Faith asked after greeting him.

Robert silently pointed across the living room to the closed door.

"Newlyweds," said Faith, laughing.

"I guess." He smiled at her. "I hope she likes to ski. If you'd told me my baby brother would marry a woman who had never skied before, I wouldn't have believed it."

Craig was the best skier in the family—by far. Just as Ben looked up to Scott and Andy, Craig had worshiped Freddy Stafford, a champion racer in his day. Craig's old room in the house in Norwell was crammed with trophies. He really should have been a ski instructor or gone into the ski patrol. Robert had a job he liked, as did Tom and Betsey. It was only Craig who still seemed out of his element.

"It must be love," Faith said.

"What must be love, my gorgeous sister-in-law?" asked Craig, opening the door and walking toward them.

"You and your nonskier wife," Faith replied.

"You bet it is, but in a few days, the word *nonskier* will no longer apply. Glenda is extremely well coordinated—and motivated. She'll be flying down black diamonds before we leave."

Dinner was a noisy and convivial gathering. Everyone seemed determined to have a good time. Dick, the paterfamilias, was in his element. The chili was a success, although both Glenda and Betsey used the lettuce and crudités to make salads.

"I have to burn some calories before I can add any," Glenda told them. Though she didn't turn down an Otter Creek—a local microbrew—and then allowed as she'd have another instead of dessert.

As chairs were pushed back and belts loosened, Faith was thinking that Dick's plan had been an inspiration. The kids would always remember this time. This time of family togetherness.

Scott and Andy had squeaked in just before dinner, earning a disapproving look from their mother, although not a scolding. They'd cleared their dishes and were on their way out the door, hoping, Faith realized, to slip away unnoticed.

"Hey, you two, where do you think you're going?" Betsey called.

"Night skiing," Scott said.

"I don't think so. Take off those parkas and sit down."

Dick stood up. A scotch before dinner, a few Otter Creeks, and the fire had turned his face bright red. "Let the kids go, Bets. We're supposed to be having fun. All of us."

"But they can go another time, Dad. It's our first night here. I thought everybody would play Pictionary or bridge the way we usually do."

"Not me, sis, I'm going skiing. Cards are for when there's no white stuff around," said Craig, heading to his room to get ready.

Robert emerged from one of the upstairs bedrooms, carrying his skis, in time to hear his brother's words. "Great," he said. "I thought I'd be by myself."

Clearly outnumbered, Betsey said to her sons, "I guess you can go, but you should have asked first."

"Mom, can I go? Can I? Please, pretty please!" Ben begged. Faith looked around for Tom, who had apparently gone next door. She was on her own. Ben was too young to ski alone, and she didn't feel like going herself. Plus, there were all the dishes to clean up.

"You can come with me," Robert said, to Faith's relief and Ben's delight. "If it's okay with your parents."

"Go get ready, but only for an hour. It's been a long day," Faith said.

Tom returned, carrying Ben's things. Her husband had been one jump, or slalom or whatever, ahead of her, Faith realized. Soon only the women and Dick were left.

Birthday or no birthday, Dick Fairchild was not the kind of man who pitched in when it came to housework. Lawn, car, the exterior of a house, yes, but washing dishes—boiling water even—no. He sat down to read the paper and was soon fast asleep.

"Sit down and relax, Marian. These will be done in a jiffy," Faith said. "Besides, there isn't room in the kitchen for all of us."

Glenda and Betsey had already started rinsing the dishes and loading the dishwasher. The cleanup was soon finished. Glenda squirted some hand lotion into her palms, rubbed it over her hands, and reached for her rings. She'd put them in a saucer next to the sink with Betsey's.

After she'd slipped on hers, she held up one of Betsey's. "This is such a pretty diamond. I love the emerald-cut setting," she said, holding the ring up to the light and sending tiny sparkles over the counter.

Business must be good, Faith thought. It was a new ring; she hadn't seen it before. An early valentine? Betsey's wedding and engagement rings were modest, bought before Dennis had made any money. This ring was at least triple their karats, maybe even quadruple. Glenda obviously had an eye for diamonds—and not simply the black ones that marked the most difficult trails.

Amy was asleep in her grandmother's lap. Faith hoisted her daughter up on her hip. She couldn't do this with Ben anymore and wouldn't be able to with Amy much longer. She said good night to everyone. Glenda and Betsey had gotten out a pack of cards.

Next door, the condo was empty. The silence was welcome, and she planned to crawl into bed with a book as soon as Amy was settled. Turning on the light, a thought suddenly occurred to her. Where was Dennis? She hadn't seen him go off with the others. He wasn't next door, and there was no one here. The place had been dark. So where was Dennis the dentist, anyway? Probably at the Pine Slopes pub, having a drink on his own. Faith didn't blame him one bit.

Faith opened her eyes. One minute, she'd been thinking about the accident, then the night before—Marian by her side; the next, she must have fallen asleep. Now Marian was gone and Tom was in her place. Tom. She sat up and he put his arms around her, holding her tightly.

"I'm so sorry, sweetheart. It must have been terrible. Are you all right?"

Yes," Faith said, realizing it was true—or would be soon. The image of Boyd Harrison's body, which had been indelible before her nap, was blurred at the edges now. She had needed to sleep; hadn't slept well the night before. She never did the first night in a new place, and that was why she had gotten up so uncharacteristically early and, in the full flush of winter wonderland romanticism, decided to go cross-country skiing before the others were awake. She'd planned to be back in time to make the heart-shaped pancakes that were a Fairchild, as in Sibley-Fairchild, family tradition. She'd brought valentine cards for everyone and thought she'd make a quick trip into Burlington to the Lake Champlain Chocolate Factory's outlet store for heart-shaped favors for tonight's dinner.

"What are the kids doing? What time is it?"

"The kids are fine. We saw your note, and I wondered why you weren't back to make pancakes, but they were so hot to get to the Pine Cones, Saps, or whatever their groups are called that I gave them some cereal, took them over, and decided to take a few runs myself. It's almost noon." He shook his head and said ruefully, "It was stupid of me to go off like that and not be here with you."

"How could you have known?" Faith said. How could anyone have known? It was such a bizarre occurrence that she was having trouble believing it had happened. "Your mother gave me some tea and tucked me in, just like Mother Rabbit, and I've been sound asleep." She kissed him, hoping he would feel the reassurance behind the gesture. The last thing Tom needed was to feel guilty on her account.

Settling back in his arms, she asked, "Did you know Boyd Harrison?"

"A little. Mom, Dad, and Craig knew him the best. He was a great guy. Lived in Charlotte, which is near Burlington, and had a law practice. But he grew up with the Staffords here on the mountain and has always been their principal investor and booster—'Mr. Pine Slopes,' they called him. Five years ago, he had a major heart attack, and he's had several close calls since then. Everyone knew this was coming, and although they're upset, they know it's how Boyd would have wanted to go."

It was essentially what Marian had said, but Faith could take it in now.

"The Staffords have posted a simple announcement in the main lodge and a couple of other places about Boyd's death from heart failure. They knew word would get out, and you know how rumors start. If they hadn't, people would be saying that Boyd had met a grizzly or that something was wrong with the trail—things that would send people packing—and that's the last thing Pine Slopes needs."

Faith did know how rumors started, and she hoped that the announcement would do the trick. People didn't want to think of anything unpleasant while on vacation, and nothing could be more unpleasant than a death on the slopes. As it was, news of a heart attack on Valentine's Day was bad enough.

She sat up straighter, suddenly restless. "What are your plans for the afternoon?"

"My plans are your plans," Tom said.

"How about the rest of the family?"

"They're all skiing, even Mom and Dad. Betsey's outfitted her guys with walkie-talkies so she can keep track of them, and Ben wants one, too. He's not skiing on his own the way they are—and his parents are not obsessed the way my big sister is, but if we do go off, we might pick some up."

Faith wished she had had one earlier.

"Why don't we go off to Burlington?" she suggested. "Get the walkie-talkies and some chocolates for tonight? We could have a bowl of soup or something at NECI Commons. I've heard so much about it. The students at the New England Culinary Institute run it. Not fancy like their Inn at Essex—just takeout and a bistro. The only thing I have to do before we leave is check in with Jean, the chef, and make sure he has everything he needs for tonight. I left the cake with him yesterday. He's quite a character."

"True. I keep forgetting you haven't been here before. It's not every day that you meet a 'French' chef at a ski resort who wears Hawaiian shirts, hip-hop gold chains, and surfer shorts with his toque. But before we go anywhere, aren't you forgetting something?" He moved his arm down to the covers and pulled them back, sliding in next to her. "It's Valentine's Day, my love."

Jean Forestier didn't have a French accent, but he did have an accent— straight from the Bronx.

"My folks moved to Mt. Vernon—that's in Westchester—when I was a kid, but you know what they say: 'You can take the boy out of the Bronx, but you can't take the Bronx out of the boy.'"

Faith laughed. She had never heard this variation on the old chestnut.

"How did you end up in Vermont?"

"I've been asking myself that for the last twenty years, and I still don't have a good answer. Maybe it's time I got out, moved someplace warm, like Boston."

"Really, did you go to the Culinary Institute, or is it the skiing?"

"None of the above. I've never had a cooking lesson in my life— please don't tell my employers that—and I couldn't ski to save my life. In fact, you'd have to if someone strapped the things on my feet. Oh, I'm sorry. That was stupid. You're the lady who found Boyd, right?"

Faith nodded. "I'm okay now. I understand he had a very serious heart condition."

"Yeah." Jean, or John—the French name was too incongruous—

seemed distracted for the moment. "A couple of conditions. But what brought me to Vermont was what usually brings a man someplace—a dame, of course. My first—and only—wife. Very romantic. She's in the Big Apple, trying to find the Metropolitan Museum of Art, and asks a passerby, me, for directions."

"And people say New Yorkers aren't friendly," Faith interjected.

"Total bullshit," Jean said, nodding his head in agreement. "Anyway, one thing leads to another and I wake up hitched. Plus, her folks have a little inn in Vermont that needs a chef, so I'm a chef."

Jean looked to be in his mid- to late fifties. He had salt-and-pepper hair as curly as gemelli pasta, and was stocky and low to the ground. His bright red shorts came almost to the top of his black high-tops, revealing a few inches of black-and-white-striped socks. Today's shirt was Meyer lemon yellow and featured hula dancers. It set off the chains nicely. Faith was amused to note that one sported a golden frying pan.

"I like your family. They behave decently. You'd be amazed at the way some people treat a place like this. It's an honor for me to be cooking Dick's birthday dinner. I'm glad you brought the cake, though. Pastry has never been my thing."

While pastry was Faith's thing, it *really* was her assistant's. Niki had created a miniature Pine Slopes atop buttercream icing, which in turn covered layers of hazelnut ganache and dark chocolate cake. It was truly a work of art. As for the rest of the meal, Dick was a meat and potatoes man, unless he found himself at the venerable Union Oyster House in downtown Boston, the Hub's oldest restaurant. In that case, he was a clam chowder, Wellfleet oysters, scrod, and potato man—choices that served him well on his first date there with Marian in 1955 and had been serving him well ever since. And he didn't like surprises. He'd called Jean himself and worked out the whole menu: "Shrimp cocktail—everybody likes it—prime rib, hamburgers for any of the kids who can't handle the big beef, cheesy potatoes—call them gratin if you want, but they're still cheesy potatoes—and string beans with almonds—okay, almandine. And no salad. I'm tired of watching all the women in my family eat salad. Plus plenty of rolls. Parker House rolls. And butter. And champagne. Lots of champagne."

Dick had called Faith early on to run the menu by her. She had wanted to cook the dinner herself, but he'd been firm. It was his party and she was going to be a guest. He was okay with the cake, especially after Faith told him Niki was going to make it.

Jean had everything well in hand for their dinner, which would be served in a private dining room at the top of the main lodge, as well as for the more eclectic menu he'd be presenting in Le Sapin's main dining room. Faith was getting ready to leave, when a man came bursting through the door the waiters used to enter the kitchen. "Hey, John, I've—" He stopped short when he saw Faith.

"Hey yourself, Tanner. This is Faith, one of the Fairchild gang. She's a caterer, so I have to mind my peas and carrots tonight. Faith, meet Simon Tanner, our awesome Aussie manager."

"Hi," Faith said. With more than a passing resemblance to Crocodile Dundee, Simon Tanner towered over the chef. "I was just leaving. And Jean, I'm sure the meal will be perfect."

"Please, don't go on my account. I don't want to disturb your shop talk," Tanner said.

"It's fine. I'm late as it is. Nice to meet you."

"Likewise—Faith, is it?"

He had only a trace of a Down Under accent, but he managed to give her name two lilting syllables. She smiled and nodded, turning to say good-bye to the chef.

"I know the plan is for us to come to the restaurant our last night, and I'm looking forward to it very much," Faith said.

"Me too, fair lady. And maybe I'll have a surprise for you." He bowed low and kissed her hand.

Unlike her father-in-law, Faith liked surprises.

"I can hardly wait," she said.

———

Loaded with walkie-talkies and an abundance of Lake Champlain chocolates, Tom and Faith were heading back toward Pine Slopes, listening to "State of the Nation" on the local NPR station. Tom was driving and Faith was looking out the window at the not-so-attractive outskirts of Vermont's largest city. Marian had offered to pick the kids up from ski school, but Faith was still anxious to get back. They'd given Ben a snowboard for Christmas, after a multitude of unsubtle hints. He was already an excellent skier and wanted to join his cousins riding goofy or daffy on a board. He'd explained these terms, which had to do with whether your feet were parallel or turned, so thoroughly that Faith had felt both goofy and daffy herself. Amy had been a more reluctant skier than Ben was at her age, and Faith wasn't about to push her. She planned to spend time with her daughter skating at the outdoor rink, which Amy loved, or hanging around the pool at the Sports Center. The complex had been redone recently and the pool was now encased in a dome. When you swam, you were surrounded by the snow-covered landscape outdoors, an enchanting sensation—like a hot-fudge sundae: toasty warmth in the midst of mounds of vanilla ice cream. Which reminded her of the chocolates they'd bought—Heart Throbs, an apt name for the dark chocolate raspberry truffle hearts, and a variation on them, dark and white chocolate cherry hearts. Tom and she had sampled an array of the factory's offerings before making up their minds, while Tom sang, "Nice Work If You Can Get In" when his mouth wasn't full.

They hit a red light and Tom braked to a stop. A strip mall and motel offered little distraction until Faith leaned over, rolling the window down for a better look.

"Hey, what gives?" Tom asked as the light changed and he pulled ahead.

"The car in the motel parking lot. I think it was Dennis's."

"Impossible. What would he be doing here? And besides, he was going to spend the day skiing with Betsey and the kids. Don't think the walkie-talkies would reach this far."

Tom had to be right, but Faith knew what she had seen—a white

Prius with a Massachusetts vanity plate that read BY GUM. How many of those were there in Vermont?

Dick had invited Harold and Mary Stafford, plus Fred, Naomi, and Naomi's daughter, Ophelia, to his birthday dinner. The last three had been delayed, but Harold and Mary, more dressed up than anyone had ever seen them, sat quietly. Faith was sure that had tonight's party been for anyone except Dick, they would have bowed out. Even though it had been expected, Boyd Harrison's death had to have been a great shock and tremendous loss for them. Dick and Marian had suggested they put the party off to another night, but the Staffords felt Boyd would have wanted them to have it as scheduled.

The rolls and butter were on the table, and a festive heart-shaped basket filled with pink and red carnations, exactly the same color as the shrimp cocktail, sat in front of the birthday boy's place. Tom was making the first toast. Faith knew what was coming. It was a Fairchild family favorite.

"May those who love us love us;
And those who don't love us,
May God turn their hearts;
And if He doesn't turn their hearts,
May He turn their ankles,
So we'll know them by their limping."

When the laughter died down, Tom grew serious. "First, I'd like to thank Harold and Mary for all the happy times we've had at Pine Slopes. And Dad." He turned toward his father and held his glass high. "Tonight is the best so far. Happy Birthday."

He sat down, acknowledging the applause—and the ribbing from his brothers, who sat on either side of him. Faith was struck by the way Marian and Dick's features had been rearranged on all four of the children, and down to the next generation, as well. It was like one of those children's flip books, where you could change the eyes, mouth, nose, hair, and chin to make a different face from the one before. Tom and Craig had the same rusty brown hair, but Tom and Betsey had the same tall, lanky frames—Betsey's only slightly softened by a curve here and there. Robert and Craig were built the same, although Craig was shorter. Marian's eyes looked back from Tom's and Craig's faces, Dick's from the other two. All four had the same broad, generous mouth as their father, the same grin, which crinkled their eyes and was impossible not to return. Glenda would bring some new genes, as had Faith and Dennis, although it was hard to predict what this might mean in the way of hair and eye color. Faith had noticed the contacts and presumed the dye job. Ben and Amy were towheads, like Faith had been at their age, but they had the Fairchild smile and build. The Fairchild boys—big, hungry guys, who seemed to burn off whatever they ate as soon as it went in—had made short work of the shrimp cocktail and were reaching for more rolls.

The Fairchild boys—and girl: Tom, Robert, Craig—and Betsey. Or "Bets," "TP" for Thomas Preston, and "Buddy" as in little Buddy for Craig, who was as much of a family mascot to his brothers as he was a family member. It occurred to Faith that Robert didn't have a nickname. Not even "Bob" or "Bobby." She'd never heard him referred to as anything but Robert. In the rough-and-tumble world that was the Fairchilds' childhood—Tom had broken his arm twice, falling out of a tree and playing touch football; fractured his leg once, jumping from the garage roof; and had managed to collect pale souvenirs of other scrapes all over his body—Robert, although a part of it all, remained, well Robert.

"Before we get to the main event here, I want to make my own toast. Now Marian, don't tell me it's not the proper thing to do."

"I wouldn't dream of it," she said, just as if she hadn't heard him rehearse all afternoon.

"First of all, I'm tickled pink to be here with all of you on Saint Valentine's Day. We made it!"

He waited for the clapping and whistles to die down.

"On the occasion of my seventieth birthday, allow me to propose a toast to the family, to the Fairchilds and the three wonderful spouses who have not merely joined us but also enriched us with their presence."

"Hear, hear," cried Craig, loudly kissing his wife.

"And to you four grandchildren—Scott, Andy, Ben, and Amy—you make us proud every day of our lives."

Amy buried her head in her mother's lap. She had never been toasted before. Ben picked up his champagne glass, which was filled with sparkling apple juice, and said, "And we're proud to be your grandchildren, Grandpa!"

Either I've a future Rotarian or a member of the diplomatic corps on my hands, maybe both, Faith thought. She clinked glasses with him.

"Thank you, Ben. Now, I know you're hungry, boys, but indulge me a little longer. One of my friends at home, Ed Martinson—you all know Ed—told me years ago about the way they toast in Norway, the old country to him. Whenever we're at his house, this is how they do it, and I'm going to do it tonight. You look straight at the person you want to toast and maybe give a little nod; then you both take a drink. I've got two glasses filled and I want to toast each of you. So here goes. Skoal!"

This time, there was no applause or catcalling. In silence, Dick looked deeply into the eyes of each person there, reaching down into each heart and soul before moving on to the next. It was a wonderful moment. When he came to her, Faith felt a lump in her throat. "Happy Birthday," she whispered, adding another toast softly to herself: "May you enter heaven late."

The prime rib and accoutrements, cheesy potatoes prominent, arrived, and Dick sat down. When he'd heard Scott and Andy ask for the beef, Ben had ordered it, too—rare, just like theirs. The huge chunk of meat was threatening to spill off the plate, and Ben eyed it with something akin to dismay. Faith was about to lean over and tell him not to worry about finishing it, when Robert whispered something in his nephew's ear, causing him to break out in a smile. He'd make such a great father, Faith thought, not by any means for the first time, and took a moment to run through her mental Rolodex of singles, despite the fact that Robert had politely but insistently refused all her matchmaking efforts.

"Just in time!" Dick cried as Fred and Naomi walked into the room. "Scotty, run out and tell them to bring the shrimp cocktails. You can eat fast and catch up," he said, beckoning the couple to their seats.

Scott stood up and headed for the door, almost colliding with the third member of the Stafford party. It was Ophelia. Faith didn't need an introduction, even though she'd never seen the girl before. The figure trailing morosely behind had sixteen-year-old female angst writ large all over it. There were visible piercings just about everywhere something could be punctured, and Faith imagined the baggy black jeans and cropped T-shirt proclaiming SHIT HAPPENS hid more. One wrist was tattooed with a barbed-wire bracelet, and again Faith suspected further decoration beneath her clothes. She wore boots with heels so high and soles so thick, they looked orthopedic. Ophelia's dark hair was short, a kind of devil-may-care nail-clipper look. She had one long magenta-streaked lock that hung down across her face, trailing to her chin.

And she was beautiful. Very, very beautiful, despite her every attempt to disguise the fact. Faith knew from the boys that she was "an awesome boarder." She was trying to shuffle into the room, but her innate grace and energy wouldn't allow it, and she almost sprang into the chair next to Andy's.

"I'm so glad you could make it, Joanie. No, no, I know that's not it. It's Miranda now, right?" Dick Fairchild was training his magnetic smile on the girl, and for a moment she was pulled in, a glimmer of one appearing in return on her lips. Then she caught herself.

"Ophelia, it's Ophelia," she said sullenly.

"Knew it was one of those Shakespeare gals. Welcome to my party, Ophelia, Fred, and Naomi. Now all the Staffords are here."

Ophelia seemed about to say something more, but instead, she started whispering to Scott, who had returned, closely followed by a waiter with the Staffords' appetizer. Faith watched Ophelia eat the lettuce, avoiding the shrimp. Then she handed the almost full plate to

Andy Parker. She shook her head when the waiter came around with the main course. She was beautiful, but she was too thin. Whippet-thin and, like the dogs, her rib cage was clearly visible. It pressed against the spandex shirt, an X ray. Ben was mesmerized by her and was leaning so far over in his chair in an attempt to be part of the older kids' conversation that it threatened to tip over.

Joan, or Joanie, didn't suit the girl. This was no poodle-skirted teen from a fifties-type sitcom. But Ophelia—an unsettling substitute, surely? Hamlet's doomed lady? It was not the sort of literary character Faith would want a daughter of hers to choose to emulate, if that was what this was. Naomi herself hadn't exactly lucked out in the name department—biblical, not Shakespearean. Faith had a vague recollection that the biblical Naomi was somebody's friend. Ruth's maybe? Anyway, adopting the name of someone who kills herself is generally a flag for the parent of an adolescent, and Faith hoped the younger Staffords were taking it seriously. Where was Ophelia's father? Not behind an arras at the moment. The walls in the private dining room were paneled with knotty pine. Was Naomi a widow or a divorcée when Fred married her? she wondered.

Plates were cleared. The noise level had increased. The room was becoming almost unpleasantly warm. Amy the dormouse was heavy-eyed amid the commotion and the heat.

"Come out on the balcony with me and let's get some fresh air, sweetie," Faith said, pushing out her chair. Amy followed her, and they went across the room and slid open the door leading to the balcony. It was a clear night.

"Look at the stars, Mommy. They're all bending down near us."

They were. Revived by the cool air, Faith kept one eye on the party so they wouldn't miss the cake's arrival. It was like watching a play, the door frame the proscenium arch. Craig tapped his glass and stood up to make a toast. He'd had a lot of wine and his words were slightly slurred, but not his emotion.

"Raise your glasses to the memory of one of the best, Boyd Harrison. Hey, guy"—he held his flute aloft—"I don't know what we're going to do without you." He sat down heavily, and Faith was surprised to see him pull out a handkerchief and dab his eyes. She hadn't known they were that close—or maybe it was the champagne. The cake was coming, and she scooped Amy up and rushed back to the table. After they sang to him, Dick gathered his grandchildren and Ophelia around him.

"You're going to have to help this old geezer blow all these candles out. Did you ever see such a cake!" he glanced appreciatively at Faith. "Okay now, one, two—"

"Wait, Grandpa." Amy tugged at his sleeve. "You have to make a wish!"

"Darling girl, my wish has already come true. You four can have my wish for me. Now blow!"

They did a thorough job, and after Dick made a ceremonial cut, the cake was taken back to the kitchen to be sliced and served with "plenty of ice cream," as per instructions.

To fill the time, Betsey stood up to make a toast. Her hair, normally pulled back in a tight knot, was loose. The sparkling wine had given a sparkle to her eyes, and her cheeks were rosy from the day's skiing. She looked very pretty, and much younger than her carefully guarded over forty age.

"To you, Daddy, the best father a girl could ever want, and also a big thank-you to the Staffords for all our years of friendship and the chance to be at this very special place. Here's to you, Harold, Mary, Fred, Naomi, and Ophelia!"

Even over the clapping and Craig's "Way to go, Bets," it was impossible to miss Ophelia's voice—or the slamming of the door that punctuated it.

"I'm not a fuckin' Stafford and never will be!"

FOUR

"Simon says this; Simon says that. Get lost—oops, you can't, because Simon didn't say so!"

Faith could hear the angry words, but without revealing her presence, she couldn't see the speaker. She was stretched out on a chaise by the side of the pool, watching Amy swim. The voice was coming from the adjoining game room.

After last night's party, everyone had slept in. Ophelia's dramatic exit hadn't produced the effect she had no doubt desired. There had been a moment of shocked silence, true—with steam coming out of Fred's ears and tears moistening Naomi's eyes—but the party didn't end. Dick had clapped Fred on the shoulder, patted Naomi's arm, and called for more champagne. "I wish I had a nickel for every time a door got slammed in our house," he'd said.

Clearly feeling his friend and mentor's pain, Craig had almost spoiled the moment by pointing out that if any of them had used the *f* word or spoken in that tone of voice to either parent, they'd have been booted off to military school—or in Betsey's case, a convent with ten-foot walls—faster than a speeding bullet. He'd been about to continue in this vein, when Tom had intervened. "Yeah, we were paragons all right. Not like today's kids." He winked at the four cousins, who had turned to stone the moment after Ophelia opened her mouth. "We owe you a nickel for every slammed door, Pop, and how about a dime for every bike and then car tearing out of the driveway faster than a speeding bullet?" Everybody had laughed, including Craig, and the party went on longer and took on an even warmer tone than it would have without the theatrical interlude. Faith watched the Fairchilds spin a cocoon of comfort around the Staffords, who had lost their closest friend only that morning and were, it was now clear, dealing with the teen from hell, or just your average adolescent, depending on one's point of view.

Harold and Dick had regaled them with a nostalgic look back at ski history, starting with a paean to the Scandinavians. "The earliest-known record of skiing dates back to 2000 B.C.—petroglyphs etched on a rock wall on an island off the coast of Norway," Harold told them. "One pictures a person on long narrow skis twice his height. Norway's Telemark region gave its name to the low, deep-kneed turn, skiing's oldest method of turning, and also produced the 'father of modern skiing'—Sondre Nordheim, who had the brilliant idea of adding a birch heel strap to the leather toe strap for greater control when descending. Skis were shortened and the lone pole used as a kind of outrigger was replaced by two shorter poles. From a method of transportation across the snowy wilds, skiing emerged as a major sport, a national pastime.

"Of course, it took awhile to catch on here," Harold had went on. "Scandinavian immigrants brought the sport with them. There was one guy, called 'Snowshoe Thompson,' who skied to deliver the mail to the mining towns in the Rockies. The mining companies even had racing teams. Imagine those logos! But Vermont is the cradle of U.S. skiing. Don't you ever forget that! Around 1900, a bunch of Norwegians or Swedes—can't remember which—were living near Stowe and started using skis to get around in the winter. It took awhile for people to stop laughing, but it caught on, and the very first ski race was held here at Mount Mansfield in 1934. Then Woodstock's Bunny Bertram invented the first rope tow in the United States—powered by a good old Model T engine—around the same time. It was kind of tiring hiking up all that way. Fred Pabst came up with the J-bar lift in '36. My dad was one of the first to try it out. First ski patrol started then, too, over in Stowe."

Dick had continued the saga. "It seemed like everywhere you looked, there was someplace to ski in these mountains. Maybe just a rope tow or maybe something more complicated. After the war, there were the 'snow trains' leaving from New York City and Boston for Vermont. The army veterans of the Tenth Mountain Division were like gods to us. They started areas, taught people how to ski, and ran the ski patrols."

"It was still pretty primitive," Harold had said to his mostly wide-eyed audience—Glenda had been half-dozing. "One of my first jobs was at Mad River Glen in 1949, foot packing. Didn't have groomers, so that's what we had to do, go up and down the trails, packing the snow down with our feet. And in the summer, we had to go back all over again and clear away any rocks. You got to know the mountain up close and personal. Course, things have changed a lot." He'd sighed, but Dick hadn't been about to let the bubbles fizzle out of his party.

He'd raised a glass and made a final toast: "Pine Slopes forever!"

The answering chorus had been everything Harold could have wished for, if the broad smile on his face and mistiness in his eyes were any indication.

This morning, after a prolonged breakfast, everyone except Faith and Amy had hit the slopes. Apparently, Glenda's private lessons were proving to be a big success, and she couldn't wait to practice what she'd learned the day before. "Roy says I'm doing amazingly well for a beginner. He couldn't believe I've never been on skis before!" As she left, Faith had noticed Glenda was wearing a different outfit—and more makeup—than the previous day. A cloud of Obsession hung in the air. *I wonder what this Roy looks like,* Faith had thought, then rebuked herself for cattiness. Glenda and Craig were obviously very happy with each other, and Glenda's enhancement of her already considerable charms was merely routine, a reflex, like the way a teenage boy buffs and polishes his first car.

Faith snapped back to the present. The argument was continuing in the next room. "You are such a baby, Josh. You just can't stand the idea of having to give up even one inch of your sacred Sports Center. You made it more than clear that you didn't want the Nordic Center here, and precious little room you've given us. What Simon is proposing is only fair— and common sense. We're the fastest-growing part of Pine Slopes, and more of a draw than your pathetic pool tables any day!"

It was a woman's voice, petulant and taunting. Faith wished she could see her. Josh had signed the Fairchilds in. He was a guy who was obviously spending his spare time using the weight-training equipment. He appeared to be in his mid-twenties, and the only thing keeping him from Mr. Universe contests was a face pitted by acne scars.

"Now, just you wait a minute. As manager of the Sports Center, it's up to *me* to allocate space. Granted we're getting more of them, but most of your Nordic yahoos only need a place to sign in and pay the trail fee. You know that as well as I do. They bring their own food to eat outdoors and don't buy anything from the Sports Bar. It's crazy to think that taking space away from the lounge for a Nordic shop is going to produce any more sales or rentals than we're already getting by having it with the Ski Shop in the main lodge! The TeleManiacs bring their own equipment, and the guests who buy or rent are more apt to do so if they see the stuff right in front of them up there."

"For your information, Simon and I have been checking out the way other resorts handle their Nordic centers, equipment sales, and rentals. *All* of them have expanded their centers and attached separate Nordic shops to them. You are so yesterday. The boomers are trading in their downhill skis for cross-country, skate, and telemarks—not to mention snowshoes—while their kids and grandkids downhill or board. They want the exercise, but they don't want knee surgery or a broken hip. We've doubled our snowshoe rentals this season. Our nightly backcountry headlamp tours are a huge success, and you know it. So, maybe the couch potatoes will have to sit a little closer to watch the crap you run on the big-screen TV. That crowd's mostly teens anyway, and they're not generating much profit!"

"Talking to you is totally pointless," Josh retorted. "Apart from the exercise room, tennis courts, and the pool, people—adults—come here to relax, have a beer, and watch a movie after skiing all day. Shoot a little pool, play Ping-Pong. You've never even bothered to check it out. Neither has Simon. But fine, move all your ski wax down here—real high profit margin there. But before anyone starts modifying this building, I want to hear about it directly from the Staffords, not 'Mr. Simon Says' Tanner and his star performer, little Miss Sally Sloane!"

"O! I can't believe you're acting like this! I wasn't happy to move from the Nordic cabin here, but it was way too small, and then I thought we were doing all right together. Simon said you'd get petty about turf, but I told him he was wrong about—"

"Simon says . . ." Josh jeered, breaking in.

"Shut up! Just shut up about the whole thing! I'm sorry you're taking it this way, but the decision has been made, so like it or lump it!"

"I'm not the one who's going to be sorry—and I'd watch out if I were you, or—"

A door slammed, cutting off whatever Josh had intended to say. Slammed doors. There seems to be a lot of that going around these days, Faith thought. But there was nothing like a turf battle to awaken the sleeping beast in every man, woman, and child. Whether it was over my side of the room as opposed to yours, a fence dividing two yards, a border in the Balkans—or the footprint of the Pine Slopes Sports Center—these wars had a way of escalating. She didn't envy the Staffords their job, or Simon Tanner, the manager, either. She wondered what would happen next. It seemed unlikely that the Staffords didn't know about what Simon and Sally were planning. Josh *would* have to like it or lump it. Amy had recognized him from last year and greeted him joyfully. He'd remembered her, too—or put up a pretty good show of doing so. Faith thought this could well be the job he'd stepped into out of school, and it certainly was his bailiwick.

"Watch me, Mommy!" Amy called. She was at the shallow end of the pool, diving for the brightly colored weighted rings Faith had brought along. On this sunny Sunday morning, they were the only ones at the pool. Everyone else was outdoors. Faith had wanted Amy to have a break, and she liked the idea of one for herself, too. Yesterday had been an emotional free-for-all, staring with her tragic discovery of Boyd Harrison's body and ending with her father-in-law's joyous birthday celebration. Life and death.

She'd swum some laps, sat in the Jacuzzi, then read while Amy stayed in the pool. Her little minnow. Skiing was still a new challenge, and Faith didn't want Amy to feel overwhelmed. Ben always roared full steam ahead into every new experience. Amy was more tentative, putting a toe in first, testing the waters. Her two were as different from each other as the Fairchild offspring—and she and her own sister—were from one another. The endless combinations and recombination of the gene pool. If it was true, as people said, that every child in a family has a different father and mother, then surely every parent has a different child. She laughed out loud as she thought this. It was the kind of illogical statement that Pix and Niki would appreciate. She'd have to try and remember it. She missed her friends. Tom was reverting to being one of the boys—in this case, one of the Green Mountain Boys—and she didn't have anyone who shared her sense of humor. Pix and Niki were also unabashed students of human nature, or gossips, to use a cruder term. Faith would have liked to run the Josh/Sally situation by them. Did Josh have a thing for Sally? And now Simon was on the scene instead? There was certainly a great deal of energy being generated in the next room, but without seeing their faces or watching their body language, Faith couldn't say what kind.

She regarded her little girl, a Nereid beneath the David Hockney blue pool water.

"Sweetie, you're turning into a prune. How about we hit the showers and go see what's going on with everybody else? If you feel like skiing this afternoon, I'll take you, or you can go back to the class."

"Okay, but just one more dive?"

"One more," Faith said firmly. This was an attribute common to all species, the old "just one more" trait—one more minute, one more turn, one more page, one more bite. At this very moment up in the backcountry, a young deer was pleading with its mother, "Just one more nibble of bark and I'll go. I promise."

On their way out, they passed Josh, who was serving steaming bowls of onion soup to a group of Trapp family look-alikes. Mama, Papa, and kinder were all in cross-country ski garb—Tyrolean ribbon trim, and could those knickers be lederhosen?—chattering away about the excellence of the trails. The Sports Bar served wine and beer, but also chili, soups, wrap sandwiches, and Ben & Jerry's ubiquitous, and always tempting, offerings. Josh looked preoccupied, and Faith was sure he wasn't pleased that his customers of the moment were living proof of Sally's argument.

When she opened the front door of their condo, Faith was surprised to hear voices, and even more surprised to find Scott, Andy, and Ophelia sprawled out on the couch, watching some sort of cartoon. She was a surprise to them, too. Ophelia grabbed the remote and turned the TV off, stood up, and seemed about to sprint for the door.

"Hi, everybody. Taking a break?" Faith said. "You don't have to go, Ophelia, and please finish what you were watching. Maybe Amy would like it, too."

"I don't think so. Anyway, we were just about to head on out," Ophelia said abruptly, still poised for flight. Her baggy ski clothes, de rigueur for boarders, hung on her skinny frame like a tent on a tent pole before it's pegged. The boys gave their aunt and cousin small smiles and almost imperceptible waves.

This could be my only opportunity, Faith thought suddenly. Betsey had the boys so programmed, even during the vacation week, that finding them alone like this might not happen again.

"I just had an idea. Why don't we go to Gracie's in Stowe and have some of those fabulous burgers Ben and Amy have been telling me about? You'll still have plenty of time to ski. I'll leave a note for your parents and Tom."

"Yeah, that would be cool," Scott said.

Andy was already up and pulling on his parka.

"Of course we'd like you to come too, Ophelia," Faith said. And she meant it. She wanted to get to know the girl better, especially because of the obvious hold she had on Faith's nephews—and her son.

"I don't eat dead animals," the girl said.

"Well, I hope you don't eat live ones," said Amy, squealing. She began to laugh so hard at her own joke that Andy had to thump her on the back.

"Good one, Ames. Better than the mouse one," Ophelia said, revealing a familiarity with her daughter Faith had not known about. Amy had a whole string of typical first-grader jokes. They featured mice, as in: "What do mice wear to play basketball? . . . Squeakers." Her riddles were worse, much worse.

"I'm a vegetarian," Ophelia explained. "You know what that is, right?"

Amy stopped giggling and answered seriously, "Yes. Their church is the brick one. Ours is wood."

"I think you mean Presbyterian," Faith said and this time it was the boys who were in hysterics. "A vegetarian is someone who doesn't eat any meat but does eat fruits and vegetables, and sometimes fish. I'm sure Gracie's has plenty of items on the menu you could eat, Ophelia, and we'd love to have you join us."

Ophelia shook her head. Whether it was the prospect of watching the others chow down on ground beef or because she plain didn't want to go, Faith decided not to pursue the matter any further, and the girl slipped out the door.

"We just have to leave the note, then stop and pick up Ben. They won't have eaten lunch yet."

The children in the ski school had cocoa breaks and a hot lunch that fell into the Kraft macaroni and cheese culinary genre. Ben and Amy adored it.

"Get ready, everybody, and we'll leave in a few minutes."

Faith went upstairs to rinse out their bathing suits, and when she opened the bathroom door, there was a distinct smell of cigarette smoke—at least she hoped it was cigarettes. The window had been left open, so it was hard to tell. She sighed. Any hint of this to her sister-in-law would produce the familial equivalent of the Cuban missile crisis. She resolved instead to keep her eyes open—wide open. Scott and Andy seemed like the last kids who'd smoke, but then all the kids you saw smoking were, too.

Driving down the mountain with a carful of kids, Faith felt a surge of happiness. Yes, the vacation had started out on a sad note, but again she thought how special last night had been. Dick had loved his party.

The cousins were singing "A Hundred Bottles of Beer on the Wall," much to Ben's delight, and Faith didn't care. Normally, even one line drove her round the bend.

Both children had described Gracie's to her in minute detail, but Faith was not prepared for the extent of the doggy decor. The small restaurant was on the bottom level of a building in the center of town. A very convincing gas version of a log fire crackled in a large fireplace at one end of the room, and a bar anchored the other. The ceilings were low and the space was filled with booths and tables—all of them filled at the moment with contented-looking diners. Tiny white lights twinkled in artificial pine boughs on the fireplace mantel and along the top of the walls. But it was these walls that drew one's eye. Every square inch was covered with dogs—photographs, prints, paintings, and posters. Fido, Bowser, Spot, Lassie, William Wegman's Man Ray, Lady, Tramp, Rin Tin Tin, Asta—dogs were everywhere. All sizes, shapes, and breeds. Show dogs and mutts. There were dogs playing cards, dogs sleeping, dogs eating, dogs sitting up, and, in Man Ray's case, dogs dressed up. A picture of Gracie, a winsome Airedale rescued from a shelter by the owners some years ago, took best in show.

When they were seated, Faith discovered the menu continued the theme. The burgers weren't named for celebrities like the ones at Bartley's Burger House's in Harvard Square, a Fairchild favorite, but named after breeds. Faith ordered a Chihuahua burger medium rare (burger with guacamole) and the Parkers went for the Boxer (burger with cheddar cheese and bacon). Ben followed suit. After careful consideration, Amy, the adventuresome gourmet—or Gourmutt, as the shop upstairs selling all sorts of doggy items was called—chose the Blue Tick Hound, asking the waitress for plenty of blue cheese. Faith also ordered a couple of things to stave off hunger until the burgers were ready. The baskets of thin, crunchy onion rings and hand-cut french fries disappeared so fast, she ordered some more. The same with the glasses of milk—it would have been simpler to have asked for a pitcher. She looked at her nephews and could see Ben in a few years. Insatiable. And funny. They were off the leash. The jokes were flowing fast and furious. She vowed that no matter what, she would let Ben—and later Amy—be as independent as possible when they got to this age. Guidance, yes; total control, no.

As if on cue, Ben piped up: "I don't think it's fair for Aunt Betsey to make Andy and Scott do things they don't want to do, Mom. I mean, I don't always want to take a bath or go to bed, but that's different. This is big stuff, like what they want to do with their *lives*." Ben was impassioned and his voice, still in the range of an English choirboy's soprano, hit a high note.

The hamburgers arrived, and her nephews dug in immediately, but Ben wasn't going to let the matter go.

"Really, Mom, can't you talk to her? Or can't Dad? She's *his* sister!"

"Ben, I don't think the Parkers want any interference in their family life; you wouldn't want someone interfering in ours."

"Oh yes I would," Ben said firmly "If my mother was acting like a tsar."

Faith remembered the fourth grade had studied Europe in the fall, and one of Ben's countries had been Russia. "Tsarina," she said, correcting him automatically; then, hoping to divert her tenacious son, asked, "How are the burgers?"

"Woof!" Amy said, her mouth full.

"Great," Scott and Andy said simultaneously, then immediately fell mute. The high spirits of moments before had vanished.

Ben had opened Pandora's box, and Faith realized she would have to deal with it.

"You do know that if you ever want to talk about anything that's going on at home or in any part of your lives that Tom or I will be happy to listen—and happy not to repeat anything you told us?" She was afraid she'd been a little too firm in response to Ben, and it was possible that one or both of the boys needed advice. She couldn't help but think of the smoke she had smelled in the condo bathroom.

The two brothers looked at each other. Scott had finished his burger. Andy quickly took a big bite of his. Clearly, he was happy to let big brother handle this one.

"What Ben's been picking up on is that we don't want to do what my mother has planned for us this summer, but there's no use talking to her. When she thinks you should do something, you do it."

"But I thought Andy liked the music camp. Didn't he go there last summer? And this Hopkins program is supposed to be excellent, Scott. You'll meet kids from all over the country," Faith said.

Andy swallowed. His newly protruding Adam's apple bulged like a boa that had devoured a mouse. "I did go and I do like it. I like it a lot, but I don't want to play the flute. I hate the flute. Last summer, I started playing the saxophone at camp, and they said I was really good, but she wouldn't listen—not even to the camp director. No, she picked the flute out for me when I was six, and the flute it will be until I'm at Lincoln Center, another James Galway or Jean-Pierre Rampal."

"How about talking to your father? Have you tried that?"

"Once or twice about a million years ago," Scott said bitterly. "He is totally whipped." He blushed. "Sorry, Aunt Faith. I just mean that he won't get involved. For me it's that I'm tired of doing schoolwork all the time, and the Hopkins thing is heavy-duty. Yeah, I'd meet new kids, but what time would I have to be with them? I wanted to have one summer for myself. I'm going to be in school or working at some job my whole life, or until I'm like sixty something, which is a long time to wait. I wanted to stay home and be with my friends."

"Especially *one* friend," said Ben, chortling.

Scott gave him a playful poke in the ribs. "I wouldn't be doing nothing. That is like the worst sin in my house, and anyway, it would be boring. So I asked at the library, and they said I could work there. Plus, I can work for the town recreation department, helping out at one of the day camps. But when I told her all this, she went nuts, kept talking about shutting doors, how it would look on my college applications—as if I care—and 'deferred gratification,' whatever that is. Anyway, hello Hopkins."

Faith stifled a groan. She wasn't very good at deferred gratification herself, never had been.

"I still think you have to give your father a try. Maybe he doesn't realize how strongly you feel." It was all she had to offer, and she knew it was pretty pathetic.

"Dad's not around much. He works late, and sometimes he even goes in on Saturdays when a patient can't schedule a weekday appointment. If he doesn't know how we feel, it's because he doesn't want to know."

Faith sought to console them with Doggie Bones for dessert—blond chocolate-chip and pecan brownie "bones" topped with vanilla ice cream, hot fudge, and whipped cream—and the conversation turned to snowboarding. Ben had moved up a group and was ready to head out with his cousins. They promised to take him to the half pipe as soon as his instructor gave them the okay.

"And Ophelia? Do you think she'd come with me? Mom, she is awesome. The best of anybody."

"It's true, Aunt Faith," Andy said. "She should be competing, and she would be if her family wasn't so fu—I mean, kind of complicated. Nobody can do a Missy Flip like she can."

"That's where you twist and flip at the same time," Ben explained kindly.

Amy was kneeling on the seat, communing with a large poster of Dalmatian puppies, so Faith felt the adult turn the conversation was taking was all right for the moment. Amy had the kind of mind that retained every word, bringing them forward at inauspicious moments.

"It seemed pretty clear last night that she doesn't feel she belongs in the Stafford family, but I don't see why. I don't really know them, but I haven't heard anything about her grandparents and parents that hasn't been good."

Scott, who was rapidly maturing before her eyes, leaned toward her, his arms resting on the table.

"Ophelia was all right with everything until her dad remarried and moved to California. Up until two years ago, she lived with him during the week in the house she grew up in and went to school in Burlington. She came out to Pine Slopes for the weekends and vacations. Now she's stuck here all the time in a school with total morons, and every time she wants to go see her old friends, Fred and Naomi have a fit. They took her car away, which they had no right to do, because her dad gave it to her, not them. Phelie never liked Fred—and face it, he is a total Dudley Do-Right—but she could stand it when she wasn't with him all the time. And he really doesn't like her, Aunt Faith. Yeah, our family has known him forever, and he seemed okay before, but I know he wishes she weren't around."

"Couldn't she go live with her dad in California?"

"He thinks she should stay in Vermont, her home, with her mother, all sorts of bullshit—sorry again. But that's what it is. The real deal is, his new wife doesn't want her any more than Fred does. And now they have a baby themselves, a boy. They have never once asked Ophelia to come out there. Her dad sends a check every month and that's it."

"And what about her mom?" Amy was losing interest in the Dalmatians, and Faith wanted to hear the rest of the story fast.

"Naomi is only interested in Fred. It's weird. My mom is too wrapped up in her kids, and Ophelia's isn't enough. Naomi does stuff like take away her car keys—probably because Fred told her to—but she has no idea what is going on with her own kid."

And that would be what? Faith thought, not sure she wanted to hear the answer.

After lunch, they walked around the center of Stowe, which took a very short time, and then stopped to browse at the country store, which combined authenticity—it had been there forever—with giftiness, a whole lot of items connected to maple syrup, skiing, and cheese. The food, the unburdening—who knows what?—seemed to bring back the good vibrations vacation feeling. The cousins cavorted along the streets like the puppies on the walls at Gracie's. Finally, Faith realized it was getting late and they'd better get back if the kids were going to have any time to ski. She wished there had been time to see the show of Judith Vivell's extraordinary bird paintings at the Clarke Galleries. They were huge canvases, captivating to all ages. Maybe they'd be able to get back to Stowe later in the week.

There was no one at the condo when they returned. Scott and Andy grabbed their gear, leaving with a hasty thanks to Faith, plus, to her delight, a quick hug from each. She had finished getting Ben and Amy ready, deciding it would be easier to come back for her own stuff after dropping them off. Just then, she saw a note that must have fallen to the floor when they'd come in.

Faith,
Come next door as soon as you get this.
Thanks,
Fred

It was written in pencil, and either he'd had the same penmanship teacher as her doctor or he had been in a terrible hurry. It took a moment to decipher the words and even the signature.

Obviously, it wasn't urgent. Otherwise, he would have waited for her at the condo. She was curious, but first she had to take the kids to their classes.

"Okay, helmets, goggles, gloves, neck warmers. Is that everything? Bathroom?"

"Mom!" Ben protested.

"Just checking. Let's go." She opened the door and stepped out into the sunshine. It was warm, and she was looking forward to being on top of the mountain without a biting wind. She might not need her French long johns after all.

Marian was walking up the path to the condo.

"Faith! Where have you been? Never mind. Just go on in," she said, motioning next door. "I'll take the kids up to the ski school."

"Didn't Tom and Betsey see my notes?" Faith asked, wondering what the rush was all about.

"Tom has been skiing with Robert all day, and Betsey has been with us, trying to get her kids and Dennis on the walkie-talkies, but they're still on the fritz."

Betsey had complained at length about the walkie-talkies at dinner the night before and was preparing to write a stinging letter of complaint to the head of the company that manufactured them. She had been unable to reach any of her family all day. At breakfast, she had replaced the batteries and was giving the CEO one more chance before she fired off her missive.

"I took all the kids into Stowe for lunch. We haven't been gone long."

"It doesn't matter now. Just go. I'll be right back. Fred will explain everything." And Marian was off.

Faith stood in the sunshine for a moment, now thoroughly bewildered. What had happened to the notes she had taped prominently at eye level on the inside of the front and back doors? The back door led directly to the slopes, and she'd figured she couldn't miss with that one; the other was just insurance. Neither note had been there when she'd arrived with the kids. Tom must have returned, assumed Betsey had seen them, and taken them down. And what was going on with Fred? She hoped it didn't involve Ophelia.

Kissing her ski afternoon good-bye, she walked next door to the Fairchilds' condo.

It was so comical to see everyone jump up the moment she opened the door and stepped inside—so many jack-in-the-boxes or puppets on a single string—that she was tempted to repeat the performance. What on earth were they all doing here? Harold, Mary, Fred, and Naomi Stafford, Simon Tanner, her father-in-law, and Betsey. For the first time, she felt anxious. But surely Marian would have said something.

Fred stepped forward. "Faith, great! We have . . . well, we have a situation on our hands."

"Let her sit down, Freddy," Harold said. "And sit down yourself. We look like a delegation from the State House. Now, here's the problem." Harold Stafford had taken command, comfortable back in the role he had played so well for so long. "Our chef has quit."

"Skedaddled," Dick said. "French, wasn't he?"

"No, from New York—the Bronx," Faith said, realizing at once that if anything, this was worse. Dick Fairchild's skepticism regarding people from the Big Apple, inhabitants of a decidedly non–New England orchard, was etched deep. He regarded his son's marriage to Faith as the equivalent of the rescue at Entebbe.

"We'll understand completely if you don't want to do this," Harold said. "It's your vacation, but if you could pitch in until we can get someone else, we would appreciate it very much."

"You would receive the same remuneration the chef did, of course," Simon Tanner interjected. Love was one thing; money was another.

Faith looked around at the faces before her, anxious faces—except for Dick Fairchild's. He was angry.

"Of course I'll help. I'd be happy to. But are you saying that John has left without a word to anyone?" She asked Simon.

"He wasn't around at breakfast—we do a brunch on Sundays—but that's not his job, although he usually comes by. We didn't start to get concerned until later. He always meets with his crew to go over the dinner menu at one o'clock. When he didn't show up, someone called his room. There was no answer, so they called me to see if I knew where he was. I went to his room and found it locked. We were afraid he might have had some sort of accident—he carries a lot of weight for a man his height—so Pete came with a master key and we went in. Clean as a whistle."

Fred took up the tale. "We know a number of resorts have been trying to hire him away from us for years, not just places here in Vermont but in other parts of New England and even out in Colorado. He used to joke about it and said he'd never leave, but somebody must have dangled a pretty penny in front of him."

Mixed metaphors aside—and what would you do, drill a hole in the penny?—Faith was still having trouble reconciling the man she had spoken to yesterday with the traitor of today. Yet he *had* said something about a surprise. What were his words? "And maybe I'll have a surprise for you." Except they'd been talking about Friday night, the last night the family would be at Pine Slopes, having a farewell dinner at his restaurant.

"Perhaps he went back to his wife's family inn? Have you been in touch with her?"

Simon and Harold exchanged an uneasy look.

"The inn has been closed for some time," Simon said tersely. "And the same for the marriage."

He clearly wanted an answer and wanted it now. Faith had no idea how long all of them had been waiting, but it couldn't have been pleasant. Every room and condominium in the resort was booked for the week. She wouldn't have been surprised to hear that the restaurant was, as well. Aside from the loss of income, closing the restaurant, even temporarily, would be a disaster for Pine Slopes. People would talk, and what was an ordinary occurrence in the restaurant world, a change of chefs, would instead become a cause célèbre. The resort's reputation would be at stake, everyone asking why the restaurant had to close. It would be the equivalent of food poisoning for a caterer—and they all knew what that meant. You might as well toss in your whisk, because the closest you'd get to food-related work would be cleaning rest rooms at Burger King.

Faith looked at her watch. "I'll need to start right away. When was the last food delivery? When's the next? How many people on the kitchen staff?"

"Whoa, lady." Simon's accent suddenly thickened, and it was charming. Faith's assistant, Niki, had spent some months Down Under, extending the trip to the point where Faith had been sure this was one little Sheba, or Sheila, who wasn't coming back.

"How about you change and then I'll take you over?" Simon suggested. "You have ample staff, and Sysco came yesterday. If anything, there's probably too much food."

Sysco was a big, high-quality supplier. This was good news.

"And don't worry about the kids," Dick said.

"As soon as Tom comes back, he can take over," Faith said. She didn't want Dick and Marian's vacation taken up with their grandchildren, much as they adored them. It was still Dick's birthday time. "They're all set until dinner anyway," she added. "Oh, dinner. There's spanakopita—you know, the Greek spinach pie—plus grilled chicken. The kids won't be hungry until later. We went to Gracie's for lunch. . . ."

"Faith, we'll manage, believe me. Between your mother-in-law and myself, we raised four kids, so I think we can deal with two!" Dick gave her a kiss and pushed her toward the door.

"We can't thank you enough," Harold said. His words were echoed in various refrains by the rest of the Staffords. "We have some good leads, and I'm sure we'll have a new chef in place by tomorrow, Tuesday at the latest."

Betsey had been quiet throughout, and now she got up and followed Faith.

"Phew," said Faith, as they stepped outside. The sun was lower in the sky, but it was still a beautiful day, and the air felt wonderful. "When I saw all of you sitting together, it looked like a wake." As soon as she spoke, she wished she could take back her words. Betsey had known Boyd Harrison well, and it was an ill-considered remark. Marian had told Faith that Boyd had left instructions for a memorial service to be held at the foot of his beloved mountain on the first sunny day in June. There would be no wake for him. Or for Pine Slopes, either. They had found a chef, albeit a temporary one.

They walked into the condo. Faith looked at her sister-in-law. She was trembling.

"Betsey, what is it? Are you all right?"

Elizabeth Fairchild Parker folded her arms in front of her chest and stood squarely in front of Faith. "No, I am *not* all right. How dare you take my children away without parental permission! And to Stowe, just to eat some lunch! They are here to ski, and if there is a change in plans, I, or their father, will make it! I know that food is next to God or something for you, but that is not the main thing. The main thing is that you are *never* to do this again!"

Now Faith was trembling. She didn't think she had ever been this angry in her life. She walked away from Tom's sister, but stopped at the bottom of the stairs and turned around.

"First of all, they are not children. They are thirteen- and fifteen-year-old adolescents. Next, I am their aunt, a responsible adult, who would never put them in any kind of danger. I thought only of providing a fun outing for the four cousins. I left notes for you and Tom taped to the inside of the front and back doors. I have no idea what happened to them. And now, finally, don't you *ever* speak to me this way again."

She went upstairs to change into whatever she could find that would pass for kitchen garb. Granted, she was low in the Hawaiian shirt, gold chain, and surfer shorts department, but she had jeans and a white turtleneck. They would have to do.

Betsey was gone when Faith came back down.

The kitchen staff was as colorful and multicultural as the chef, that Hawaiian-Franco-Bronxian. Faith had heard how difficult it had been for the Staffords to get help, especially in recent years. There was the problem of where to house people if they didn't live locally, and Pine Slopes was small. It couldn't compete in salary, benefits, and perks with the larger places. This explained why the housekeeping and kitchen staff was primarily from South America this year.

"They're almost all university students," Simon explained. "It's summer for them, remember, and this is an ideal way for them to practice their English, have an adventure."

Faith seriously wondered how much of an adventure it was coming to a land of ice and snow to make beds, chop onions, and vacuum floors far away from not only a metropolis but a town. Yet the Peruvians and lone Bolivian in the kitchen seemed a cheerful bunch. She tried out her Spanish on them, which may have accounted for the broad smiles and giggles that greeted her. She'd stick to English.

They got straight to work. Despite his casual attire, John had been extremely well organized. Besides the standard nightly menu, which featured what the average diner would look for—a recognizable form of chicken, a recognizable form of seafood, surf 'n' turf, and pasta primavera—he'd listed the specials for several weeks ahead. Was it always this way? she wondered. Or did he know he was leaving?

The crew had started the prep work for dinner. Again, John had trained them well, and Simon walked her through the drill. It wasn't hard, especially since Le Sapin only served dinner.

"We're booked tonight, but we can take some walk-ins. Sunday is a turnaround day, so people often decide at the last minute not to cook in their condos, but to come here instead. They're generally later than other diners, so we can turn over some of the tables three times.

"And Faith, I know the chef stays until the bitter end, but you're to get out of here once the last dessert is served—or even before. I leave it to you. These guys know how to clean up and close down. I'll be in and out. Harold, too."

"Thanks, but it will be fine." Faith wanted to tell him that this was child's play for her—a small restaurant in the hinterlands of Vermont. She'd done larger cocktail parties even in the Aleford area—forget New York. But she didn't want to brag. Plus, there wasn't time.

Tom appeared at five o'clock with Ben and Amy.

"I know, I know, you're very busy. We're leaving. Came to do this." He gave her a big hug and a kiss, the kids between them like the filling in a sandwich. "You can't imagine how grateful the Staffords are. You saved their lives, or livelihood, I should say. It could have gotten pretty ugly tonight when people showed up and found out the cupboard was bare."

Her husband looked wonderful after these two days of skiing with his brothers. Relaxed, slightly tanned. She had been planning to tell him about Betsey, but he looked too happy. Besides, there was very little Faith could tell him that he didn't already know.

After they left, Faith walked out into the main dining room to check on everything. She'd read that Queen Elizabeth did this before every banquet at Windsor or Buckingham Palace, making her stately way down past the gilded chairs, eyeing the line of gold plates, perhaps pointing out a slightly out-of-kilter vermeil fork to one of the white-gloved servants following in her wake, who would align it correctly for "Ma'am." Faith twitched a tablecloth that had caught on the arm of a chair and then stood back. Everything was ready.

She could hear laughter from the Pine Needle Pub across the hall. Like the Sports Bar, it served some soups, chili, burgers, and a few sandwiches and desserts. But mostly it was a place to have a drink and look out the picture windows at the slopes. It was beautiful now, the lights on for night skiing—fascinating to watch the skiers come down, all of them made graceful by the glancing light and deep shadows.

Faith walked to the door leading out into the hall and looked over at the pub. In the deep shadows, well away from the windows, sat her sister-in-law Glenda, a Viking prince across from her. They were practicing the Scandinavian skoal, eyes locked, but both their glasses were empty at the moment. A waitress went by and the prince called out, "Two of the same."

"Sure, Roy," she answered.

FIVE

The back door was opening slowly. The fluorescent light over the sink that they left on as a night-light was enough to pick up the motion. Instinctively, Faith ducked behind the counter, clutching the glass of orange juice she'd come down to get—sleepless even at 1:30 A.M., jazzed from the night's work, jazzed by a whole lot of things.

She wasn't afraid—yet. All she had to do was scream and the three adults upstairs would be alerted. No, she wasn't afraid, just curious.

The frigid night air swept into the room as the door opened wider. It must be windy outside, she thought. Not a night fit for man nor beast. Nor burglar. But it was absurd to think it was a burglar. There was nothing in the condo worth taking—no plasma TV, no high-tech computer equipment. The cutlery was Betty Crocker box tops stainless and the plates yard-sale mismatches. Any major jewelry was firmly on the owners' fingers. Besides, it was Vermont, a place where the bovine population had exceeded the human population in number until recently. The most rural state in the Union—with a minuscule crime rate.

A low voice asked, "Everything okay?"

There was no reply. The other person must have gestured. She heard the door shut. Soft footsteps were stealthily creeping toward the kitchen area. She moved farther back into the corner where the counter met the stove, crouching down even lower. She had a pretty good idea who it was now, and she wasn't sure she wanted to be seen. The figure passed by and headed straight for the bedroom down the hall.

She was right! It was Scott.

As soon as she heard him close the door, Faith raced to the window at the rear of the condo—her slippered feet gliding noiselessly over the carpet—and looked out. She was just in time to see a figure walking slowly away. When it reached the spotlight outside the last unit, Faith saw it was Ophelia—hatless, seemingly oblivious to the cold, that unmistakable purple streak of hair blowing straight back in the wind, a pennant.

"Damn," Faith said softly. This was more information than she wanted to have. What was she supposed to do? Sneaking out and then back in like this was a rite of passage for kids Scott's age, but what was he up to with Ophelia? If Faith told Betsey, she'd ground him for life, and certainly the family vacation would be ruined. If Faith didn't tell Betsey and Betsey found out that Faith hadn't told her, Faith would be grounded for life, and the family vacation ruined. What about confronting Scott? She didn't feel comfortable about doing that, either. *She* wasn't his mother. What would she say to him?

As the disquieting thoughts made an untidy pile in her mind, she continued to watch Ophelia. Where was the girl going? There weren't any houses or condos in that direction—only woods. She couldn't be camping out in this kind of weather, although Faith knew there were plenty of diehards who did. But why would Ophelia pitch a tent, with a warm bed nearby? When Fred's parents retired, the younger Staffords had taken over the house Fred had grown up in. It was a small stone Arts and Crafts–style lodge built near the main lodge, but far enough away for privacy. The original owner of the resort's 260-plus acres had built it some time in the twenties as a retreat from his mansion overlooking Lake Champlain.

Wherever Ophelia was heading, it wasn't home.

Faith felt sorry for the girl. She'd had multiple disruptions in her short life, starting with her parents' divorce. Faith remembered something a divorced friend of hers had said some years ago when Faith had naïvely commented that the kids must be happier without all the tension in the house. "Your husband—or wife—could be an ax murderer, or, more commonly, the two of you could be having knock-down-drag-out fights every night, and your kids would still want you to stay together. And what's more, they always will. Yes, you may be doing it for them and it may be the right and only thing to do, but there's always a place in every kids' minds where they're praying that mom and dad will get back together—and I'm talking about six-year-olds and sixty-year-olds. Hope never dies."

This would explain Ophelia's attitude toward Fred, and, by extension, the rest of the Staffords. Her father's remarriage, move, and subsequent abandonment of her—if Scott was to be believed—had only made things worse. Taking her away from her friends must have been the last straw. Pine Slopes was the booniest of the boonies. You couldn't even get cell phone reception here, an adolescent girl's lifeline. Maybe that's when Joanie became Ophelia—and maybe a whole lot of other things, too.

The girl had disappeared into the woods, and Faith realized she was still holding her orange juice. She drank it and considered whether to get something to eat. The restaurant had been packed, and although she'd left before the cleanup, she'd worked straight through from 5:00 P.M.—they ate at ungodly hours in New England, she'd discovered as a new bride—until 11:00, when a group she assumed to be New Yorkers stopped ordering more desserts. She'd been too busy to eat, then, back at the condo, too tired. Everyone had gone to bed, exhausted by the day's activity. Faith had been relieved. She had no wish to see Betsey. She knew at some point she'd have to say something to her sister-in-law and smooth things over, but not yet.

Tom had stayed up, reading in bed, waiting for her.

After a very satisfactory greeting, he'd told her that the Staffords had a lead on a chef. Faith was pretty skeptical that they could find someone so soon at the height of the season and was sure she'd be on call for a few days. Maybe they could trace John and hire whomever he'd bumped.

She'd started to tell Tom about Betsey's over-the-top reaction to the boys going to Stowe for lunch, but he'd started talking about Boyd Harrison's will, and she'd shelved Betsey for another time.

"He wasn't married, was an only child, and his parents had been dead for quite some time. But he did have a major beneficiary. The problem for the Staffords is that they owed Boyd quite a lot of money. He'd put some capital into the resort outright, but some was as a loan. And now it has to be paid back to the estate. Apparently, this isn't someone with an interest in the resort or working out some sort of repayment plan. I'm surprised the Staffords didn't foresee this possibility, especially given Boyd's health."

Faith had been, too. "Or Simon, he's a sharp cookie, and he must have known about the arrangement. He keeps the books. Maybe they all assumed Boyd had forgiven the debt in the will."

Tom had agreed. "Maybe he planned to, but nothing was specified. He was a lawyer, you know. It sounds a little like the old saw about shoemakers' wives going barefoot. . . . At least he had a will.

"The other problem," Tom had continued, "is that the Staffords and Boyd were still just at the talking stage about some new snowmaking equipment—essential if a resort is going to survive. Global warming makes golf resorts, not ski resorts, happy. Nothing was on paper, just a verbal agreement that he'd put up half the money. Fred was hoping to get a deal at the end of the season from one of the manufacturers."

"No wonder they're frantic about losing their famous chef; they can't afford any losses," Faith had said. "How did you find out about all this anyway?"

Tom, unlike his wife, did not make it his business to ferret out information, especially this kind of information. Presumably, his mind was on higher things.

"Craig. You know how close he is to Freddy. It's not a brother or father thing. Hard to explain. Soul mates, maybe. I think the happiest times of my brother's life have been here at Pine Slopes. Both of these guys could have made the Olympic team. Fred couldn't afford to; Craig . . . well, you know Craig."

Faith did. Her brother-in-law, much as she loved him, lacked the self-discipline—and willingness to accede to the authority of a coach—required for this ultimate challenge.

Tom had continued. "I'm worried about how hard Craig is taking Boyd's death. It's almost as if he feels Boyd did it on purpose, which is nuts. But he keeps talking about how Pine Slopes could go under and what a disaster that would be. Thinks that Boyd should have left everything to Freddy and Naomi, or Mary and Harold. He's very angry." These last words, although dramatic, had been said with a yawn, and they had turned out the bedside lights. Besides not telling Tom about the eruption of Mount Betsey, Faith had also figured it wasn't the time to tell him about Craig's wife, Glenda, and her Nordic god of a ski instructor.

Her thoughts returning to the present, Faith decided against warming up the lone piece of spanakopita—the layered combination of feta cheese, spinach, and flaky phyllo dough had obviously been a success (see recipe on page 236). She put her empty glass in the sink and went back upstairs for what she fervently hoped would be some kind of night's sleep.

The woman's body was facedown in the pool, arms and legs splayed out. The water, as still as the figure, was stained red, uneven rivulets of color against the blue tile. Her long blond hair floated at the surface in gory squidlike tendrils.

Sally Sloane screamed and raced to the phone, first dialing 911, then Simon at the lodge.

"Don't go in there!" She dropped the phone and tried to block the families emerging from the locker rooms and rapidly approaching the pool.

The vacation week had started in earnest, and the resort was packed—particularly the Sports Center on this overcast morning, as people awaited the meteorologist's prediction of a clear, sunny afternoon to hit the slopes.

"What's going on?" Josh asked. He'd been checking people in at the front counter and handing out towels, keeping a close tally to shove in Simon's face when they met later to talk about the facility. Every piece of equipment was in use; there was even a waiting list for the treadmills. If anything, they needed to expand the exercise facility. Josh was a fair telemark skier himself, but he wished the Nordic Center had stayed in the quaint little cabin by the trails and kept out of his place.

His place! He looked at Sally. She had shut the door to the pool and was blocking the entrance with her body, all one hundred pounds of it. What the hell was she doing?

It was pandemonium. Parents were rushing their kids back to the locker rooms. They couldn't go outside in their bathing suits, and outside was where everybody wanted to be.

"Josh! Thank God!" Sally cried. "There's a body in the pool. Someone must have come in early, one of the lap swimmers. And she's . . ." She started to sob. "Dead!"

Josh made his way over to her and put his arms around her. "Have you called the police?"

Sally nodded. "And Simon. He should be here any minute."

"You should have called Fred." He dropped his arms.

A line of large plants obscured the view of the pool from the rest of the Sports Center, but there was nothing in front of the door.

"Move out of the way, Sally," Josh said.

"You're not supposed to disturb a crime scene until the police get here." She'd stopped crying.

"Move over, you idiot! Now!" Josh pushed her to one side and opened the door. Watching him go close to the pool, Sally turned her head away. She didn't want to see that ghastly figure again.

Josh was back in a few seconds.

"Everyone, please listen," he said loudly. "I'm afraid our Nordic director has made a mistake—a very natural mistake. What she saw in the pool is a stupid prank. The body is one of those inflatable ones—the kind I don't really want to talk about in front of children. It's not real. There is no one in the pool, alive or dead." He glared at Sally.

"I think I'm going to be sick," she said, and bolted from the room.

Josh repeated his statement. There were a few guffaws and some people wanted to go look, but Josh locked the door. Whatever it was, it still looked very real—and it was going to be a bitch to clean up.

"Please stay and use the rest of the Sports Center. In the bar, I'll be offering food and drinks on the house."

He saw Simon come in with the woman who had been in the pool with her little girl yesterday. They seemed to be together. He deliberately turned his back on them and called the police. Maybe he'd be able to stop them before they came charging up the mountain road, sirens blaring. The way his life was going lately, though, he doubted it.

Faith had awakened tired and determined the best cure would be to get some exercise. Tom took the kids to ski school and Faith agreed to meet him for a morning of skiing together after she checked in with the kitchen. She had planned to call Niki this morning to tell her what a success the cake had been and to check on a recipe for mushroom soup (see recipe on page 233). This one was a delectable combination of fresh and dried mushrooms in a rich broth. She wanted to serve it as one of the specials, but the call could wait.

No sooner had she arrived in the kitchen than the phone rang. Juana answered it and immediately began shrieking. The rest of the help clustered around her, and after a sea of Spanish, one of them said to Faith, "A dead body—all chopped to pieces—in the pool!"

Faith promptly turned around and went back out the door. Word had apparently not spread yet; outside, everything looked normal. Running, she almost collided with Simon at the top of the stairs that led from the lift ticket booths to the road down to the Sports Center.

"You heard?" he said.

She nodded, and he matched his pace to hers.

On the way, they encountered a stream of people and a torrent of confusion. One woman grabbed Simon. "Mr. Tanner! What's going on? Is the woman in the pool dead or not?"

A teenager ran by, laughing. "A sex toy! This is some cool place!"

What on earth could he mean? Not stopping to find out, Faith kept going.

Inside the Sports Center, they could see Josh on the phone, and the place was relatively calm. But the people who were left were expressing a full range of emotions.

"I'm packing, and we're getting out of here right away! What if Tommy had seen it? I thought this was supposed to be a family resort!"

"The poor Staffords! Didn't they just lose his brother or someone over the weekend, and now this? It must be those young snowboarders. I blame the parents."

"It certainly looks real, from what you can see through the door. We should pull this on Harry next summer. You know the way he feels about that precious pool of his!"

"Josh." Simon was striding over to the phone as he spoke.

Faith went to the glass door and looked through. There wasn't much to see except what was apparently a blond wig, now streaked with red, floating on the surface of the grotesquely red water. It was a horrible prank—and an easy one to carry out, she thought. The extremely realistic party girl was available on countless Web sites in countless forms, but Faith didn't think the nearest stores—convenience, liquor, or "Made in Vermont" outlets that sold cheese, maple syrup, wooden bowls, things with cows on them, things with moose on them, and endless crafts—ran to this sort of item, although in a free-spirited state like this, she could be wrong. Faith peered more intently at the "body"—and it was quite a body, from what she could see. If she hadn't come with her own curly locks, a wig could have been glued in place. Blow her up, toss in a Baggie of fake blood—or some homemade concoction with food coloring—punctured for a slow ooze, and then throw the lady herself on top.

But when? It would have to have been after Josh opened up. A sign on the front entrance indicated that the facility was protected by an alarm system. He would have activated it when he closed up last night, then shut it off this morning when he came in. What time was that? She'd have to ask him. What made the most sense was that someone had hidden in the Sports Center and spent the night, slipping out once Josh had dealt with the alarm. There was a door from the pool to an outside deck that was used in the summer—Pine Slopes was a year-round resort, catering to hikers, leaf-peepers, and skiers alike. The deck was buried in mounds of snow. It would be a simple matter to check if someone had been able to get out that way. Or the merry prankster could have been wearing sweats and blended right in with the crowd—blended in, then out.

Sally returned, pale and fighting back tears. She went straight to Simon's side.

"I'm so sorry. She—it . . . looked so real!"

"You did exactly the right thing, calling for help immediately. Anyone else would have made the same assumption, and I hope would have reacted the same way in such an emergency. Don't beat yourself up, luv." Simon gave her a hug. "Why don't you take the morning off? When you get back this afternoon, it will all be gone."

Josh was glowering.

"Why didn't you at least go a little closer? Anyone would have been able to see it wasn't a real body!"

"Josh, that's enough!" Simon said crisply, the Brit in his Aussie accent coming to the fore. "Sally is not to blame. Someone else is, and when I get my hands on him, he's going to be very, very sorry."

"Or her," said Fred, who had come in and was approaching the group. "I'm afraid this has my stepdaughter's name written all over it."

"But Ophelia couldn't have," Faith blurted out. "I saw her late last night. That is, I saw her outside near our condo. I'd gotten up to get a drink. A drink of orange juice." It wasn't coming out right, any of it. "I mean, whoever did this had to have hidden in here overnight."

"Not necessarily," Josh said. "After I opened up, there were plenty of times when I was away from the front desk and wouldn't have seen any-one come in or out."

"But they'd be so noticeable," Faith said. "Carrying that . . . that thing around. It had to have been done at night."

Simon was getting impatient. "We can figure out all the whys and what have yous later. Now, we need to clean up this mess and calm every-body down. How about a Hawaiian pool party or something, if not to-night, then tomorrow night? Get people back in the swim." He grinned.

It was a good idea, Faith thought. But it might take a little more than a few mai tais to get her in there.

Josh had managed to stave off the sirens, but the police arrived to check out the situation, and Faith found herself superfluous. Plus, she re-membered her husband. Tom had probably heard about this by now and assumed she'd be here, but he'd still be eager to climb into the chairlift.

As Faith left, the police were questioning Sally, and it looked as if she wouldn't have her morning off after all. Josh and Simon were standing on either side of her. Faith had the distinct impression that without the girl in between, the two men would be at each other's throats.

Faith tracked Tom down in the cafeteria. He and Robert were eating fries. They were laughing about something. Dick really did do a good thing, she thought. These two, in particular, seldom had a chance to spend any time together, let alone revert to the malt shop stage. Robert was drinking a Coke, and Faith half-expected to see some erupt from his nose. The paper cover from the straw was nowhere to be seen, and she was pretty sure it was on Tom's lap.

"Hey, it's about time!" Tom said. "I know, I know, you had to go down to the Sports Center to find out what's going on, but now it's time for some of my kind of fun. The sun's out and the slopes are calling us!"

"I'm sorry, but—"

Tom put up his hand. "Say no more. I'm a very understanding hus-band, right, bro?"

"You're the perfect husband—and Faith's the perfect wife. Now let's get out of here," Robert said.

They were tossing out their trash when Scott came running up to them, wild-eyed and panting.

"You have *got* to talk to Fred Stafford. He thinks Ophelia put that dummy in the pool. She keeps telling him she had nothing to do with it, but he won't believe her! He is such an asshole."

"Hold on, nephew," Robert said, pulling him over toward an empty table. They all sat down. "First, what makes you so sure Ophelia didn't do it? She made it pretty clear the other night that she has no great love for the Staffords."

"I know." Scott looked miserable. "Sometimes she gets a little out of control, but she would never do anything like this. Plus, how could she? I mean, she would've had to have a key to the Sports Center and know how to disarm the alarm. Or maybe she just walked in there this morning with the doll," he added bitterly.

"Look, we don't know who did it. It was a very stupid—no, make that very *harmful*—prank. Fred's upset. But his relationship with his stepdaughter is a family matter. We can't tell him what to do," Tom said.

"I knew you'd say that!" Scott pushed his chair back angrily. "If Phelie wanted to hurt this place, she wouldn't just put something in the pool."

"Come ski with us. Put us all to shame," Robert coaxed.

"That's a great idea," Tom said. "Ben wants me to take up boarding. I can rent one and you and Uncle Robert can get me started."

"Not today," Scott said, his tone indicating that it wouldn't be any day.

Faith had been silent, wishing there was something she could do. Tom was right: They couldn't interfere in this. Craig was the only one who was close enough to Fred for it to be appropriate, and Faith was sure Craig would be even harder on Ophelia than her stepfather. It would be that convent with the ten-foot walls for sure.

Scott stood up and gave them what might have been a wave. His face was still flushed.

"Be with you in a minute," Faith told the two men, and followed her nephew out of the cafeteria.

"Look, Scott, it's not that we don't understand—or care. For that matter, I don't think Ophelia did it, either. Unfortunately, this is the way some people get their kicks, and there's obviously a very sick individual staying here at the moment. But what I wanted to say to you is that I've already told Fred that I don't see how Ophelia could have been involved, and when I see him later, I'll mention it again."

Scott's face brightened. "Thanks, Aunt Faith. Phelie needs all the help she can get."

"And Scott, even if this hadn't come up this way, I'd intended to mention to you in private that I think you had better stick to your curfew."

He looked surprised.

"I was having trouble sleeping last night—or rather, very early this morning."

Her nephew looked embarrassed. "We weren't doing anything. I mean we weren't messing around, if that's what you—"

Faith interrupted him. This was getting to be more than a need-to-know situation. She just wanted him to watch out for himself. Ophelia definitely needed help, but Faith definitely didn't want Scott the Saint Bernard to be the one to rescue her. Why was it that a certain type of teen, including herself at that age, was a magnet for peers in need? In her case, it had been a Heathcliffe look-alike with a serious drinking problem. She'd thought she could save him. She'd thought wrong.

"We're here to have a fun week, and I know she's your friend, but spend time with the rest of the family, too. Someday you'll be glad you did. I know, I know, I sound like a preacher's wife. Funny thing."

This brought a smile to his face and one to hers, as well. She *had* sounded like a preacher's wife. She'd better be careful.

Something bleeped deep within the folds of Scott's oversized boarder's pants, and he fished out a walkie-talkie. Faith had forgotten about Betsey's tracking devices.

"I'm outside the cafeteria talking to Aunt Faith. . . . No, I don't know where he is. Probably with Dad. . . . Yes, yes. . . . I said yes. . . . Sorry. Bye."

"I have to go look for Andy. Andy wanted to check out the pool, so I'll see if he's there. Anyway, well . . . See you."

Scott was getting better-looking each year, taller, broad-shouldered, his curly dark hair even thicker. A heartbreaker, you'd assume, but more likely his heart was on his sleeve. Oh, that she could keep Ben from all this!

As she walked back to the condo, she noticed that a resort employee was taping bright red notices on various locations. Faith looked at the one now prominently posted outside the deli. It was a severely edited version of the pool incident, with the standard request for information about the perp or perps. The bulk of the notice announced that tomorrow night would be Nordic Night at the Sports Center. Apparently, Simon had changed his mind about a Hawaiian night in favor of this theme. Josh must be livid—and maybe that's why Simon did it, Faith speculated. She read on. Besides all the glögg you could drink, there would be Little Viking swimming games in the pool, a Land of the Midnight Sun tennis tournament at the indoor courts, screenings of Xtreme X-Country videos, and a Norwegian Bachelor Farmer look-alike contest. The whole facility, including the sauna, would remain open until midnight. Out-doors, a horse-drawn sleigh would be available for rides through the woods, and headlamp snowshoe and ski tours would continue all evening. The last line read "Feast on Scandinavian fare at Le Sapin's special smor-gasbord! Reservations suggested." Faith frowned. It wasn't that the change would be difficult—Swedish meatballs, salmon with a mustard dill sauce—and she'd send someone out to pick up some other ingredients for more dishes, especially yellow split peas for a traditional soup. They had plenty of locally smoked ham to dice up, the other essential ingredi-ent. Desserts could be renamed, and Niki could fax the recipe for princess cake, although not everybody liked marzipan. She could replace that with another icing. No, it wasn't the task that annoyed her; it was not being asked. Unless they'd found a new chef, someone hailing from Oslo? She mulled this over as she made her way back—as well as the incredibly in-appropriate choice of color for the notice: bright red. Just like the water in the pool.

It had been fun skiing with Tom and Robert, but she'd left them for a soak in the oversized tub in the master bedroom suite before heading over to the restaurant. She was glad they were in this unit, although the elder Fairchilds' was nice and considerably larger. The owners of this condo were obviously more hedonistic than Tom's family, who thought a five-minute shower was the first step on that downward path and a whirlpool like this one, the descent into the very maelstrom itself.

Now she was stretched out on the very comfy chaise lounge, a phone cradled in her hand. The window nearby overlooked a spectacular view of the valley and Mount Mansfield beyond.

"Dick loved the cake! Didn't want to cut into it at first, then of course he was happy he had, 'cause it was so yummy. I'm glad we took some pictures."

On the other end, Niki said, "What's wrong? Is it that sister-in-law of yours? You've got that fake 'These are a few of my favorite things' tone in your voice."

It was very difficult to fool Niki. But where to start?

"Let's just say it's not the vacation I thought it would be."

"But you thought it was going to be the vacation from Hades. Don't tell me it's worse than that!"

"Okay. Not worse, just different—and there have been some very nice parts. Saturday night was nice. The cake *was* perfect, and this isn't Julie Andrews speaking. But early that morning, I was cross-country skiing in the woods and I found a friend of the resort's owners dead from a heart attack, and—"

"Faith, not another body!"

"Natural causes, completely natural causes. He had a very serious heart condition and was some kind of walking time bomb."

"Still, you poor thing. It must have been horrible. This is why I never get up early unless I have to. Come to think of it, you never get up early, either. Didn't you and Tom used to flip for Saturday mornings when the kids were babies?"

"I was awake, and it looked so beautiful out. All those pine trees, the snow, no one around. Nature beckoned."

"Well, next time, tell Nature to take a hike. It's very dangerous."

"Then the chef walked out yesterday, and they haven't been able to—"

"Find anyone to replace him or her, so naturally you're doing it. Faith! What's going on? Isn't this a business? They could get some temps from NECI."

"It's complicated because the owners, the Staffords, are such close friends of my in-laws, and I think they were afraid to take a chance on even a very qualified student. The place is full and the restaurant's booked every night. But they have a lead, and I'm only doing it one more night. Really, it's a snap. Only dinner, and it's a great crew. They're all from South America. I'm learning a lot of Spanish—well, kitchen Spanish."

"Do you want me to come up? We don't have anything until the Tischler bat mitzvah next Saturday night."

"No, really. It will only be for one more day, and you need time to finish the wedding plans."

"Look, I'll pay you to call my mother and tell her there's an emergency and I need to help you out."

Niki was getting married in June. She had wanted a December wedding, but her mother had other ideas. She'd also wanted a simple ivory slip gown, but was ending up looking, as she said, "like one of those crocheted dolls my aunt Alcina makes to go over the spare roll of toilet paper." For years, Niki had managed to alarm her large Greek family with her choices, only to fall head over heels in love with the man of their dreams—a Greek-American Harvard MBA who carried pictures of his nieces and nephews in his wallet. Niki was seriously thinking of getting in touch with HBO to offer the ceremony and reception to the producers of *My Big Fat Greek Wedding II.*

"The only thing I need is for you to look up how much chicken broth is in the Apology mushroom soup and call me back." They called the soup this because the recipe had come from their friend David Pologe, whose last name was pronounced like the word's last three syllables, hence "A Pology" mushroom soup. It was a way to differentiate it from the scores of other mushroom soup recipes they'd collected.

"Okay, but please no more bodies, no more jobs. You're supposed to be having fun."

Faith decided not to mention the party playmate in the pool, but she needed to tell her friend about Betsey.

"What a witch! Or more like the woman definitely needs some magic bullets, little round white or pink ones."

They laughed.

"Promise you'll tell me if I ever get that involved with my kids. I keep wondering what she's going to do when they leave for college. Somehow, I don't think Dennis is going to be willing to take their place." She flashed on the picture of his car outside the motel. Maybe he'd just been asking for directions.

Faith gave Niki the number for the resort's kitchen and said goodbye. She wished Niki were here, but this was family time. Although she considered Niki part of her family, she wasn't part of the Fairchild clan. Faith hadn't wanted to tell Niki that one of the main reasons she didn't mind pitching in at Le Sapin was that it was a whole lot more fun in the kitchen with her new friends than dealing with the ties that bind. Niki would have understood, but Faith felt more than a little guilty.

W
ho on earth is that woman? Has she been here before?" Faith asked Eduardo. He'd been on his way out the door with the woman's salad, but Faith had pulled him back into the kitchen to add the requested extra croutons, which she had almost forgotten. There was no new chef on the horizon, and Faith was on duty again. She had also met with the staff to plan the following night's Scandinavian soiree. With a

silent apology to the Nordic nations, she'd replaced boiled potatoes with oven-roasted and twice-baked ones. And no one would miss lutefisk, or several kinds of herring, unless there was a Minnesota contingent among the guests. Apart from these alterations, the smorgasbord would be as authentic as she could make it.

"She's been here a couple of times before, twice with a tall, skinny old man. Silver hair. Ask Mr. Tanner. He knows her," Eduardo said. The young Peruvian was majoring in English, and Faith had come to rely on him as an occasional interpreter. His bright eyes, with their suggestion of mischief, didn't miss much, and he was also her main source for gossip. It was Eduardo she'd taken aside on Sunday to find out if any of the kitchen help knew where John Forest was. They hadn't. They also hadn't had any idea that he was planning to leave.

"He was so good to work for," Eduardo had said. "Alessandro, the short one—we call her 'Tiny,' because there is another Alessandro working in housekeeping, and she's tall—was teaching him to play some Bolivian love songs on his guitar. He was always playing for us and singing all these American ones. My favorite was 'Wake Up Little Susan.' He seemed very happy with his cooking and his music. But life is not always what it seems."

Apparently, Eduardo was a philosopher as well as an Everly Brothers fan. Faith had no musical talents, so entertaining the crew as John had done was out, but she'd found an oldies station and helped everybody as they tried to sing along. It *was* a cheerful place to work. The kids were great and as eager to learn how to butterfly a leg of lamb as they were to learn about the existence of the homonym—and its nuances.

The lady who had caught Faith's eye was seated alone tonight, her tall silver-haired friend somewhere else. After Eduardo went through the swinging door, Faith continued to look out the small round window into the dining room, a small corner of which was now staked out as Forever Woodstock. Dark hair that was competing with gray for space streamed past the woman's shoulders from a center part. She wore granny glasses tinted rose and a peasant blouse exuberantly embroidered with a rainbow of flowers never seen in nature. The drawstring of the blouse had loosened, revealing one bony shoulder and a small daisy tattoo. Strings of beads were knocking against the table, and as Eduardo served the salad, she cavalierly flung them over her shoulder, where they encountered resistance from her long silver and turquoise earrings. She stood out from the Patagonia /EMS/L. L. Bean crowd at the other tables, just as a woman dressed in anything but black stands out at a New York cocktail party.

Eduardo had said she'd been in before. Was it recently? Someone's eccentric old grandmother or aunt brought along to get her out of the house—and her time warp—for a vacation? Or was she a local? This made more sense. Vermont was a haven for the Flower Power generation— witness Ben & Jerry's Cherry Garcia ice cream and the abundance of tie-dyed shirts for sale in their gift shop. Witness also the fierce independence that periodically expressed itself in the secession of individual towns. Killington had recently voted to reunite with New Hampshire—it had originally been part of the Granite State in 1761, not joining what was then the Republic of Vermont until 1777. So what if they were thirty-five miles from the border? It was the principle that mattered, even if the states involved didn't pay any attention to the act.

Faith was curious to find out more about this interesting creature with a penchant for croutons. If there were a lull in the kitchen, Faith would go over after the main course was served and ask her how she'd liked it.

It wasn't until the woman was taking the last succulent bite of her tarte tatin that Faith was able to leave the kitchen. A couple at another table stopped her on her way. It was the best onion soup they'd ever had, even in Paris, they told her. Always nice to hear, but by the time she reached her quarry, Lucy in the Sky with Diamonds had stood up. She tossed her long hair back over her shoulders and rearranged her beads. Up close, Faith was impressed with how attractive the woman was, although obviously she was someone who would never see fifty again. She had cheekbones Audrey Hepburn might have envied and smooth clear skin. Yes, she was a caricature. Now that she was standing, Faith noted that, as she had suspected, the rest of the outfit was one of those long wraparound skirts made from an India-print bedspread. But no, she wasn't a joke.

"I hope you enjoyed your dinner," Faith said.

"Very nice. Very nice indeed." Her voice was slightly husky, hovering between an alto and a tenor. She gave the chef a gracious nod and a Mona Lisa smile before sailing off, leaving patchouli, incense, and definitely Mary Jane in her wake.

Eduardo had been smiling even more than usual throughout the evening, and now Faith had her answer. It must have been a pretty potent contact high. No wonder she'd enjoyed her meal so much—munchies. The breadbasket was empty; even the little bags of oyster crackers had been devoured. Le Sapin had a dense chocolate brownie à la mode on the dessert menu, but it was the wrong kind. Faith would have to get out her Alice B. Toklas cookbook to satisfy this palate.

The moon was bright, an altogether-different sphere from the one over Manhattan. Faith was glad she didn't have to choose between the two kinds of radiance, each special in its own way. True, she didn't see the Chrysler Building gleaming in its rays or hear Gershwin when she looked up at this shining orb, but the treetops shimmered and the deep silence was musical in another way, deep music—music you had to listen very hard to hear. She'd worked later than last night, helping clean up, charmed by Alessandro's—or rather, Tiny's—beautiful singing voice. Maybe she could sing for the guests one night in the pub or down at the Sports Center. Faith was surprised Simon hadn't thought of it. He was on top of everything, but perhaps she'd been too shy to sing when he was around. I'll let him know, and the Staffords, Faith resolved. Fred and Naomi had come by around 4:00 P.M. and apologized for not letting her know about Nordic Night. They had thought Simon had told her; he'd thought they had. It was only when Marian had said to Harold and Mary that she thought they needed to communicate with Faith a bit better that it had all come out. Faith hadn't complained to her mother-in-law, but she had mentioned to Tom she was slightly annoyed—and Tom had told his mother. Round and round it goes, Faith had thought, listening to the Staffords. Fred was positive they would have a chef by Wednesday. Naomi'd nodded vigorously in agreement with her husband. Faith had been tempted to grab her to get her to stop, or suggest she find a spot on a dashboard. Did Ophelia ever call forth this kind of approval from her mother? Simon was going to Middlebury tomorrow to check the chef out, Freddy'd said. Faith had assured them that all was well—and it was. Naomi'd stopped bobbing and they left.

She took a deep breath of the night air. She would never want to have her own restaurant—it owned you—but it was fun to pretend for a few nights.

She was at the back door of the condo when she saw a flash of movement under the farthest spotlight—the one that had revealed Ophelia the previous night. And it was Ophelia again. She'd probably dropped Scott off—well, it was before midnight; surely Betsey wouldn't be upset by that. Faith had only a hazy idea of what curfews were appropriate for what ages. She'd never had one. Jane had simply expected them to behave sensibly, and Faith's father wouldn't have noticed. She and Hope, especially Hope, mostly had.

Faith reached for the doorknob, then impulsively decided to follow the girl. It wasn't cold, and she knew she wouldn't sleep until she found out where Ophelia was going at night. Was there a party in the woods?

She walked quickly and went where she'd seen Ophelia go the night before. The moonlight was better than any flashlight. Wherever Miss Ophelia was heading, it was someplace she—or others—went frequently. There was a well-defined path in the snow.

Faith couldn't see her, but she could see the tracks Ophelia's boots had made. She knew she would have to be careful not to get too close. She didn't want to be spotted.

It was a lot farther than she thought. She looked at her watch. She'd been in the woods for at least ten minutes. A mouse or a mole—impossible to tell—scurried across the path, startling her. She pressed on. This was no time to turn back. Ophelia hadn't been carrying any equipment, so she wasn't headed for the backcountry—no midnight trek on the Catamount Trail to Stowe, thank goodness. Faith was beginning to get tired just walking fast. It had been a long day.

She decided she would go another five minutes, then call it quits and come back when it was warmer and she had a few more ounces of energy.

The clearing took her completely by surprise. One moment she was in the dense woods, and the next she was stepping into a fairy tale. The cottage was dark brown and had white gingerbread trim; the curlicues gleamed like boiled white icing. Lights blazed from every window, sending bright golden ribbons across the snow. Smoke was coming from the chimney. It was all Faith could do to keep herself from knocking at the door and collapsing into the cozy armchair she was sure must be pulled up in front of a fireplace. The time of night, and the house's location, precluded any notions of canvassing the neighborhood for its opinions on genetically altered veggies or posing as the Welcome Wagon lady. She was about to creep forward and peep through one of the side windows, when the front door opened. Ophelia walked out onto the porch. She had traded her parka for a long purple suede coat.

"You forgot the keys, silly!" a voice called from inside, and a woman appeared behind her. Ophelia turned and took them, gave the woman a quick hug, and said, "Thanks! See you later." As she moved down the steps, Faith had a clear view.

It was the Flower Power woman from dinner. And there was a man in the shadows behind her.

She had barely taken this in when a vintage VW van came chugging down the drive from the back of the house. It was painted pink and covered with bumper stickers and decals. Ophelia was at the wheel.

Faith hoped she had plenty of bread crumbs with her.

SIX

Not sure who that would be, Mrs. Fairchild." Pete Reynolds turned the tap off and stood straight. He'd been bent over the tub in their bathroom while Faith studied the stripes on the wallpaper, avoiding the sight the pull of his heavy tool belt exposed.

"Works like a charm now. You won't have any more problems. Every once in awhile, you have to clear all the hair out of the trap."

Faith was surprised. Not by the hair in the trap. She'd figured that was why the tub wasn't draining, but she hadn't wanted to tackle it herself, since it wasn't her property. No, she was surprised that Pete didn't know who the mystery woman in the woods was. He lived a mile down the road and had apparently been raised by wolves in the forest surrounding the resort—this according to Tom when he'd described Pete's long-standing connection to Pine Slopes.

"We've been getting a lot of newcomers these past years. Hard to keep track."

"You'd remember her if you ever saw her: tall, long dark hair with some gray streaks, dresses like people did in the sixties—you know, beads, granny glasses."

Pete laughed. "Sounds like half of Vermont. The other half dresses like me." Pete's work clothes—Dickies—were soft from many washings and permanently spotted with remnants of maintenance jobs—chimneys to chairlifts.

"Thanks for fixing the tub," Faith said, giving up. It seemed that humanity was less interesting—and diverse—to Pete than machinery.

"Give me a call if you need anything else." Pete hitched up his pants and went downstairs.

Faith thought she'd grab the time to take a bath, now that the tub was operational. The kids were at the ski school. Amy was doing very well and had proudly demonstrated her "pizza slices" when Faith had dropped her off. Ben had started to scoff at Amy's lack of poles, but Faith had loudly talked over him and bustled him off to his group. She'd reminded him that none of the children, including himself, had started out with them. It was easier to teach balance and control without adding pole techniques—and being low to the ground to start with, kids didn't have far to fall.

They'd waved to Glenda, who was surprising her husband by getting up early to take her lesson and hit the slopes.

"My little sleepyhead has turned into my little snow bunny," Craig had said when he and Robert came to get Tom, accompanied by the elder Fairchilds. Recalling how close the little bunny had stood next to her jackrabbit ski instructor in the bar, Faith had wished that the little sleepyhead would return. A flirtation, a fling, call it what you would—but if Craig found out, he would be devastated.

Betsey had announced that the Parkers would be joining Dick and Marian for a postbirthday day of cross-country ski touring, ignoring the sullen looks her boys gave her, as well as missing the slightly pained glances her parents had exchanged—glances that said, There goes our time alone together. Faith had noted with amusement that Dick took the silver heat-reflecting space blanket from his day pack. No off-trail canoodling on this outing. As he was fond of saying, "I may be getting older, but I'm not getting colder."

At the last minute, Dennis had decided to catch up with his brothers-in-law, who had just left. Faith had expected Betsey to protest, but oddly, she had looked relieved. Seizing the moment, Scott and Andy had tried to follow their father's lead, but the only concession Betsey made was that they could come back at lunchtime.

"We'll certainly have enough to eat," she'd told her parents brightly. "It will just be the three of us! And I made some egg salad sandwiches just the way you like them, Daddy, with plenty of mayo. And cupcakes for dessert." Betsey had proclaimed the entire week "Birthday Week," and she was sticking to the theme. Faith had no doubt that Betsey's pack also included party hats and favors.

Pete had arrived as the others were leaving. Now everyone was gone. Faith reveled for a moment in the silence, a precious commodity this week, then measured some lavender and aloe bath salts into the tub and turned on the taps. She went into the bedroom to get clean clothes, stripping off the sweats she'd been wearing since she got up, and was startled to hear the doorbell. Who was it now? She turned off the water, pulled her clothes back on, and went downstairs.

It was the head of housekeeping, Candy Laverdiere, and she was emptying the kitchen trash into a large Hefty bag.

"Oh, sorry, Mrs. Fairchild. I didn't know anyone was here. I rang the bell, but there was no answer."

"It's just me. Everyone else is off, and I'm being lazy."

"From what I hear, I'd say you're anything but. I don't know what the place would have done if you hadn't stepped in for John."

Faith had met Candy on Friday when she'd come by with fresh towels. They had bonded instantly when Faith told her that as far as her family was concerned, they would let her know when they needed clean ones and that it was not necessary for the staff to change them every day, or make their beds. Taking out the trash and vacuuming the downstairs— even with their boots off, Faith had known the dark green carpeting would get gritty—was all they'd need. Candy had relaxed visibly and confessed to Faith that she was extremely shorthanded. Betsey had come in at that point and, fortunately, had agreed with Faith. "I have tried to teach my boys to be conscious of the planet. We have timers on our showers, and between recycling and composting, we end up with barely enough trash to fill a teacup!" Faith had tried, without success, to picture this, but at the time, she'd been glad Betsey was going along with the plan. Now she realized she had another chance to find out who lived in the cottage in the woods—and maybe something about chef John. His whereabouts continued to puzzle her. She'd pumped the kitchen staff, but it was a dry well. None of them had any idea where he might be, had never heard him mention the name of another restaurant, nor had he had a lot of phone calls or a visitor—nothing that might suggest who had wooed him away.

Pete might be oblivious to the animate part of his surroundings, but Faith was sure Candy wasn't. This was one of those gender differences that made Faith particularly glad to be a woman.

"Let me give you a hand, and then I hope you'll have time for some coffee."

"I *always* have time for a cup of coffee, Mrs. Fairchild. Every time I go to donate blood, I'm afraid they're going to find Maxwell House instead."

Faith laughed and went upstairs to get their dirty towels and the Parkers'—Betsey had said she'd put theirs in their tub. "Please call me Faith," she said over her shoulder.

Soon, steaming mugs in hand and a plate of Faith's sweet, crunchy oatmeal lace cookies (see recipe in *The Body in the Moonlight*) between them, the two women were chatting away.

"How long have you been working at Pine Slopes?" Faith asked.

"Oh Lord, off and on for more than twenty years. I started when I was in my teens. Then I got married, and my husband was in the army, so we moved around a lot. Finally, I told him we had to pick a place. It wasn't good for the kids. My oldest—that's Jessica—was starting to have problems at school. Always being the new kid, and she was shy to start with—not like her two brothers. They'd have a few fights on the playground and everything would be hunky-dory. Jessica would just come home every day and cry."

Faith nodded. "So you moved back to Vermont?"

"Well, some of us did. Me and the kids. I expect Ralph will retire one of these days, and then Richmond might look better to him. But I can't complain. He's a good provider. Never misses a check, and spends time with us when he can."

"So you're not divorced?"

"No. I guess that might seem a little strange, but there was no reason to. I never wanted anyone else—getting used to one man is more than enough, in my book—and neither did he. At least not yet. You know when they get to his age, they start wanting to trade a forty for two twenties."

Faith hoped Ralph would go for a sports car instead. She liked Candy and her blunt humor.

"Do you still have kids at home?"

"Only my youngest, Jason. He's sixteen. Jessica's a kindergarten teacher in Burlington, and Ty followed his dad into the service. I wasn't happy about it, not with the world the way it is these days, but what could I do?"

Faith tried hard not to think about the way the world was—at least not during all of her waking hours. It was tough not to, especially when she thought about her kids' future, and that of all the other kids scattered across the globe.

She got up and poured some more coffee in their mugs. Candy didn't seem in a hurry to leave, but Faith figured she'd better get to the point.

"Do you know who lives in the house in the woods beyond the last condo? It's some distance in. I was taking a walk and came across it. Seems a bit isolated. A woman came out on the porch, but I didn't want to intrude."

"That's Gertrude Stafford's place, and she has plenty of 'intruders,' not that I've ever been invited. Wouldn't go if I was."

"Stafford? I don't remember anyone mentioning any Staffords other than Harold, Mary, Fred, and Naomi."

"And you won't." Candy leaned over her mug, moving closer to Faith. "Gertrude—and don't ever call her 'Gert'—is Harold's sister. She's much younger, sixty-six or sixty-seven, although to hear her tell, she's still in her fifties. Anyway, she was what her folks called 'the extra dividend.' Harold was ten or eleven at the time, and they'd assumed he was it. My mom says all of them spoiled her rotten when she was growing up. Never heard the word *no*. When their parents died, Harold bought out her share of Pine Slopes. It had just started up. She wasn't even around—out in California, living on a commune. I think that was the time. Or maybe it was the one in New Mexico. She came to the funeral wrapped from head to toe in some kind of black lace, with a big red rose pinned to her chest. Of course, I wasn't there, but people still talk about it."

"It doesn't sound like this is her sort of place. What's she doing here?"

"Where else is she going to go? Especially at her age? She doesn't have any money. Never worked that I've heard about. Oh well, there was her folksinging career. She'd go on about that. Opening for Bob Dylan. Give me Patsy Cline any day. My kids laugh at me, but country is *my* music. You wouldn't believe what Jason listens to."

Faith would and was dreading it.

"Part of the deal was that Harold would build her a house wherever she wanted on the mountain and give her so many acres to guarantee her privacy. She's never had much interest in the resort, although she's always been a wicked good skier. Just comes and keeps to herself in the woods.

"I don't like to speak ill of people," Candy said with relish, Faith noted, "but it's no secret that Miss Gertrude Stafford is no better than she should be. My mother wouldn't let us go to the Gingerbread House— that's what we all call it—and I told my kids the same thing. Let her be a free spirit, but I didn't want her dragging any of my three down. Why the police haven't raided her parties for drugs and underage drinking is beyond me, unless the Staffords pay them off, which would be no surprise."

"You said 'Miss'—she never married?"

"Oh, she probably stood in a field someplace holding a bunch of daisies and exchanged vows more than once, but nothing legal. There were always men. You'd see her with them in Stowe or Burlington. Sometimes here at the restaurant. But none of them lasted more than one season—that is when she was around at all. There would be years when we wouldn't see hide nor hair of Gertrude. No, there was only one man who was a steady. And he was local. We all thought she must have slipped him some kind of potion when they were kids. They grew up together, and he never had eyes for anyone else. She led him a merry dance, though. And he could have had anybody. It was a damn shame." Candy almost spat the last words out. "And now he's gone. One of the sweetest men on earth."

Faith didn't really have to ask Candy who it was, but she needed to hear it out loud.

"And that was . . ."

"Boyd Harrison. The guy you found in the snowdrift."

She had her answer, and it left her with more questions than she'd started out with, Faith realized. At the door, she thought of her futile conversation with Pete and the nagging doubt it was raising.

"Pete has worked here a long time, too, hasn't he?"

Candy smiled. "Probably was stringing the rope in the old rope tows when he was a toddler."

"He does seem pretty tied to the place," Faith quipped.

"That's the word for it. Pine Slopes and this mountain are his wife, mistress, child—you name it—all rolled up into one. It's his world and all he has in this world. The Staffords may own it, but Pete keeps it going, always has. It's a human being to him, and he'd protect it with his life—or yours. If Pete thought someone was hurting the place, he wouldn't think twice about getting rid of him, or her."

Faith closed the door behind Candy, her last words echoing, joined by another refrain: If Pete was as tied to Pine Slopes as Candy—and others—indicated, why had he said he didn't know who lived in the chalet in the woods?

Tom had suggested meeting for lunch at the pub, and the idea of sitting by the big windows, eating onion soup—she'd modified John Forest's recipe only slightly, less salt, more cheese—getting glimpses of Ben and Amy skiing had appealed to Faith. After a relaxing soak in the tub—maybe there *was* something to the claims on the label of the bath salts, which promised everything from Zen-like tranquillity to baby-soft skin—the idea was even more appealing. She reached for the hair dryer and was about to turn it on, when she heard Scott and Andy's voices downstairs. She opened the door and called down, "Hi, hope you had a good time. Are you going to the cafeteria for lunch, or do you want to eat something here? There's chicken gumbo soup and plenty of stuff for sandwiches."

"Thanks, Aunt Faith," Scott answered, "but Mom gave us some of the sandwiches she packed. We'll eat those; then we're meeting Phelie. Were you here when Dad was?"

Deciding that her hair could wait, Faith went down to continue the conversation face-to-face. Why did Scott think his father had been there? But then, why not? Everybody else in the greater Burlington area seemed to have been in and out.

"I've been here since you left, but I didn't see your father. He must have come in while I was in the tub. What makes you think he was here?"

"This is his neck warmer. Mom gave us each one in our stockings at Christmas, and Dad's is blue. Oops, I mean Santa put them in our stockings." Scott and Andy laughed.

"Don't slip in front of Amy. She's still a believer," Faith cautioned.

"We know, we know—also the Easter Bunny, the Tooth Fairy, and Tinker Bell," Andy said.

"Anyway, Dad was wearing his when he left, but if he didn't leave a note or anything, I guess we can meet Phelie." Scott paused. "Mom didn't say we couldn't, but she doesn't like her. The walkie-talkies are working now, so we'll tell her where we are. Dad, too."

Where you are, but not with whom, Faith thought. The surest way to drive any child into the arms of an undesirable peer was to make it forbidden fruit. This wasn't something she'd picked up from Pix; it was instinctive. She thought of her assistant, Niki, searching out beaux all these years who were guaranteed to get a rise from her parents—the vegan biker, the sixty-year-old unpublished poet, the apparent pilot of the Jefferson Airplane, who was still circling. Maybe he'd been one of Gertrude's conquests, too. After each initial meeting, Mr. and Mrs. Constantine would dramatically bar Niki from ever bringing her swain to their doorstep again, thereby prolonging each affair beyond Niki's natural inclination.

"That sounds fine." Faith wasn't getting involved in this one. "I'm meeting Tom for lunch; then I have to go to work. It's Nordic Night, and we have a lot of specials to get ready."

"Yeah, we know. Mom is getting all excited about it. She wants everyone to go on a sleigh ride."

There was little excitement in Andy's voice.

"I know Ben and Amy want to go down to the Sports Center for the games early. Tom's taking them. I'll suggest that he try to organize the sleigh ride then."

And get it over with, she added silently. The two boys shot her grateful looks. Maybe raising teenagers wasn't going to be as hard as she feared. It was a question of choosing battlegrounds, deciding what was important. A sleigh ride versus whatever they, especially Scott, were up to with Ophelia. Faith would forego a tussle over the former to find out more about the latter any day. She hoped it was just night skiing.

A light snow was falling—the kind where each large flake looked as if a child had cut it out of paper. Faith was tempted to stick out her tongue to catch some. She had heard that the Eskimo peoples supposedly have fifty-six words for snow, which made sense when you were as immersed in the white stuff as Faith was. English was sadly lacking at times like this.

The activity at the resort provided a sharp contrast to the leisurely morning. Skiers of all ages, shapes, and sizes were everywhere; their brightly colored outfits stood out against the white slopes. The Staffords must be relieved, Faith thought. Yesterday's pool incident was today's funny story. If any guests had left, it wasn't apparent in the lift lines or the people Faith could see crowding the base lodge. She walked in and went to the second floor, where the pub was located. Tom hadn't arrived yet. Faith snagged a table by the window and sat down to wait. She had a lot to tell him, starting with Gertrude.

Gertrude! Hamlet's mother. Ophelia's prospective mother-in-law. Mother figure. Gertrude Stafford, Earth Mother. When had Joanie changed her name? Faith thought back to the way the two had embraced on Gertrude's porch last night. Mother/daughter. Doomed to madness and death in the play.

Tom joined his wife in time to see his daughter triumphantly snow-plow—or pizza-slice—her way down the bunny slope. He was also in time to see his sister-in-law walking arm in arm with her ski instructor away from the bunny, and every other, slope, and also away from the condos and lodge.

"Maybe they're signed up for the Pilates class in the Sports Center?" Faith offered. There were many ways to increase one's flexibility and endurance, after all.

"I don't think so—and you don't think so." Tom frowned. "Why did she have to pick this week? Everything's been going so well."

Faith had to remind herself that her husband had been spending the majority of his time skiing down various mountain trails, all of them black diamonds. She also reminded herself that Robert wasn't the only one in the Fairchild family who put blinders on whenever anything untoward was going on with his kin. Parishioners—the entire rest of the world, in fact—were quite another matter, but Tom turned turtle when it came to his sibs.

"Maybe Craig won't find out. That is," she added hastily, "if there *is* anything to find out."

"Could they be any more flagrant? Of course he'll find out—whatever it is. Let's just hope he can keep his cool, so Mom and Dad don't know."

"Your dad, sure, but your mom probably knows more than we do."

"And we all thought Glenda was going to help Craig settle down."
Tom sounded bitter.

After one look at Glenda, Faith had never entertained any notions
that her future sister-in-law would be the kind of wife to settle a husband
down, but she had kept the thought to herself then, and she kept it to herself now. Time to change the subject.

"The week has certainly turned out well for Pine Slopes. We're completely booked for the two smorgasbord seatings tonight, one at six and
one at eight, so people can get to the Sports Center activities. We've commandeered the pub, too, even though the tables are smaller. People said
they didn't care. After the pool prank, things could have been dicey.
Whoever thought of this mini Nordic festival was a genius. I'm pretty
sure it was Simon."

"I heard that, too. He's been a real plus for Fred. They make a good
team." Tom reached for his wife's hand. He gave it a squeeze. "You're in
the thick of things, as usual. Have you heard any scuttlebutt about who
pulled the prank? Kitchen talk?"

"Most of the kitchen talk is in Spanish, but I have learned that *la
piscina* means 'swimming pool,' which I got from knowing that it's *piscine*
in French. Aside from that, nada. And it was only right after the phone
call that anyone mentioned *la piscina* in my hearing. I'm sure they've all
been talking about it when I'm not around, and it's probably already
headlines in Lima and La Paz."

"According to Craig, Fred still thinks it was his stepdaughter, despite
what you said about seeing her the night before. Craig thinks it was
Ophelia, too. But he'd think whatever Fred did. I worry sometimes about
how easily influenced my little brother is. Fred's a good guy, always has
been, but you know Craig's made some half-assed decisions in his young
life on the say-so of others."

Faith had lived through them, along with the rest of the family, and
had even kicked in to bail him out several times. There'd been the
organic-vitamins franchise, a surefire bet; a dubious dot com; and, most

recently, a condo development that turned out to be slated for a former hazardous-waste dump site.

It was mesmerizing watching the skiers through the window, and Faith hoped she'd be able to get a lot more time on the mountain herself. Ben was skiing today, not boarding, and they watched him come speeding down, crouched low in the tuck position, a look of pure joy on his face.

"That's my boy!" Tom said, beaming.

"Yes indeed," Faith replied.

They'd both ordered onion soup, and Tom decided onion rings were the perfect redundancy, which—oddly enough—they were.

As they ate, Faith returned to their speculations about the vandalism at the Sports Center. "Means, motive, opportunity. We should be able to figure this out."

"Before we start, do I have to be Watson again?"

Faith smiled indulgently. Of course he did.

"Let's count Ophelia out and focus on who has a key to the facility and knows the alarm code."

Tom's mouth was full, so Faith continued. "Josh, as manager; Sally, as Nordic director—those are definite. Then, Fred—and by extension Naomi—and I'd imagine Harold. Fred may be in charge now, but Harold still plays a major role here, I've noticed. Simon would also have access. Who else?"

"Don't forget Pete," Tom said.

"That would be impossible. Okay, that's seven right there. I don't imagine Candy would need the alarm code, but she might have a key, being head of housekeeping."

"So we've established means for eight people. But what about the other two—motive and opportunity?"

"In this case, means equals opportunity. Any one of them could have entered during the night or early that morning. For example, Josh could have staged the whole thing before Sally arrived."

"But why? Doesn't he live and die for the Sports Center? Craig says he's always after Fred to get more equipment, allocate more of the budget for Sports Center activities. I get the impression that the whole ski thing is secondary, scenery for people to look at while they work out or swim."

Noting that Craig seemed to spend a lot of time talking about Pine Slopes with Fred—and vice versa—Faith agreed with Tom and told him about the argument she'd overheard Sunday morning between Josh and Sally over the decision to put the Nordic rental and retail shop in the Sports Center.

"Maybe he went off the rails and put the dummy in the pool as a symbolic gesture," Tom said. "He knew Sally would find it. Maybe he wanted to frighten her off his turf."

"Possible, possible. I certainly can't think of a motive for any of the others. They're all people who've literally and figuratively invested their lives in Pine Slopes. They wouldn't do anything to tarnish the resort's image."

Tom had finished the onion rings. Faith looked at her watch, knowing she should be getting to the kitchen.

"The only thing that makes sense is what I've said from the start. It wasn't a person who had legitimate access. Someone hid in one of the locker rooms—it would be easy enough either in a shower or toilet stall— put the dummy in the pool, and then slipped out the front door when Josh was in the weight room or somewhere else. The person wouldn't even have had to leave; he or she could have mingled with the crowd in a bathing suit or ski clothes. I wonder if Josh noticed any Nordic skis in the rack outside when he came in that morning." Faith had a sudden vision of a "wicked good skier" gliding to the Sports Center with a loaded backpack, spending the night, then gliding home to the Gingerbread House in the woods the next morning. It was the type of joke that would appeal to a latter-day Keseyite, especially if she was still on the bus, metaphorically and psychedelically speaking. Faith would have to somehow ask Sally and Josh if they'd smelled anything out of the ordinary that morning, something sweet and low-down.

————

E*stá muy rico,"* Faith repeated slowly. Apparently, she was close, because her whole crew clapped.

"Now you guys say it in English," she said. "It's very tasty." This was easy, and they went on to "*Ya está*": "It's ready." By the time I leave Le Sapin, I could be fluent, Faith thought, as she gave the Swedish meatballs—the place was fast becoming an outpost of the UN—one last pinch of freshly ground nutmeg before declaring them done. She'd made them the day before—essential with this recipe (see recipe in *The Body in the Cast*). The thinly sliced cucumbers with plenty of dill, white vinegar, sugar, salt, and pepper had spent the night in the fridge, too. The salmon was ready for poaching, and the traditional mustard sauce with more dill was all set. Two vats of yellow split-pea soup with plenty of fragrant diced ham were simmering on the back burners. In addition, she'd made a kind of Scandie coleslaw with finely shredded red cabbage and diced apples, with just lemon juice and a pinch of sugar and salt for dressing. She'd varied Janssen's temptation, that smorgasbord stable, replacing the anchovies, not everyone's favorite, with smoked trout, which would do nicely with the strips of potato and onion. The board would further groan with a selection of cheeses, a green salad with Danish blue cheese dressing, a chicken liver pâté that mimicked the traditional Swedish *lever-pastej,* and plenty of bread and rolls from the Red Hen Baking Company in nearby Duxbury. For dessert, she'd modified the marzipan princess cake and added several other confections renamed for the occasion, such as Northern Lights Delight, a rich sponge cake layered with lemon custard, and Lapp It Up sorbets in a variety of flavors. Since coffee was the national beverage throughout Scandinavia, she'd also done a mocha cheesecake.

The Sports Center would be serving the soup, and she'd given Josh her recipe for glögg: dry red wine, sugar, cinnamon, cloves, cardamom, and orange zest heated together, but not boiled. Unfortunately, they didn't have any aquavit—a vital ingredient. The glögg would still warm the cockles of one's heart, just not set it afire the way it would have with the aquavit, literally "the water of life." A shot of the 100-proof authentic Nordic liquor had been said to bring back the dead. They'd be offering glögg at the restaurant and in the pub, too.

Eduardo poked his head out the kitchen door, "Señora Confianza, phone for you. *Su esposo.*" Eduardo, along with the rest of the South Americans, had settled on "Mrs. Faith" for their boss's name, despite her initial request that they simply call her Faith. "Confianza" was definitely growing on her, and she'd made them write it down. Confident, faithful. Maybe she'd switch. Maybe she'd learn to tango, too.

Faith went into the kitchen and picked up the phone.

"What's up, honey?"

"Do you think you could get over here for a few minutes?" Tom sounded extremely agitated, and Faith could hear several angry voices in the background. The loudest was Betsey's.

"What's wrong? It's not one of the kids is—"

"No, everyone's fine. But the condo's been burglarized."

"What! How can this have happened? There've been people around all day! Has it been trashed?"

"No, thank goodness."

"And the kids? Do they know about it? Where are they?"

"The kids are with Mom and Dad down at the Sports Center. Pete and his crew made a sled run for the junior Vikings. And they don't know about the break-in. We won't be able to keep it from Ben, but no one will say anything to Amy. Dennis called the Staffords, and they're on their way over. We're trying to establish the times people were here, so it would help if you could come, too." He lowered his voice. "Betsey's gone bonkers. It would also help if you were here to calm her down."

Faith hadn't mentioned the Betsey blowup to Tom. It hadn't seemed necessary. She and her sister-in-law were now on speaking terms—Betsey's lips clenched perhaps a bit tighter than usual, her vowels and consonants a tad more clipped. Despite this crack in the veneer, Faith was definitely not the person to calm Mrs. Parker down.

"Why is she so upset, apart from the fact that it's horrible to go through something like this, as well we know." The Aleford parsonage had been completely cleaned out several years ago, and Faith still had nightmares about coming home to find the back door smashed in, not to mention the response of the first policeman to arrive on the scene: "Was it like this when you left?"

"One of the missing items is the diamond ring Dennis gave her for Valentine's Day."

"I'll be there as soon as I can," Faith said, a string of expletives in a variety of languages coursing through her mind. Out of all the diamond rings in the world, why, oh why, did it have to be her sister-in-law's?

Betsey jumped up from the couch and started shouting questions at Faith the moment she walked through the door. "What time did you leave here? Were you alone this morning?"

Valiantly suppressing the urge to request that her sister-in-law stop treating her as a suspect, Faith walked in and sat in a chair next to Tom.

Craig was pacing back and forth in front of the fireplace. Glenda was sitting on one of the stools by the breakfast bar. Scott and Andy, whom Faith had incorrectly assumed would be with their grandparents, were sitting on the bottom stair and looking guilty as hell. Betsey sat back down, and Dennis put his arm around her shoulders. Faith assumed it was the pose her entrance had interrupted. Robert was standing near the back door, as far away as he could get without actually going through it. As a family reunion, it could have been staged by Albee or O'Neill.

"What did they take?" Faith asked, deciding to ignore Betsey for the moment.

"Betsey's ring and Scott's laptop are all we've determined so far. You didn't bring any good jewelry, did you? I've had a look in our room. Nothing seems disturbed, but I don't know what you brought," Tom said.

"Only what I'm wearing now and the silver necklace I wore Saturday night." The latter was a sterling collar made by Maine silversmith Ron Pearson. Faith considered it her all-purpose ornament, liking the way it rested on her collarbones, whether she was wearing a V-necked T-shirt or a scoop-necked cashmere top, as she had for Dick's party. "Oh, and my glass beads, the ones from Penrose." Ricky Bernstein's studio was out in Sheffield, Massachusetts, and was always a favorite destination. While both items could be replaced, the feeling of loss could not.

"The silver necklace and the beads are in the drawer."

Faith was relieved, but only for a moment. "What about our camera—and you brought one too, didn't you?" she asked, looked anxiously at Betsey and Dennis.

"I had ours with me," Betsey said. "I wanted to take pictures of our picnic, and Tom says *yours* is where he left it." Another accusation: Why hadn't Faith suffered any losses?

"I think what happened," Tom said, "was that someone saw us leave, took a chance and came inside, grabbed the ring and the laptop, and then left. Maybe he went upstairs and didn't see anything worth taking. The camera is still up on the closet shelf in the gym bag I packed it in." The Fairchilds tended to take the camera along on vacations, with every intention of using it to record their experiences, then, when it remained untouched, vowed on the way home to take lots of pictures next time.

Faith had learned from their burglary that speed was of the essence to a thief, also portability and salability. Other than their camera, which wasn't a new one, the only thing of value in the condo that fit the bill was Scott's laptop. The TV, VCR and DVD player were good ones and fairly new, but the owner had secured them to the large unit that housed them. Betsey's ring outshone everything else, literally—but why hadn't she been wearing it?

"Where was your ring? Why didn't you have it on?" Faith asked.

Betsey flushed angrily. Faith could tell she'd been crying.

"I took it off to wash the breakfast dishes. Everyone else seemed to have other things to do," Betsey said pointedly. Another accusation: If Faith or Glenda had done the dishes, Betsey would still have her rock.

"Then I was busy making sandwiches, Mom and Daddy came, and

we left. You must have seen it in the saucer by the sink. I can't imagine why you didn't put it somewhere safe."

"I wish I had seen it, Betsey," Faith said, meaning it with all her heart. It was terrible to have something stolen from you. What Faith had regretted losing most from their break-in was her charm bracelet, each charm a gift from her parents. It had to be even worse when you'd left the item in plain sight.

"I didn't see it, either," Glenda said quickly. Craig stopped pacing and went over to his wife.

"Of course you didn't, darling."

Glenda's chin was raised, and there had been a slightly defiant note to her denial. But before Faith could wonder about it, the Staffords arrived in full force—Harold, Mary, Fred, and Naomi Stafford, that is.

Fred rushed over to Betsey and Dennis.

"I am so, so sorry about this. In all these years, we've never had anything like it happen before. People take VCRs, even microwaves from the kitchenettes in the hotel units, but not often, and we can usually track them down. Occasionally, some ski equipment left outside will disappear, but even that almost never happens. And since people live up here year-round, we don't have a problem with off-season break-ins. Simon is down at the Nordic events and can't get away, but he'll be stopping by later."

Naomi took Betsey's hand and sat down on the couch. Naomi was an armful, and with Dennis on the other side, Betsey was squashed in the middle. "Fred tells me your ring was a Valentine's Day present from Dennis. We're going to do everything we can to find out who did this and get it back!"

Betsey started to work the room. "He gave it to me early. It was a complete surprise. Just the most beautiful ring there ever was. To make up for not having a big engagement ring. I've only been wearing it a few days, so I didn't miss the feel of it on my finger, not the way I would my other rings."

Naomi nodded sympathetically.

"When did the police say they'd get here?" Faith asked, breaking the mood. She had to get back to the kitchen. There was no telling what her crew might think were authentic Scandinavian touches.

"We, uh, haven't called the police yet," Fred said. "We wanted to have all the information first."

Faith thought this was what the police usually did. Gather information.

"Well, I was here all morning. Scott and Andy were eating lunch when I left. Then Tom came back with the kids in the late afternoon. That's as much as I know. Oh, Pete fixed the tub, and Candy came by with linens. But aside from it being preposterous to suspect them, I was still around."

"And the doors weren't locked?" Harold asked.

"With the kids coming and going, besides all of us, we've been leaving the place unlocked," Tom told him. "I really didn't think there was anything of value. I gather from my parents that the owners do the same thing. Mom and Dad do, too. Pine Slopes isn't the kind of place where you think to lock your doors."

"Fortunately, both the ring and the laptop are insured for their full value," Dennis said. Faith was startled for a moment by his voice, which was deep and strong. He spoke so rarely at family gatherings that she'd always assumed whatever he said would be in a whisper.

"That's not the point," Betsey snapped. "The ring, fine, but how is Scott supposed to do his work this week? And what about everything on his hard drive?"

"Mom, I don't have that much to do, and everything on the drive is backed up on CD-RWs. Don't worry," Scott said.

"I'm not the one who should be worrying," she shot back. "If you don't pull that *A*-minus in French up to an *A,* what college do you think will take you?"

Scott leaned back against the stair and didn't say another word. Faith saw Robert start to inch his hand toward the doorknob. He was out of here, and so, she decided, was she. She started to get up, then stayed where she was when Tom started to speak.

"We need to report the theft to the police, Fred. I think we have the facts now. I know Pine Slopes isn't responsible for missing articles, especially from individually owned condos, but the insurance company will need a report."

It was Craig who responded—almost out-Betseying Betsey.

"Fine," he shouted, knocking over an empty chair. "Call the police and let it get out all over the States and Canada that your stuff isn't safe at Pine Slopes. Why don't you just hang a 'Closed' sign up at the turnoff and be done with it!"

"Craig, I think you're overreacting a little here, and I'm sure the Staffords agree that the authorities have to be notified." Tom walked over to his brother and put his hand on Craig's shoulder. Craig shrugged it away. Tom picked up the chair and sat in it.

It was the Staffords turn to speak, but aside from a few uneasy glances, none of them appeared to have anything to say.

Dennis stood up, and Betsey toppled toward the empty space.

"Look, I think Craig is right. The place has had a string of bad luck lately—I don't have to spell it out—and this is the kind of thing that gets blown out of proportion. I'll call my insurance agent and see what they need for documentation. Reporting it to the ski patrol here may be sufficient. And son"—he walked over to Scott and tousled his hair—"I think you just got a couple of days of real vacation. You were smart to back up your work. It's always a good idea." Before his wife could vent, he placated her. "Maybe Scott can find some French-speaking kids to talk to, practice on. Seems I've been hearing every language under the sun these last few days."

And so the matter was closed. Robert dropped his hand from the doorknob and stepped into the room. The Staffords all stood up, and Faith put her coat on.

But Betsey wasn't finished. Unless Dennis could find a graduate of the Sorbonne who specialized in tutoring English-speaking students, his gesture wasn't cutting any *glace* with his wife.

"Fine and dandy. Everything's settled. But what about the criminal? How very, very convenient that your laptop has magically disappeared, Scott. Wasn't that the plan all along? But then there was my ring just lying there—a golden opportunity to make some money for drugs or whatever else she's into."

"Shut up, Mom! Shut up now!" Scott yelled.

"There was one of those stupid Japanese *anime* tapes in the VCR when I put my exercise tape in. She left a calling card. Little Miss Ophelia!"

Faith looked at the Staffords, particularly Naomi. This was her daughter whom Betsey was excoriating. Why didn't Naomi say something?

"You know, sis, I think you might be on to something here. What do you think, Fred?" Craig asked.

"I think we'll look for Joanie and talk to her." His face was grim. "Better wait before you call the insurance people, Dennis."

"Nooooo!" Scott screamed. "You don't know her. Just because you hate her, you think she's doing all this shit! The pool, and now this. She's the most honest person I know. More honest than any of you! Yeah, we watched a tape while we ate lunch, but if we'd wanted to hide that we were all here, wouldn't she have taken it with her? You have no proof. No proof about the pool and no proof about this!"

Andy's head was in his lap, and Faith was pretty sure he was crying.

"Sometimes you may think you know someone, when in fact you don't, son," Fred said wearily. "And as for proof, we found that hat of Joanie's, the orange-and-blue one that looks like a jester's, in the women's locker room right after that dummy was discovered. Joanie said she hadn't been in the Sports Center for a week or more, so how did her hat get there all by itself?"

"I hate you! All of you! You probably put the hat there yourself, Fred!"

"I want you to apologize to Mr. Stafford this instant, Scott. Then go to your room!" Betsey said. "I think we've heard enough from you on this subject. This is a family matter—a Stafford family matter."

"No way. Everything I've said is true." He was walking toward the back door.

Betsey was beside herself.

"You'd better not open that door, young man. If you leave here now, you will be severely punished. Joanie has been even a worse influence on you than I thought, but then, as she showed us at Daddy's party, she's no better than a little slut!"

The words hung in the air. Scott let out a roar and seemed about to head for his mother, then turned and raced out the door.

Robert followed him.

Faith was still shaking when she went back into the restaurant's kitchen. The inviting smells and organized chaos immediately calmed her down. She could imagine a scheme whereby Scott's laptop disappeared for the week, only to be found mixed in with the dirty laundry or some such place. She was avoiding the room the cousins were sharing, except to tuck her kids in at night and wake them in the morning. Their clothes were up with Tom's and Faith's. These brief forays had been enough to remind her that smells, especially boy smells—no, make that boy funk—change mightily with age. It would be plausible to find the laptop buried under a pile of socks and underwear. But the ring was something else again. She couldn't see Ophelia taking it, even with Scott and Andy aiding and abetting. What would they do with it? They couldn't sell it, unless Ophelia had contacts with a fence in Burlington. And it wasn't exactly Ophelia's style—an oversized diamond cocktail ring. It was Glenda's style. And Glenda had been acting oddly, but then, she was hiding a Lord of the Ring. She'd admired the gift several times, but Faith had viewed her comments more as broad hints to Craig than anything else. Yet, what if Glenda had gone back to touch up her makeup, found the condo empty, and, acting on impulse—her usual mode of behavior— took the bijou? She'd never be able to wear it in front of the family, or even her husband, but perhaps it would be enough to take an occasional private peek, like those billionaires with their hot Vermeers and van Goghs.

And Betsey. Faith knew she would have to tell Tom about the other day. His sister needed help. Faith wasn't sure what Tom could do, but this was a woman on the edge. As Faith was leaving, Betsey had raced up to her, grabbed her arm so hard that Faith was sure she'd be sporting a bracelet of bruises from Betsey's fingers for the rest of the week, and hissed, "Not a word about any of this to my parents!"

"Señora Confianza, is something wrong?" Eduardo asked anxiously.

"My sister-in-law lost something and thought I might know what happened to it, but everything is fine." And it was. The smorgasbord beckoned; Faith had people to feed.

"Ah," Eduardo said. "My mother lost a necklace that my grand-mother gave her when she was married. For two days, the house was loco. First this person was the thief, afterwards that person. Even my father was accused! Then she put on a dress to go to church, and there was the neck-lace caught in the collar. I am sure it will be the same with your *familia*."

Faith wasn't so sure.

SEVEN

Simon Tanner was sitting at the kitchen counter, attacking a large portion of meatballs and roasted potatoes. He'd passed over the cucumbers and the rest of the other veggie dishes Faith had prepared for the smorgasbord. Like her father-in-law, the Aussie was obviously a meat and potatoes man. He'd come by to tell her that the new chef would be arriving in the morning, and she'd insisted he stay for some dinner. The 6:00 P.M. seating was in full swing, and she didn't have much to do, except keep an eye on the pots.

"This reminds me of all the tucker I had here with John," Simon said in a wistful tone. "I would never have figured him for a bolter."

"And no one has heard a word from him or where he might be?" Faith asked.

Simon shook his head. He wasn't bad-looking. Her initial Crocodile Dundee impression, cliché though it was, remained. Simon was tall and slim, his collar-length sandy hair streaked with gray. He sported cowboy boots, and Faith was sure the rest of the outback regalia, including the hat and vest, were in his closet. It was hard to tell how old he was. He'd spent a great deal of his life outdoors, Faith guessed. His tanned face showed it.

"Who knows? Maybe he went to some restaurant in New York City. That's where he was from. Maybe he was tired of winter."

This possibility hadn't occurred to Faith. She'd call some of her chef friends in Manhattan and see if there was a new kid on the block. It nagged at her—the not knowing, just as not knowing always did.

And here was Simon. There was a lot she didn't know about him.

"What brought you to this part of the world?" She placed a large piece of chocolate mousse cake in front of him. It wasn't Scandinavian, but she'd included it, along with a few other non-Nordic offerings that she knew people would expect at a buffet. She'd told herself that it was fusion cuisine. If you could have Franco-American, you could certainly have Franco-Norwegian.

Simon was obviously a chocolate lover, and half the cake disappeared rapidly before he answered her question.

"I was one of those guys who followed the snow. My mum and dad died when I was a teenager. My sister was married with a bunch of kids. I was the last thing she needed, so I started working my way around the world from one mountain to the next. It was great while it lasted. No worries." He took another bite of cake.

"But why Vermont? Why Pine Slopes?" It must seem pretty tame for someone who has skied the Alps *and* the Andes, she thought.

"One day, I looked around me and all my mates had moved on to other things. I was the old man in the crowd. It was time for me to move on, too. The only thing I know anything about is skiing and ski resorts. I picked up a few courses in management, so I'd look good on paper, then began sending 'all about me' letters around. Most places wanted me to head the ski school, or teach skiing. Been there, done that. Pine Slopes wanted a manager. End of story."

Faith was sure there were lots of chapters that had been edited out, but she was equally sure Simon wasn't going to reveal any more than he had.

"Thanks for dinner. It was brilliant. And thanks for working this week. Giving up your vacation time was a lot for us to ask, but I don't know what we would have done if you hadn't been here." Simon reached across the counter for Faith's hand. She wasn't sure whether he was going to kiss it—she flashed back to John's gesture—or shake it. Simon shook it.

"Time to get back to the salt mines, better known as the Sports Center. It's almost time for the Hagar the Horrible weight-lifting competition."

"You certainly don't want to miss that," Faith said, laughing.

"No—especially because I'm judging it."

"Josh must be entered, then, since he isn't judging," Faith said.

Simon frowned. "Josh hasn't been too keen on Nordic Night. He's tending the bar and serving out snacks."

Eduardo entered with one of the large chafing dishes, followed by two of the other waiters, who were carrying more empty ones.

"They are like animals out there!" Eduardo cried, then fell silent and put the dish on the counter. The other two did the same and stood waiting.

"Aren't you boys supposed to be doing something?" Simon asked, zipping up his parka. "And *mucho gracias*, don't be calling our guests, 'animals.' See you, Faith."

He left before Faith could explain that she had told them she'd be doing all the replenishing. They had to save enough for the next seating. And animals—the insect variety, as in locusts—were exactly what people were like at an "all you can eat" affair.

"What can I do?" Eduardo asked, frown lines puckering his smooth brow.

"Nada until I refill these. Don't worry. Simon didn't know what my instructions were. He came by to tell me that the new chef will be here tomorrow morning."

"But we want you to stay, Señora Confianza!" Juana said solemnly. Her words reflected the expressions on all the other faces in the kitchen.

"And I wish I could. I've loved working with all of you, but I have to go home, back to my job, at the end of the week. So I need to be with my family here." As she spoke, Faith realized how much fun she *had* been having. She wouldn't have minded if the new chef hadn't shown up until

Friday. Tom and the kids were one thing, but she wasn't looking forward to quality time with the rest of the family, especially after the ugly scene a few hours ago. Tom had said he would call from the Sports Center to tell her what was going on, but so far, he hadn't. She toyed with the idea of slipping down there, but she needed—and wanted—to stay right where she was, far from the scene of battle.

"I'll be here to meet him with you and tell him how lucky he is to have such a well-trained crew." Faith assumed this was the chef from Middlebury. She'd forgotten to ask Simon where he was coming from or what kind of cuisine he specialized in. The chef was a man, because Simon had said, "He'll be here around ten o'clock tomorrow morning."

She glanced at the clock. The next seating could linger, but these folks would have to be moved along. She hated to do it, but there wasn't any choice.

"You'll have to start busing the empty places and stop offering coffee refills. Of course, if someone asks for more, that's different. We won't refill any of the main dishes completely. They should be on dessert by now, but there are always some endless pits that have to keep going back for more, so take these out." She refilled the platters with a judicious amount.

"When you have time, you have to tell me what an 'endless pit' means," Eduardo said. "I know *endless*, and a pit is what is in the middle of some kinds of fruit. I learned that from John. But an 'endless pit'?" He shrugged expressively.

"I'll explain later. There are two kinds of pits, and they mean very different things."

"Like *dice* and *dice*," a tall boy named Vincente piped up. "John taught us that, too."

Faith began to wonder what else John had taught them.

Tom called at 8:30. Amy had crashed, and he was back at the condo.

"She was asleep as soon as she got her nightie on, so I skipped teeth tonight. She can brush them twice in the morning. Is this a bad time?"

"No, it's fine. The second wave has arrived, and my new amigos are dealing with everything nicely. But Tom, they've found a chef. He starts tomorrow. This is my last night."

"You sound disappointed."

Faith hastened to cover herself. Tom had sounded disappointed, too.

"Not exactly. It's just that I've been having fun with them, not to mention being a real restaurant chef—you know, sort of like that old TV show *Queen for a Day*. But I'm looking forward to hitting the slopes with all of you and being with everyone at the condo."

"Liar." Tom laughed. "You may want to hit the slopes, but the togetherness part is a fib, and I don't blame you. I was glad to have Amy as an excuse to leave. There's something rotten in the state of Fairchild. Even Dad is picking up on it."

"Betsey?"

"To start. I know my big sister is bossy, but something else is going on. She insisted we all go on the sleigh ride she organized, even though it was cold, and the horse blanket was very horsey, and not too warm, unless you want to count the heat generated by the smell of manure. Fortunately, it wasn't long."

"What's happened with Scott? Was he there?"

"My brother Robert, who, I'm beginning to think, is the sanest of us all—and certainly the most sensitive—apparently didn't let his nephew out of his sight after Scott charged out the back door. Robert's taken both boys to dinner and the movies in Stowe. More 'woof-woof' burgers, as Amy calls them, at Gracie's, and then on to that funky theater."

The small Stowe cinema had a tiny loge with comfy seating, where patrons could order a beer or wine and hearty movie snacks.

"Scott will have to come home at some point."

"Not in this life, if he can help it. Apparently, Dennis and Betsey had words about the way she handled things this afternoon. Now Dennis has vanished."

"Maybe he's with Robert and the boys."

"Possibly. I didn't think of that, but it makes sense. Scott will slide into his room tonight, and then we'll have the fun of watching him avoid his mother for the rest of the vacation."

Faith giggled. "Guess he'll be turning off his walkie-talkie." She was at the point where she had to laugh or cry about the whole debacle, and it was infinitely better to laugh.

"He doesn't need to; they've never worked well. Betsey is furious about that, too. Anyway, being with Mom and Dad seems to be what she wants. The three of them are in the Scrabble tournament. I'm not sure that's a Nordic game, but it's on the program. And speaking of Nordic, I wish you could have seen some of the getups people were wearing, in the fond belief that they were imitating real Vikings. One guy was decked out in some kind of caveman outfit made of fake fur, and he had an ice bucket decorated with cardboard horns on his head. If his arms and legs were anything to go by, he didn't need the fake fur, by the way. Then we also had a six-foot-tall Brunhilde—quite a bit of confusion between Wagner and Grieg tonight—complete with an aluminum-foil breastplate."

"Maybe I can duck down for a few minutes. What's Ben up to?"

"He's as happy as a Swede with a boatload of herring. I just made that up. Pretty cute, huh?"

"Very cute, but who's keeping on eye on him? Craig and Glenda?"

"More like Craig. Glenda bowed out after the sleigh ride to shower and change. They're signed up for the Land of the Midnight Sun tennis doubles tourney. Maybe she's back down there by now."

And maybe she's not, Faith thought. She'd look in the pub after she finished talking to Tom.

"Craig entered this strongman thing and is in the finals. Ben wanted me to try, and now he knows what a hernia is. He and Craig were sledding when I left. Mom said she'd bring him up here before ten, or earlier if she gets eliminated."

"Sounds like a rollicking time."

"*Uffda,* as they say in Oslo. Wish you were here, honey. I haven't seen much of you lately."

"I know," Faith said. Tom and she needed a vacation to recover from this vacation.

Tiny came running into the kitchen.

"A very big man has just taken all the meatballs! The people behind him in line are very angry. ¡*Dios mio!* What do I do?"

"Got to go, sweetheart. Meatball emergency."

Faith had planned to freeze a large quantity of the leftover main courses, but she'd obviously underestimated these peoples' appetites. She filled a chafing dish with the intended leftovers and sent Eduardo out with it, instructing Tiny to remove the one that was almost empty.

There were a great many things she had trouble imagining people doing in this world—some of which she could hardly bear to think about—but on a very basic level, taking more than one's fair share ranked high.

By the time she remembered to check the Pine Needle Pub, there were only a few stragglers in the dining room, and even fewer at the tables in the pub. But each stool at the pub's bar was filled—and Glenda and her ski instructor occupied two of them.

Before she could duck out, Glenda spotted her sister-in-law. Cool as one of the cucumbers Faith had sliced wafer-thin and mixed with her dill sauce, Glenda called out, "Faith, hello. Come meet Roy, my wonderful teacher."

Glenda was wearing a tight silver Lycra top. The low light in the room seemed to make it shine more, not less. She'd obviously showered and washed her gleaming hair. She smelled like expensive perfume, nothing equine, and something else, something basic. They made an arresting couple. Roy was, if anything, more striking than Glenda. His hair was white blond, too, and his eyes were as clear and blue as the North Sea. And like the North Sea's treasure, the oil that had made Norway so rich, Roy projected power—an ample store of health, athletic prowess, and sex. This was someone who should be on a Calvin Klein billboard in Times Square, not squiring snow bunnies around a small family-oriented ski resort in the wilds of Vermont. What was his story? Or, Faith corrected herself, saga.

"Faith, meet Roy Hansen. Roy, this is my sister-in-law Faith. She's the one I've been telling you about who took the chef's place. She knows how to cook."

Glenda clearly thought Faith's accomplishments fell somewhere below giving a good manicure and above changing spark plugs. Roy got up and extended his hand. He had perfect posture.

"I'm very pleased to meet you, and I have heard about what you have done for Pine Slopes. The smorgasbord you prepared tonight was wonderful. If I closed my eyes, it was like Christmas Eve at home."

Faith shook his hand. It was warm and smooth. He wasn't wearing any rings. As in the skoaling tradition of his countrymen, he was looking straight into her eyes. She reached up to pat a loose hair into place and realized she was still holding his hand. Dropping it, she said, "I'm pleased to meet you, too. I know Glenda has been very happy with her lessons. And thank you. I didn't have much notice for tonight, so there's a lot missing—herring, lingonberries, Jarlsberg cheese, reindeer steaks."

She was babbling; saying dopey things, but he was having a dopey effect on her. I'm tired, thought Faith. Time to go home. But she stayed.

"Roy is from Norway," Glenda said, happily stating the obvious.

"A friend of ours and her mother had a wonderful trip there several years ago, mostly on the west coast." Pix Miller and her mother, Ursula, had gone to Norway to help an old friend of Ursula's locate her missing granddaughter. The trip *had* been wonderful, if you consider finding a body in a fjord and getting locked in a sauna with the heat cranked up to a murderous level wonderful. But Pix kept talking about going back. The people were so nice and the scenery was gorgeous. And the food, especially breakfast! Faith decided not to go into all this with Roy.

"I am from the west coast myself. A place called Ålesund. You would like it very much. It is very beautiful, and many tourists come to us in the summer. Winters are not so nice."

He spoke English with a faint British accent—Scandinavian children learned British English in school—and a slight lilt softened his vowels, making even this simple statement lyrical.

Glenda had had enough time away from center stage. "I'd love to go to Norway. Maybe next summer. If Craig can't get away, I'll go by myself. Roy says there are all these awesome places to hike to, and you stay in little cabins. All I'd need is a backpack."

And a steamer trunk for your cosmetics, Faith added silently.

"I have to get back to the kitchen. It was a pleasure meeting you, Roy."

"You, too, Faith." Once more, he reached out his hand, and once more she took it.

"It wasn't any fun down at the Sports Center," Glenda said defiantly. "A smelly sleigh ride, then watching Craig lift weights. I told him I might end up here."

Faith was positive that was a lie—what about the tennis match?—but she smiled at Glenda and said, "Maybe he'll join you later."

"Maybe he will," Glenda said, pouting. "He hasn't met Roy yet, and I'm sure the two will hit it off."

Hit was the operative word here. Faith pulled her hand away from Roy's and went back to help close the kitchen. It would be an early night for once.

After regrets had been expressed on both sides, she left, promising to have breakfast with the kitchen staff before the new chef arrived. Outside, it was another clear night, and warmer than usual. She walked quickly toward the condo, eager for some time alone with Tom. If Ben had come back, he'd be in bed, and the Parkers would still be occupied with their various activities. Betsey was a killer Scrabble player and had memorized all those lists of obscure two- and three-letter words you needed to know to score a gazillion points by laying down one tile. With luck, Faith could scoot up to their bedroom, join Tom, and firmly close the door.

There must have been another killer player. Betsey Fairchild Parker did not look as if she'd won anything. She was stomping up the stairs to the condo alone, obviously put out. Faith hung back. Luck was not with her, but she could improve the odds by waiting a little before she went in.

It was warm, but not that warm, so she opened their car door, sat in the driver's seat, got out her keys, and turned on the heat. This is really childish, she told herself. But she didn't move. Lights went on downstairs. Tom must have gone to bed, Faith realized. She'd wait until Betsey did, too. Faith hoped her sister-in-law was tired after expending so much emotional energy. It hadn't been a good day for Bets. Losing the ring was terrible, but she'd get another one. Bigger, even. It was the scene with Scott—that was far, far worse. Had she lost her son, as well? Faith thought about suggesting to Marian that she talk to her daughter. Generally, Tom's parents didn't interfere in their children's lives—as Faith's hadn't, either. Maybe it's a generational thing, Faith mused. She couldn't imagine keeping her mouth as tightly shut as the Fairchilds had during some of Craig's misadventures. But she also couldn't imagine opening it the way Betsey did each and every day. She'd clearly crossed the line from normally interested/involved parent to paranoid/obsessive—and Faith was the last person who could point this out, however tactfully. Marian was the embodiment of tact. She could do it. Faith looked at the kitchen window and saw that the lights were still on. What was Betsey doing? Drowning her sorrows in chai? Why didn't the woman go up to bed, already!

A car came down the road from the woods. Faith sat up and looked in the rearview mirror. It was Gertrude Stafford's hippie mobile. There was no mistaking that paint job, the Eugene McCarthy daisies, and the various "Make Love, Not War" genre bumper stickers. Ophelia was driving, and Gertrude herself was in the passenger seat.

Without thinking twice, Faith backed up and followed them down the mountain. It beat waiting for the lights to go out in the condo.

At the bottom, where the road to Pine Slopes connected with the main road, they turned right. Ophelia was a good driver, used turn signals, and obeyed the speed limit—or perhaps this was as fast as the aging van could go. It was easy to keep her quarry in sight. They passed through Richmond. Faith turned on the radio. Randy Newman was singing "Baltimore." She was a long way from Baltimore—a great crab-cake town—and this thought produced another. The two ladies might be planning more than a night out. Something of a longer duration. The head housekeeper, Candy, had said that Gertrude left for many months at a time. This might be one of those times. Ophelia seizing the chance to run away? "Ain't nowhere to run to . . ." Newman's distinctive gravelly voice sang. But he was wrong in this case. The Canadian border was only a few hours north.

Ophelia had said she wasn't a Stafford, but had Naomi had Joanie's name changed to match hers once she married Freddy, or had Ophelia kept her father's? Having the same surname would make it easier at the border—and they were sure to be stopped. Then again, Gertrude struck Faith as the kind of person who would know all sorts of ways of getting from Vermont's Northeast Kingdom straight into Canada without en-countering the fuzz. From the glimpses she'd had of life chez Stafford, Faith was surprised Ophelia hadn't split long ago. Once again, she felt an-gry that Naomi was either consciously or unconsciously ignoring the cries for help her daughter was broadcasting so loudly and clearly. Faith thought wearily of the chain of events that would follow if indeed the two were about to make their own buddy movie. She'd have to get Scott to find out whether Ophelia returned home tonight, and then tell the Staffords. Or should she call the Staffords now? She was loath to sound the alarm, in case this turned out to be just a pizza run to Mr. Mike's in Burlington. The van turned onto the interstate, and Faith decided to fol-low them only long enough to confirm things one way or the other.

The car was warm, the song suited her mood, and she let her mind drift back over the day's events. The big question was who had broken into the condo, and when. Ophelia's night flight could be a reaction to the suspicion—loudly voiced, Faith guessed, by Freddy—that had fallen upon the girl. Scott had been so passionate in his defense of his friend. His was a passionate age.

Nothing made sense. If the computer hadn't also been missing, Faith would have been tempted to believe that the ring had fallen down the garbage disposal. Things like that happened. They could pinpoint the time, since Candy definitely would have noticed a sparkler like that when she came in. And Pete before her. Then the kids said Dennis had been there. And what about the kids? Easy enough to have knocked it into the drain and then been afraid to fess up. It made the most sense, in fact. Then give the computer to Ophelia for cover. Andy and Scott were smart boys. Just ask their mother.

The van had its blinker on. They were getting off the interstate. Faith quickly changed lanes and followed suit, feeling greatly relieved. No Montreal or other Canadian port of call tonight. They were on the Williston Road, heading into Burlington. Maybe it *was* a pizza run. They passed the motel where Faith had seen Dennis's car on Saturday. She noticed now that the motel had a coffee shop attached to it. Anxious to get out of walkie-talkie range, he might have pulled in for some apple pie and a cup of joe.

They were coming into Burlington. Williston Road turned into Main Street, and Faith sped up. There was more traffic, and she didn't want to lose them. They were in the "Hill" section of town. Burlington, on the shores of Lake Champlain, had been an important port in the 1800s. In the latter part of the century, wealthy businessmen and industrialists had covered the Hill with grand Italianate, Queen Anne, and Colonial-style mansions. Now these were UVM fraternity and sorority houses, as well as campus buildings used by the university and by Champlain College. The van's blinker went on again, and it appeared that one of these architectural grande dames was their destination. Faith pulled over to the side of the street and watched as the women came to a stop. A few seconds later, they got out of the van. Under the street lights, she could see that Ophelia was carrying a guitar case and Gertrude was taking a hit. She carefully stubbed the roach out in a snowbank and put it in her pocket. Ready to rock 'n' roll.

A frat party? Wasn't Gertrude a little old—and Ophelia a little young? Well, maybe not Ophelia. A townie as hot-looking as she was would be more than welcome. Every maternal alarm bell in Faith's body went off at once. Naomi Stafford had to know that Ophelia was virtually living at Gertrude's—Gertrude, that terrific role model. Again, Faith asked herself, Could Naomi be so dense—or uncaring?

There was a steady stream of people going into the large house. It was as imposing now as the man who built it must have been. Faith pictured him in his top hat and swallow-tailed coat, standing on the broad veranda in front of his symbol of success, the symbol of his power. Ego incarnate overlooking the wide waters of the lake. Tonight, Faith could see lights from the New York side shining far across the expanse. It would have been a black void in those earlier days, but a generation of like-minded entrepreneurs had taken care of that.

It was time to go back to Pine Slopes and bed. She now knew where Ophelia went some of the time, not, as Faith had supposed, to hang out with her Burlington friends, but to chauffer Gertrude to gigs. Faith wondered if the folkie had updated her Joni Mitchell/Joan Baez repertoire to techno or rap. A foursome passed on the sidewalk and turned to go into the house. Oldies. Not as old as Gertrude, but the men's beards were flecked with white, as if it were snowing, and the skin on the women's faces was poised between the tautness of youth and the soft lines of middle age. For the second time that night, Faith did not bother to pause between thought and action. She got out of the car and slipped in behind them. They were through the door. She had passed.

Passed into a time warp. Although, she reflected, what could possibly have changed in that college ritual known as "getting wasted"? The music was loud, the room was stifling, dancers who could find a spare inch of space in which to move were gyrating wildly, and major amounts of alcohol were being consumed. Another kind of Nordic Night.

There was no sign of Gertrude and Ophelia. It seemed an unlikely venue for a hootenanny. But Faith had seen them enter. Initially, curiosity had drawn her in, but the more she looked about, the more she wanted to make sure Ophelia was all right. Gertrude was not the chaperone Faith would have selected for the girl, or for anyone else. She wiggled her way out into the hall, dodged a few gropes—not even slightly flattering, as the gropers, feeling no pain, wouldn't have known Faith from Grandma Moses—and went upstairs. A couple of the doors were locked, but one room wasn't, and she backed out hastily after ascertaining that the individuals hunched over a desk, doing lines, were neither Gertrude nor, thank God, Ophelia. After walking in on a couple who had obviously been studying the *Kama Sutra* more religiously than their college texts, she decided to forgo the living quarters and head for the basement, retracing her steps until she found another set of stairs.

She heard her before she saw her. Gertrude's voice wasn't bad. It wasn't good, either. But she was pushing it for all it was worth, wailing out a Janis Joplin number, which was going over big. Whether this was because her audience was totally stoned or totally unacquainted with the real thing, Faith didn't know.

The frat house had turned the space into a coffeehouse. A few people were even drinking coffee—or something from mugs. The air was filled with smoke, the lights low, and Gertrude was perched on a high stool, a single blue spot above picking up the gold threads of her elaborately embroidered caftan. She cradled the mike, holding it close to her mouth—in a close approximation of what Faith had walked in on upstairs. Ophelia, carved in stone, sat at her idol's feet, holding a bottle of Poland Spring water—not Southern Comfort—her hand on the cap, ready to offer succor at a moment's notice. Two more bottles stood at the ready. Faith didn't have to worry about being spotted. The girl was gazing at the singer with total devotion. It would have taken a major calamity to distract her, and even then Faith imagined the two figures, one singing, one listening, continuing on, oblivious to the flames, falling beams, or other disasters surrounding them. The guitar was off to one side. Faith had missed the opening number. "If I Had a Hammer"?

Gertrude finished the song, wailing, "Call on me, darlin', just call on me." Ophelia's hand shot up, and without looking down, Gertrude drank, smacked her lips, and dropped the bottle back into the waiting receptacle.

The room had exploded with applause, whistles, and the occasional "We love you, Gert!" Apparently, the nickname was all right on campus.

"Thank you, thank you so much. You're a lovely audience." The huskiness in her voice was more pronounced tonight than it had been when Faith had had that brief interchange with her in the dining room at Le Sapin. Could be the cigarette smoke. Or the joint? Today's marijuana was not your father's reefer. Stronger several times over, usually laced with something else, and harsher. Maybe Gert grew her own.

Two skinny undergrads of indeterminate sex had provided backup. The only resemblance to the Holding Company was their hair—long and frizzy, the old "put my finger in a socket" look. One of those guys who were always around at things like this came up and fiddled with the mike, twirled some dials on the sound system, then crouched in readiness, a bookend to Ophelia. The girl seemed safe enough. The only liquid in any proximity was water—and she probably wouldn't even drink that, saving it for the diva instead. Gertrude was the only person in the room—perhaps the only person in the world—who mattered to the girl.

Some more people drifted in; a few left.

"I knew her, you know," Gertrude said softly into the mike, sharing a secret just with them, just with the people lucky enough to be in this room on this particular winter night. Cosmic. "Out in the Haight. Janis. A wild thing. Beautiful. None of the photographs ever captured her essence. Who she really was. We didn't deserve her, and she left us. We killed her."

This was not quite the story Faith had heard, but it played well with the audience. Gertrude appeared to be about to say something more, but then she closed her eyes—the better to commune?—and transformed herself into Donovan, rasping out "Mellow Yellow" to the appreciative group who joined in lustily every time the only two words they knew came up.

It was quite a performance, but Faith had seen enough.

———

Tom was a heavy sleeper, but a child's cough or cry in the night—or, in this case, his wife's step on the carpeted floor—wakened him immediately.

"Hey, you. Where have you been? A farewell party with your *compadres?*"

Faith walked closer to the bed.

"Phew. That must have been some wingding. You stink, my love."

Hoping she wouldn't rouse him, she'd planned to jump into the shower and get rid of the smell of cigarettes and beer that clung to her body.

"It's a long story. I'll tell you all about it in the morning. What's been going on here?"

"Not much. Mom and Dad brought Ben home, and he fell into bed almost as fast as Amy had, but I did get him to do his teeth."

The Fairchilds were very big on teeth. It was the first thing Marian ever noted about anyone, Faith had observed. "She has good teeth," or "He has a very white smile," she'd say. Maybe they had been in the placebo group in the Gardol study when they were kids. Had happened to be sitting on the wrong side of the classroom that day.

"That's a relief. What about Betsey—and Scott?"

"Betsey came slamming in, ripping because some teenager from North Carolina beat her in Scrabble. I went down when I heard the door, figured it was you. I thought maybe I could get her to calm down and talk a little, but no hope. She did agree to a cup of Sleepytime tea, but the moment I raised my availability as a listener, she was off again. 'Thank you, Tom. Thank you *very* much.' You know how she says it. And 'I have my own pastor, should I be in need of any advice, which I am not.' So I poured myself a brandy and went to bed. I don't know if Scott and Andy are home or not. I presume so, because I did hear Dennis come in, and he must have been with them."

"You go back to sleep. I'm going to take a quick shower. Sleep in if you want. I'll take the kids in the morning. I promised the crew I'd have breakfast with them. They're making me something special, and then I'm going to brief the new chef."

"I would have thought you'd seen enough of them tonight." Tom sounded slightly annoyed.

"I wasn't with them. I was . . . well, I'll tell you tomorrow. Now I just need to get this smell out of my hair and get to bed." Faith wanted her husband to be alert and understanding when she explained that she had spent a few hours tailing an aging hippie and her acolyte to Animal House.

She had turned on the taps and started to undress, when she was seized by a question that had to be answered immediately. She turned the water off and slipped out the door and down the stairs. The light over the sink kept her from knocking into the furniture. She slowly turned the knob to the kids' room and pushed the door open. There was enough light to see four mounds. She stepped in and listened contentedly to the soft breathing coming from the bunk beds. She was about to leave, when she realized that there was no noise at all coming from one of the bottom bunks. She peeled a corner of the sheet from the lump on the pillow. The old rolled-up blanket trick. If he were sleeping next door, he wouldn't have tried to make it look like he was here. He wasn't with Ophelia the roadie. So where *was* Scott?

A re you *sure* you want to go?" Faith asked her children. Wednesday had dawned cold and bleak. "You can come with me and hang out in the kitchen for a while, then go with Dad to the Sports Center. Or this morning might be a great time to take the Ben & Jerry's tour." She thought for sure this last suggestion would do the trick. It was a lousy ski day.

"Mom," Ben explained patiently. "How am I ever going to learn to ride the rail all the way if I don't stick with my lessons and practice?"

Faith now knew this was Ben's description of going down the rail slide on his board in the Terrain Park, not hopping a freight car bound for Frisco.

"Yeah," Amy piped up. "And how am I going to get good enough to ski with Ben if I don't go?"

"You're never—" Ben started, then catching his mother's gaze of disapproval, did a 180 and finished, "going to get better if you don't practice. You're right, Amester. Besides, Mom"—somehow, he was managing to invest his prepubescent voice with David McCulloch–like measured tones—"a lot of kids won't be there, so we'll have like private lessons."

"Don't say *like*," she said automatically, then resigned herself to bundling all of them up for the outdoors. It would have been nice to linger in the condo a bit longer, but she knew when she had been beaten.

This was the Fairchild side, as in the "Let's bike to Alaska" dream Dick mentioned all too frequently.

She left Amy with her group inside the lodge and walked up to the main lift with Ben to meet his. The lift had just opened, so there weren't many people in line. Faith watched idly as skiers reached for the chair and sat back. One, two, three—they moved slowly up the mountain. Four, five, six—they swayed slightly side to side, skis up like toothpicks. Then suddenly, the lift stopped.

The people waiting in line grew still, eyes on the lift. The slight morning breeze, which had made small eddies in the snowy surfaces of the slopes, died down. Then suddenly, everything in front of Faith was almost literally turned upside down as she watched in horror with everyone else. Swiftly, inexorably, the chairs on the motionless lift came sliding down the cable, crashing into one another and spilling their contents to the ground. One man jumped, his arms outstretched like some kind of rara avis. Screams filled the air and the people in line frantically pushed their way under the ropes, streaming down the slope toward the lodge as others were racing up. Ben grabbed her arm.

"*What's happening? What's wrong?*"

She pulled him close to her, wrapping him against her body as she turned him away from the ghastly sight.

"Something's wrong with the lift. Help is coming, so don't worry." She struggled to keep her voice calm.

The first ski patrol snowmobiles, stationed close to the lift, came roaring by.

Faith stood, immobilized. It had been like any accident: slow-motion seconds that seemed to go on forever, then fast forward and chaos.

Some of the people on the ground were getting to their feet. The members of the ski patrol had one man on a stretcher and were moving a young girl, a boarder, onto another. For a moment, Faith thought it might be Ophelia, but when they took her helmet off, a mass of dark brown curls tumbled to her shoulders. She looked scared, but she was nodding.

Faith had to get Ben away.

"Let's go back to the condo. The ski patrol is taking care of things. The lift stopped before the chairs were too high off the ground, and it looks like no one has been badly hurt, thank God."

"But what happened, Mom? Why did all the chairs slide like that?"

"I don't know, sweetheart, but we'll find out."

"This isn't something that happens a lot, is it?" he asked anxiously. "I never heard of it happening."

"No, the lifts are very, very safe. They're inspected all the time. When we find out what happened, we'll know more. But you shouldn't worry about going on them." Faith resolved to take Ben down to one of the other lifts at the resort as soon as they knew what was going on. This had been an accident. A freak accident.

Pete was walking away from the lift. He looked grim.

"Stay here a moment," Faith told Ben, pointing to one of the ski racks outside the lodge.

She caught up to Pete. "What's wrong with the lift?"

"Nothing's wrong with the lift," he said. "Someone wedged the bull wheel—that's what keeps the lift running. Be all right for a while until you got to the wedge, then just like someone picking up the end of a curtain rod and letting all the rings slide off."

"So it wasn't an accident?"

"No, Mrs. Fairchild, it wasn't an accident."

EIGHT

And going back to work would be the worst thing in the world, I guess? Especially when you're sooo busy at the gym and the mall! I thought you'd want to help, that being married meant helping out when times were rough. Looks like I thought wrong."

Craig Fairchild's voice was suffused with sadness. It was far worse than one of his blowups. Faith wished she hadn't walked in on this particular scene. Neither Glenda nor Craig had noticed her. Perhaps she could slip back out. She'd come to her in-law's condo, expecting that Tom would be there with the rest of them, but apparently they were all still on the slopes. Both Amy's and Ben's ski groups were down at the Sports Center—far away from the scene at the base of the mountain.

It had been total chaos until the staff managed to get the word out that the problem was an easily repairable equipment malfunction and that there had been no serious injuries. Bruises, some aches and pains, but only the young snowboarder had sustained anything worse—unfortunately, she had broken an ankle. She'd be laid up for the rest of the season. The Staffords lurched into damage control once more and suspended lift fees for the rest of the week for those staying at Pine Slopes and gave a free day to everyone else. Craig had been in the thick of things, racing around, reassuring people he knew and people he didn't. "I plan to be first on the lift the moment Pete gives the okay," Faith had heard him declare over and over. Ben had wanted to stay, but fortunately Steve, one of his instructors, came over and told them about the change in plans for the morning. Faith offered to take Ben down to the Sports Center while Steve rounded up the others. Then it was "Hurry up, Mom. Steve said to get down there right away." And Faith reflected, not by any means for the first time, how one's children will always behave better for total strangers and certainly for ski gurus than for their parents. It was both reassuring and disheartening.

While she was fulfilling Steve's wishes, Craig must have returned to the condo. And now here he was, engaged in a bitter argument with his wife. Glenda was wearing a pearly white ski outfit today, lustrous and formfitting. It was trimmed with pale gray fur at the color and cuffs. A hat of the same fur—fox?—was on the floor. Pulled off in irritation? She tossed her hair back, and it seemed to crackle, as if a flashbulb had burst. The full effect was intimidating, a reincarnation of Narnia's White Witch. Craig was standing face-to-face with his wife, and Faith had a sudden impulse to pull him away, lest Glenda turn him to stone with her icy touch.

"Don't start laying this on me!" Glenda's voice was louder and not a bit sad. "I'm not the one who's losing everything we own!"

Faith closed the door firmly behind her. She didn't want to hear any more. No, that wasn't it. She definitely wanted to hear more, but at any moment, one or the other would spot her, an eavesdropper, a voyeur.

"Hi, the ski school has moved down to the Sports Center for the morning and I wanted to let Tom know, but he's not next door. Do you know where he is?"

Craig shook his head. "I haven't seen him since the accident, but I'm late for a meeting with Freddy. If I run into Tom, I'll let him know."

"Thanks. I left a note next door and I'll leave one here, but I don't seem to be having much luck with that form of communication. Tell him

I have to brief the new chef and then I'll be free. If he doesn't meet me at the restaurant, I'll come back here."

"Okay," Craig said, and turned to Glenda. "We'll talk later. I won't be long." He reached out to give her a kiss. She took a step backward and sat down.

"I don't know what my plans are. But yes, we *will* be talking."

Looking grim, Craig left, and Faith started to follow him. She'd already called the kitchen once to tell them she was running late for the surprise breakfast the crew had prepared. She didn't want to keep them waiting any longer, especially since the new chef would be arriving soon.

"You heard, didn't you?" Glenda said. It wasn't an accusation. More a point of information.

"Some of it," Faith admitted.

Glenda stood up and walked over to the bookcase. She reached behind a book and took out a pack of cigarettes.

"I'm trying to quit, but not today. Do you mind?"

Faith did mind—minded that Glenda hadn't been able to stop and minded the smell—but she nodded. It was Glenda's life, and as she had amply demonstrated, she was a big girl who made her own decisions.

"He's stripped what little savings we had, taken a second mortgage on the house, and borrowed money from anyone stupid enough to lend him some just to put a bundle into this two-bit resort. I'm no Donald Trump, but even I could tell him that he'd have been better off standing on the Bourne Bridge and throwing it all into the Cape Cod Canal. But it's always 'Freddy thinks' or 'Freddy wants.'" Glenda's smoking matched her invective. She'd take a drag, pulling the smoke deep into her lungs, expel it forcibly, and wave the cigarette, stained deep red from her lipstick, into the air with a punching motion, as if Craig were close at hand.

"Oh dear," Faith said, inwardly noting the inadequacy of the words but unable, after all that had been happening since her arrival at Pine Slopes, to come up with anything else. "Do Dick *and* Marian know?"

"I doubt it. I don't think anyone knows—and I don't want anyone to know. *Capice?*"

Faith capiced.

"What he has to do is get it all back. If we have to, we can sue the Staffords. Undue influence."

Glenda probably watched a lot of Court TV, besides *The Apprentice*, Faith speculated. She was right about the influence part, though. Craig would do anything for Freddy, and that meant doing anything for Pine Slopes. It was clear now why he'd pressed his father to have the birthday celebration here; also why Craig seemed to know so much about the inner workings of the place—and care so much. He was losing his shirt.

Investing in a ski resort was all well and good if you could afford the possibility that you might be saying good-bye to the money. True of any investment, but especially one so dependent on the will of the gods. If it snowed, you'd make money. If it didn't . . . And even if it did snow, there were other factors, and those had been coming fast and furious at Pine Slopes: the loss of the chef, the prank at the pool, today's sabotage—still a secret, from what Faith had observed. The break-in at the condo was being kept under wraps, too. And then there was Boyd Harrison's death. Although terrible in itself, its ramifications—the calling in of the loans—were a further disaster.

"Look, I know you probably think I'm a terrible wife. That I should stand by my man and let him deal with this himself."

"No. Of course I—"

"Let me finish. I know how you Fairchilds stick together. This family is like a club. Dick's the president, Marian's the secretary, and the rest of you show up for meetings. Maybe there's a secret handshake. For sure, there are a lot of inside jokes. It hasn't been easy being the newest member. But the thing that's made life the hardest is the bill of goods Craig sold me. I thought he had money, a lot of money. He had a great car—and hefty payments every month, I found out too late—took me to nice places, and flashed his Amex card around. He was *known*."

Faith could picture it all—all too well.

"When I met the family, I could tell there was money there, too."

"But—"

"Give me a break, Faith. I know church mice get more than Tom does, but you come from money and make a lot of money. What are you wearing today? I'll bet you anything it's not from the Gap. Then there are the Parkers. They live in a mansion. My family lived in a place the size of Betsey's Great Room, and there were six of us. Dick and Marian are the types who have their money safely stowed away, making more money. Marian walks around in sweaters my mother would give to the Salvation Army, but on Marian they look right. Because she can buy any sweater Talbot's sells, but sews up the holes in her old ones instead. Think about it. They own three houses. Could you blame me for assuming that Craig was like the rest of his family? A clever businessman, money in the bank? I almost forgot Robert. That seems to happen a lot in the Fairchild Club. Maybe he's the one I should have gone after. He's definitely got bucks, and he's as good-looking as Craig, maybe better."

Faith had to get to the restaurant kitchen, but she couldn't leave Glenda like this.

"It *is* a hard family to fit into. I think all families are, even for those born into them." Maybe especially for them, she added to herself. "But everyone was truly pleased when Craig married you. He's been so happy, and I suppose we took it for granted that you were, too. He's done a stupid—no, make that terrible—thing. One of the rules of marriage is that you have to talk to each other about decisions like this. I think Craig wanted to surprise you. Make a huge profit and buy you a house like his sister's." Or a ring, Faith thought, and again kept the thought to herself. "He's like a little boy in some ways."

"Well, I'm not sure I have the time or patience to wait for him to grow up. I love Craig. He's very sweet and good to me, but I can't trust him."

Enough was enough. Glenda had just admitted she'd married Craig for his money. From the remark about the size of her house, it was clear she had come from a poor background, but that was no excuse. A reason, but not an excuse. Faith looked her sister-in-law straight in the eye.

"Can he trust you?"

Glenda turned red, angrily stubbed her cigarette out against the fireplace, and threw the butt in with the logs.

"I think you'd better mind your own business, Faith. I'd watch out if I was you."

For the second time that week, Faith found herself trembling with rage at one of her sisters-in-law.

"Is that a threat of some kind?"

Glenda picked her hat off the floor and put it on, deliberately turning her back on Faith.

"Take it however you want."

The kitchen smelled heavenly, and Faith felt the morning's events melt away like a late-spring snow. The appetizing fragrance would make a great first impression when the chef arrived. If whatever it was tasted as good as it smelled, there could be a new addition—something with a Latin flair—to Le Sapin's menu.

"Ah, Señora Confianza, we have been keeping your food hot for you," Eduardo said. Faith knew they must have been watching the clock anxiously, and yet from their relaxed poses at the counter and against the wall, it was as if they had all the time in the world. A nice feeling. No "Where have you beens?" to greet her. No guilt.

"Sit down, sit down," Alessandro said with a flourish, leading Faith to a place setting on the counter.

"I hope you like this. It is a dish from Peru." Eduardo put a plate in front of her. She could smell onions, garlic, and the sauce had tomatoes in it. There was also a hint of peanuts. What could it be?

"I know I'll love it."

They gathered around to watch her take the first bite.

"*¡Riquisimo!*" she declared—and it *was* delicious.

The dish was fantastic. Faith thought of what Calvin Trillin's daughter used to say when she was younger: "My tongue is smiling."

"Okay, what is this? And I hope there's more."

"It's Peruvian. *Llapingachos* with Salsa de Mali (see recipe on page 234). We eat a lot of potatoes in Peru. First, we mix mashed potatoes with onion and cheese, add a little salt and pepper, and make little flat cakes, which we fry. Then we put the sauce on—tomatoes, garlic, more onion, and peanuts. We used peanut butter today, because we could not find any peanuts to chop up, but it tastes almost the same."

Peruvian potato pancakes. Faith loved the whole idea.

"Before you leave, we will make you some Bolivian *salteñas*," said Juana. "We make round circles of piecrust and put all sorts of good things on one half—chopped beef, onions, olives, tomato, garlic, rice, sometimes hard-boiled egg—then we fold it over and bake it in the oven. You can buy them anywhere. People are always happy to walk around eating *salteñas.*"

"I'd like that. Every culture had a kind of food like your *salteñas*—sandwiches, of course, but Cornish pasties are even more similar, and then there are Italian calzones, Chinese dumplings, and Polish pierogies. Portable food to take to work or for a picnic." Faith scraped the last morsel of potato cake from her plate and was promptly rewarded with another helping. She looked around at her crew, so young, so eager.

"There was a problem with *la silla del ascenso,* the chairlift, yes?" Vincente asked with poorly disguised casualness.

"Yes, but it's probably been fixed by now, and no one was seriously injured. One girl has a broken ankle. It was very lucky that it didn't happen later in the day."

Eduardo and Vincente exchanged glances. What do they know about all this? Faith wondered. As help—and foreign help, in addition—they had a kind of presence that might have caused them to learn more about what was happening at Pine Slopes than others. A built-in Harry Potter cloak of invisibility. People would talk in front of them, assuming they didn't understand and mostly not noticing them in the first place. Like the chairs, tables, cutlery, they were just there at the restaurant. Not people, but things.

Faith looked at her watch. The chef would be here any minute. There was nothing to do to get ready, though. The kitchen was gleaming, and she'd prepared a list of possible specials for next week. They still had John's list and were a day ahead, since Nordic Night had bumped duck à l'orange and butternut squash ravioli with brown butter and sage.

"Have you been able to get time to ski? On you days off?" she asked.

Alessandro giggled. "On our days off, we work, but I tried skiing. The snow—*la nieve*—is too cold and hard. I was falling always."

"What do you mean you work on your days off?" Faith was startled. The Staffords might be having trouble, but there were laws about this sort of thing.

"We want to. When Mr. Tanner said he needed us to, we were glad. It means more money for us to take home."

"So, Mr. Tanner is your boss. The one who assigns the jobs and the hours?" It was what Faith would have expected. Simon *was* the manager, but she wondered if the Staffords were aware of what he was doing.

One of the swinging doors from the dining room opened and a man walked in. Faith stood up.

"Hello," she said, walking toward him. "You must be the new chef. I'm Faith Fairchild. I've been covering for a few days. And this is your crew—a very well trained and—"

"Yes, I must be the new chef, and no, I don't have all the time in the world to chitchat, lady."

He looked like Nick Nolte on a bad day and was twice his size. Sampling his own wares had added rolls of fat to his large frame. He wasn't wearing anything resembling chef's clothes—no crisp white jacket or checked pants. He wasn't carrying a bag with his knives or other favorite implements. There was no long white apron or even a toque in sight. He was wearing jeans that might have been clean several weeks ago and a flannel shirt—not one of your better-known tartans, perhaps belonging to the K mart clan. His wide black leather belt was cinched tightly, causing his belly to cascade over it, pulled by gravity toward his knees.

"I understand you were at a restaurant in Middlebury?" Faith was aware of the dismay in the room. She was feeling it, too. Yet, perhaps he was an eccentric, like John with his Hawaiian shirts. A gem in slob's clothing?

"Huh? Yeah. So, let's get this show on the road."

"Well," said Faith brightly—too brightly. "As I was saying, this is your staff. They are all very well trained. Over there is Eduardo; then next to him is Alessandro, not to be confused with Tiny, who is also named Alessandro. . . ."

"Lady," the man said wearily. "Are you still here? I know what to do, and as far as I'm concerned, they're all named María or José. Makes life easier. They'll get the picture."

From their faces, the utter lack of any expression whatsoever, Faith knew they already had. Her heart was sinking. What could Simon have been thinking of when he hired this guy? Surely there had to have been someone else?

She made one last try. "Here's a list of the specials for this week, and here's our regular menu. I ordered from Sysco yesterday, and we also have some local suppliers."

He looked at the lists she'd prepared and opened the menu. She realized she didn't know his name. Didn't want to, either.

With a swift motion, he crumbled the lists in a ball and tossed it into the trash can, closing the menu.

"We'll keep the steaks, add more pasta, and fry all the fish. That's what people want."

"But this is a French restaurant! Some of the dishes borrow from other cuisines, but the customers expect primarily French food. I'm sure you know the kind of reputation Le Sapin has."

"This is a ski resort, isn't it? That's what I know. After coming down the mountain all day, people want meat and potatoes. There's your French for you—french fries. Now put on the exhaust fan and open a window one of you. It stinks in here."

"If you need any help—"

Cutting her off seemed to delight the new chef. "I won't. Now, lady, are you still here?"

Eduardo opened the door for her, and out of sight of his new boss, he gave Faith a look of such longing that it was all she could do to keep from firing the man herself and taking his place.

What she did do was go straight to Simon's office.

The manager's office was strategically located on the top floor of the main lodge, a site that was almost exactly in the center of things indoors, with a view of everything happening outdoors at the base of the mountain. Her questions—and irritation—mounting, Faith realized she would have to take a number. Stepping through the door at the end of the corridor, she saw an unmistakable creature slip out of the office and head for the stairs across from it. She was grinning broadly. What business could Gertrude Stafford have had with Simon? As Gertrude was heading down, Craig and Freddy were sprinting up. The look of intense hatred on both the men's faces as they passed Gertrude shocked Faith. None of the three paused to exchange pleasantries, and the two men were in Simon's office before Faith had a chance to say anything. There was no telling how long they would be there, but she decided to wait for a few minutes. She sat down outside the door. It had been a busy morning and she was very tired. The floor was hard and cold—like Alessandro's description of the ski slopes. But Faith didn't care. She leaned back against the wall. Vacation? What vacation?

"Look, Simon, we know you're doing everything you can—Nordic Night was a great idea—but Dad wants us to have another try. You're the only one who can possibly get through to her."

Freddy's voice was coming loud and clear through the door. In their haste, they hadn't closed it completely. Faith edged closer. If anyone came out suddenly, she'd simply tell the truth. She was waiting to talk to Simon about the new chef.

"I *have* been talking to her, believe me. I'll keep on, but we have to face facts. Gertrude's not going to change her mind. What Boyd left her is *hers*."

Faith was stunned. Gertrude was Boyd's heir? Although, remembering what Candy had said about their relationship, it made sense. What didn't was Gertrude's adamant refusal to wait until Pine Slopes was in better shape. Mary and Harold Stafford seemed like such kind—and reasonable people. Couldn't they persuade her? Freddy and his little shadow, Craig, were too angry to be of any use. And Naomi? She seemed to exist on the margins here. Faith had no idea what the woman did all day.

Craig was speaking now, and the desperation in his voice would have made his situation evident even if Faith hadn't talked to Glenda.

"Look, I don't care about a profit. I just have to get back what I've put in. If I don't, I stand to lose my house—and my wife."

"Mate, I'd like to help. I wish I could give it back, but it's not there. You know that. I explained it to you. I also explained the odds when you said you wanted to invest. This is a risky business, and everything's that happened this week shows why. But we'll break even, and there's still the Canadian school vacation week—we're completely booked—and with luck we'll have snow through March or even into April. People love spring skiing. We'll be turning them away."

"I think we should try to give Craig back at least some of his money. He has a mortgage payment coming up, and after all the support he and his family have given us over the years, we should be helping him out."

"Too right. We can do that much. We'll scrape it up from somewhere, but meanwhile we have to find the bastard who wedged the bull wheel and put sand in the tank of the newest groomer."

"*What?*" Freddy yelled. "Nobody told me about this!"

"Pete discovered it yesterday. I assumed you knew. Fortunately, he noticed something was wrong right away, so it should be back in service by the weekend. That's what your father told me."

"It's like someone is out to get us," Craig blurted out. "How hard would it be to wedge that bull wheel? Could a sixteen-year-old girl do it? She could pull all the other stunts all right."

Faith had straightened up at Freddy's cry. What was going on? Could

Ophelia be behind this? The fury was there, but Scott was so sure she wasn't involved. But then, he would have to be. A passionate partisan.

"You're sure the will can't be contested?" Craig asked, coming back to Gertrude when no one took him up on the Ophelia suggestion. There had been a short silence. Faith had no idea whether it was because the men didn't suspect Ophelia or because they wanted to discuss it when Craig wasn't around.

"Sure as can be. Remember, Boyd was a lawyer. He left everything signed, sealed, and delivered to her. That's the way he wanted it, apparently," Simon said.

"I knew about them," Freddy said. "Everyone did, but I never thought he'd cut us out. Mom and Dad didn't, either."

Faith heard a chair scrape. Someone was getting up. She scrambled to her feet and moved farther down the hall, out of earshot, but not before she heard Simon's last words.

"Gertrude was the love of his life, Freddy boy. It's down there in black and white in his last will and testament for all the world to see."

The two men stepped into the hall.

"Hi," Faith called, coming through the door at the end of the hall once again. "Craig, did you see Tom?"

"Yes, and I told him if you weren't in the kitchen, you'd be at the condo." He tried for a smile. Faith's heart ached for him, and her hand ached to slap him up the side of his head. Why was he always doing these stupid things? Putting all his snowballs in one basket like this? And without consulting any of them? She realized with that question, she had her answer. "Buddy," as in "Little Buddy" was the club mascot and had never achieved anything on his own. They'd bailed him out, scolded him gently and not so gently, but they'd never treated him as an equal, an adult. Of course he kept plunging into new ventures, blindly hoping that *this* one—planned all by himself—would be the one that would elevate him to full club membership. She had a sudden image of Betsey's missing ring, and Scott's fancy titanium laptop. Craig had brightened considerably at the notion of pinning the blame on Ophelia. Both items would more than cover his mortgage and credit-card bills for the immediate future. Was he holding them in abeyance, in case he couldn't get his money back from the Staffords? Was Craig the thief? He was desperate enough. He knew the items were insured. Faith looked at his face, usually so open and honest. Craig never had a thought or emotion that couldn't be read there. But not today. After that brief attempt at a smile, the book was shut tight, leaving an unfamiliar blank.

"Thanks," she said. "I need to have a quick word with Simon and then I'll be over."

"Pete's reopening the lift at noon. It was fixed earlier, but he said people wouldn't trust anything that didn't take at least a couple of hours to set straight. I'm going up first with Freddy."

"And we'll be right behind you," Faith said. She had absolute faith in Pete, in more ways than one. He hadn't told her about Gertrude for some reason, but the man was an astute judge of human nature. It was true: If he'd announced the lift was safe fifteen minutes later, not a soul would have believed him.

She knocked on the manager's door.

"Come in," Simon said.

Faith had been in Simon's office only once before and had been impressed then, as now, by its appearance. The large window overlooking the slopes was a constantly changing dynamic backdrop to the furniture, which Faith recognized as coming from Thomas Mosher—clean lines and beautiful woods. An extraordinary Aboriginal painting hung on the wall—undulating curves of color. Simon was working on a Mac G5 with a large flat-screen display, state-of-the-art.

"What a wonderful piece," Faith said, gesturing toward the painting.

"Yes," Simon agreed. "It was from my parents' collection, and I was the lucky one when we drew straws. It's by Helicopter Tjungurrayi of the Balgo Hills. Got his name as a kid when a helicopter flew him to the mission there for treatment."

Faith had had the impression that Simon came from a working-class family, one that wouldn't have an art collection, but she hadn't really gotten very far in her exploration of his roots. Perhaps they'd simply been people with a good eye.

"But you didn't come here to discuss Abo art, although I'm always happy to have a chin-wag."

Faith liked it that the manager was so direct. It made things much easier.

"I'm worried about the new chef."

"Wendell?" Simon raised an eyebrow. He really was good-looking, and this gave him a slight Cary Grant air. A Mercedes in the outback.

"He's completely changing the menu, and I'm afraid we'll lose customers." Faith noticed she had adopted the royal *we*. Well, it was "we." Even the short amount of time she'd invested in Le Sapin had left her feeling like part of the operation.

"Every chef likes to put his or her own stamp on a menu. You know that, I'm sure."

"But this may be the wrong stamp. Fried foods, pastas, steak, none of our specialties, nothing French, except the fries."

Simon laughed. Faith hadn't meant her last words to be funny, but she could see how he might have interpreted them as a joke.

"Let's give him a chance. He came highly recommended."

"But was he the chef or sous-chef in Middlebury? Has he had charge of an entire restaurant and staff? Because that was the other thing: He didn't seem very sensitive to the staff."

Simon laughed. "Those kids don't need a sensitive boss. They're here to make money and pick up some English. Believe me, they're a tough crowd. I don't know what wool they were pulling over your eyes—probably llama's—but don't worry about them. They'll be fine."

Faith doubted it, but there was nothing she could do. She got up. It was getting close to noon and she had to change into her ski clothes. Craig was right: It was important that they all go on the lift.

"I told him to give me a call if he needs any help."

Simon walked around the desk and opened the door for her.

"Don't worry. You got gypped out of your vacation. I want you to enjoy the rest of your time here and stay out of the kitchen. Wendell knows what he's doing."

That's what Faith was afraid of.

It was one thing to say how important it was to be one of the first people on a chairlift that you had seen send its passengers crashing down the mountain only a few hours earlier, but quite another to do it. As Tom and she followed Fred and Craig, Faith had a sudden impulse to wait and take a later chair—the way some couples insist on taking separate planes. But she pasted a smile securely in place and sat back, the tips of her skis pointed toward heaven, and said a quick prayer. She wondered if Tom was doing the same. His lips seemed to be moving slightly. At least the weather had improved. It was another picture postcard–perfect blue sky, a sunny day in the Green Mountain state.

Tom took her hand and squeezed it.

"Okay, honey?"

"Okay."

"You didn't have to come, you know."

Not exactly the best time to tell her this, swaying from side to side, moving farther aloft. Faith had known she didn't have to come, but she'd wanted to. Or rather, she felt she had to stand up—or sit down, in this case—and be counted. And she told Tom so.

She concentrated on the scenery surrounding her. The emergence of the sun's rays had been benevolent, a good omen, and when she looked over her shoulder, she saw that the lift was filling up. We have such faith in technology, she thought. Here in the Estados Unidos. Americans believe everything can be fixed—especially if the sun is shining.

She'd filled Tom in on Craig while they were changing into their ski clothes, and he had been even more dismayed than Faith. She'd also given him a somewhat abbreviated account of her conversation with Glenda.

She was two for two with her sisters-in-law at the moment. She felt a sudden longing for her own sister, Hope, or Niki or Pix. For a female who liked her.

"Should we offer to help Craig out?" she asked. They were high above the treetops now and she was swallowing any panic that dared make its way from the pit of her stomach to the bottom of her throat.

"We don't know anything's wrong, remember? And anyway, I'm not sure that's the right thing to do. Glenda should go back to work. And if she does, that will cover their mortgage, especially if Freddy and Simon come up with some money. I think we'd better leave this one alone for now."

"And if Glenda doesn't get a job?"

"Oh Faith, I don't know. Can we forget about them, forget about my whole family for a couple of hours and just be the two of us?"

"Sounds like a fine idea to me," his wife said, although in practice it might be difficult. Just as Craig, Faith, and Tom had turned out in support of Pine Slopes this afternoon, the rest of the family had been right in line behind them. Faith looked back: Marian and Dick, Betsey and Dennis, Robert, Scott and Andy. Only Glenda was missing, still on the lower slopes. Faith thought about those collective nouns: an exaltation of larks, a pride of lions, a parliament of owls. They were a phalanx of Fairchilds.

Stepping off at the top, she heard a raucous birdcall from the top of one of the tall pines that lined the slope and remembered another term—a murder of crows.

Energized by the afternoon's skiing—it had been glorious—Faith left Tom reluctantly to go shower and change before picking the kids up. He had been right: They needed time together, and he'd been happy to stay with her, tailoring his style and pace to hers. He loved to ski on the woodland trails, as did she. Looking off into the backcountry, Faith was sorry she hadn't had her father-in-law's foresight and packed one of those space blankets inside her parka. At the end of their last run together, they'd met up with Dick and Marian. Marian was ready to call it a day, but Dick wanted to stay out with his sons.

"The day I can't keep up with these brats is the day I take up knitting," Dick said.

"Knitting is very relaxing, but perhaps you're not quite ready for it yet," his wife said before she and Faith walked off toward the condos.

"Pix has a great-uncle who knits his own socks," Faith said as she and Marian walked along. She didn't remember how this had come up in conversation with Pix and Ursula, but what had surprised her more than the unusual activity for a male was the matter-of-fact way the two women had accepted it.

"Odd, but not all that odd for that generation of New Englanders," Marian commented. "But let's get away from knitting. While we have a moment, I want to talk to you about Craig and Glenda," She paused, slowing her usually rapid stride.

"Oh dear," Faith said for the second time in only a few hours. Again the words were inadequate, but the others that sprang to her lips would have been inappropriate. She'd heard Marian say "Darn" once when she'd knocked a pitcher of lemonade over, and then again when she'd discovered the snowplow had uprooted an azalea.

Darn. It had been such a lovely afternoon. She'd almost managed to forget about the new chef, and she *had* managed to shove Craig and Glenda into a file drawer extremely far back in a dusty corner of her mind.

"Exactly my sentiment. I'm afraid they got married before they really knew each other well enough to make that kind of commitment, and now that they are getting to know each other, they may not be so thrilled with what they're finding out."

"It was a pretty hasty marriage. They'd only met a month before, right? Sometimes those things work out—that bolt from the blue, head over heels kind of love. . . ." Faith was thinking about the first time she saw Tom, standing by the buffet at a wedding reception she was catering at the Campbell Apartment in Grand Central Station, one of the city's hidden treasures. In the 1920s, John Campbell had transformed a huge space off the west balcony into a Florentine palazzo/office, adding a pipe organ and grand piano for the nights when he and his wife entertained. Restored with many of its original furnishings, including a Persian rug thirty feet wide and sixty feet long, it was a wonderful place for a party. Tom had been intensely interested in her miniature saucisson en brioche, then intensely interested in her. By the time the horse-drawn carriage in Central Park had reached its stop opposite the Plaza Hotel later that night, they'd known they were meant to be together for the rest of their lives, although it was more than a year before they actually tied the knot.

"And sometimes they don't," said Marian, finishing for her. "Craig's current money problems have brought things to a head sooner, perhaps, than they would have otherwise."

Faith wasn't surprised that Marian knew about Craig's investments.

"I think Glenda is pretty upset that he didn't tell her what he was doing," Faith said. She didn't consider the conversation she'd had with Glenda one of a confidential nature. Besides, Marian probably knew all about it, too. Did she know about Betsey's behavior, as well? Faith hoped this little talk wasn't going to lead to a thorough examination of her relations with her sisters-in-law, although Marian was not a "let your hair down," "put your cards on the table" type of person. Faith was somewhat startled that Marian was bringing Craig and Glenda up at all. Alongside the Fairchild motto "Live Actively or Die" was its corollary, "Let Sleeping Dogs Lie."

"And she has a right to be upset. A marriage where the spouses don't tell each other important things like this—you notice I didn't say *everything*, Faith, because that's important, too—is resting on a pretty shaky foundation."

Marian must be extremely worried to be talking this way, Faith thought. Her mother-in-law never gave, or took, advice. It was one of the things Faith adored about her. Faith could only remember a few times when Marian had spoken so categorically.

"Umm." Faith nodded. It was the only response she could think of.

What's happening to my brain? she wondered. She seemed to be having trouble starting the engine, forget getting out of first gear.

"I'm mentioning all this because we have to keep an eye on Craig. She's going to leave him. It's just a question of when, and we'll have to be ready to pick up the pieces."

Before her conversation with Glenda—and before Roy Hansen—Faith would have been stunned at her mother-in-law's words. Words Marian repeated with emphasis as they reached the condos and went their separate ways.

"She married him for better, not worse, and she'll be taking off one of these days, unless by some miracle Craig manages to get back everything he's put into Pine Slopes, or wins the lottery. Such a waste of money, but you can't convince him of that. Or his father, either. 'Think of the likelihood,' I tell Dick, and he only says, 'Somebody's got to win, why not me?' " Marian sighed.

Faith had bought a lottery ticket once, didn't win, and never bought another one, so Marian was preaching to the choir.

"See you at dinner," Faith said, giving Marian a hug. "Maybe things aren't as bad as we think."

Marian hugged her back. "You know they are, sweetheart. And by the way, don't say a word to Dick. He doesn't suspect a thing, and I'd hate to spoil his birthday fun."

Why am I not surprised? Faith said to herself when she opened the door and saw Glenda sitting on the couch in the living room with her jacket on and two suitcases on the floor next to her. The "when" of Mrs. Craig Fairchild's departure was being answered possibly sooner than Marian expected.

"Good, you're back. I hoped it would be you," Glenda said, turning Oprah off with the remote control. What had the topic been, Faith wondered. "Women Who Marry in Haste and Don't Want to Repent at Leisure"? "She Doesn't Tell; He Doesn't Tell: Where's There's No Fire, There's Smoke"?

"What's going on, Glenda? Why are you all packed?" Faith asked.

There was no way she was going to get her shower, she realized dismally. It had been difficult all week to squeeze in time in the tub or shower. Just another aspect of her "vacation."

Glenda's chin jutted forward. Her tight leather jacket and pants emphasized her breasts, elbows, and knees. She'd just done her nails. They were filed and painted a shiny crimson. The woman was a mass of sharp points.

"Roy is driving me to the bus station in Montpelier. I'm getting out of here, and I need someone to tell Craig."

"Oh no, not me." Faith backed toward the kitchen and sat down on one of the stools. Definitely not me, she said to herself. Glenda could do her own dirty work. A Dear John letter, a phone call from the bus station, or how about telling him face-to-face—a novel idea?

"I could leave him a note or call him later, but it's better if he hears it from someone in person." Glenda had obviously given the matter some thought.

"And that can't be you, because . . ."

Glenda looked at her, seemingly puzzled that Faith would ask such a stupid question.

"I have no idea when he's going to be coming back from skiing, and I want to get the seven o'clock bus. As it is, it's going to be tight. We probably won't have time to stop for a bite to eat."

"Glenda!" Faith couldn't help herself. "If what I'm hearing is correct, you're talking about leaving your husband, not just cutting out on this vacation, and all you're worried about is catching a particular bus and getting something to eat!"

"I told you we probably *wouldn't* have time to get something to eat," Glenda explained patiently. "But, yes, this is good-bye. I thought I explained it all this morning. Craig has destroyed my trust in him. I can't live with always wondering what half-assed thing he's going to put our money into next. He's never had a real job and never will. I need someone dependable."

And rich, Faith added to herself.

"I know you think I'm some kind of a heartless bitch to be going off like this, but I've thought the whole thing through. I called my friend Marcy, and she thinks I'm being very practical. Why drag things out when I know where this is going? And it's kinder to Craig not to have some big deal 'I'm outta here' scene. This way, I leave, get my stuff from the house, file for a quickie no-fault divorce, and that's that."

It was a pretty short "To Do" list, and Faith was sure Glenda would squeeze the health club in somewhere.

Not being able to reassure her soon-to-be ex-sister-in-law as to what she thought of her, Faith was determined to stick to her original refusal. Hadn't Glenda ever heard of killing the messenger?

"I'm not going to be the one to tell him. You either have to leave a note or tell him yourself and take a later bus. There must be one after seven going to Boston."

"Tell who what?"

Both women had been so intent on their conversation that they hadn't noticed Dennis come in. Even if they had noticed him, they wouldn't have. He was that kind of person.

But Glenda seized upon him, literally grabbing his hand and upping the wattage on her strobe smile.

"Dennis. Perfect! Much better for a guy to tell him."

"Nice to see you, too, Glenda," Dennis said. Maybe he does have a sense of humor, Faith thought.

There was a knock on the door. Glenda hastily called out, "Come in," and Roy Hansen stepped into the room. The condo was filling up rapidly.

Looking uncomfortable, the Viking prince kept close to the door and said, "Maybe this is not a good time?"

"No, it's perfect. I'll be with you in a second." Glenda directed her beam toward him, then back at Dennis. "Look, Faith will explain every-thing. Roy is driving me to the bus. Things haven't exactly worked out for Craig and me, and I need you to tell him I've left." She stood up and reached for her suitcases.

"Wait a minute!" Dennis said. "You want *me* to tell your husband you're leaving him? I mean, is this for good? You just got married!"

Glenda nodded. "Faith will explain everything." She was moving toward the door, and Roy, Scandinavian gentleman that he was, had grabbed her suitcases.

"No, thank you," Dennis said emphatically. "I'm not getting involved in this."

Glenda gave Roy a pained look, which clearly said, See what I have to deal with?

"It doesn't really matter. I was *trying* to be thoughtful. If he comes back and I'm not here, he might worry. Do whatever you want, but if he starts sending the ski patrol looking for me, you might tell him not to bother. I guess I can ask you to do that much." Sarcasm was not Glenda's style, but she managed to pull this last bit off. Faith realized she was right. They, the team of Faith and Dennis, would have to tell Craig, or he would report his wife missing.

"I'll be staying with Marcy, and I'll call him about the divorce. It will save money not to use lawyers. Say good-bye to everybody for me. It was a fun couple of days. I never thought I'd learn to ski."

And with that, Glenda Fairchild walked out of the door and out of their lives.

Dinner was a subdued affair. Initial attempts at light conversation had proved as leaden as the vegetarian lasagna Betsey had prepared. After the first bite, Craig had made no attempt to eat any more. He was opting for a liquid diet of Otter Creek. After Glenda left, Faith and Dennis had gone next door and told Marian what had happened. Then the skiers had arrived back all at once. Faith had taken Tom aside, and he'd ended up being the one to break the news to Craig.

"It's cold out. Too cold to walk down to the Sports Center. Why don't you kids go next door and watch some videos?" Faith suggested. "There's popcorn." Even Amy had picked up on the tension and the fact that there was someone missing at the table.

"Where's Aunt Glenda?" she'd asked when Betsey had started serving.

"She had to go home early," Tom had said, and then ignored Ben's whys until the Parker boys picked up the cue, diverting Ben with promises of a full morning of boarding on Saturday, their last day.

The movie idea seemed to be going over well. "Okay, Mom, can we invite Phelie?" Amy asked. Little feet dared tread where none, even angels', would.

Before Betsey could say anything, Marian said, "I think that's a wonderful idea. You can call her from next door. We'll all be here if you need anything."

The kids left. Giving up on dinner, the adults cleared the table, stacked the dishwasher—Dick rinsing, mirabile dictu—and then sat back down while Faith set out mugs of coffee and tea, along with a big plate of sugar and spice cookies. Soon everyone was cradling a mug, but and no one had reached for a cookie. There was no talk of night skiing. There was no talk at all.

Then Craig let the dam burst open.

"Okay, I've been an idiot again. I've lost all my money, my house, and my wife," he said in a choked voice. "I thought Pine Slopes would be a safe bet. I *know* the owners. They'd never screw me over the way the others did. It's been a nightmare. One thing after another. Freddy doesn't know what to do. *Harold* doesn't know what to do, and that's never happened before. Simon may be able to get me enough so I don't lose the house." He ran his hands through his hair, pulling at the roots. "Nothing as bad as this week can happen again. We can still pull it out, but it could be too late for me. It's too late for Glenda, that's for sure."

Dick walked over and sat on the arm of the easy chair his son was slouching in.

"Everybody goes through bad times, son, and, yes, you've had more than your share of them, but don't you *ever* call any kid of mine an idiot." He put an arm around Craig's shoulder.

Faith thought she had never loved her father-in-law as much as she did at this moment.

Craig sat up straighter.

"You can't keep bailing me out, Dad. All of you. I can't accept any more help."

"Nobody's talking about that, and I'm proud to hear you say this. But there's help and there's help. About Glenda—well, she was a knockout, but maybe the two of you got hitched too fast. It hurts and it's gonna hurt, but your mother is a good listener. Keeps her mouth shut, too, which is more than I can say about myself. Talk to her. And then as far as the rest goes, I think it's time you finished reviewing and took the licensing exam. Time for you to join Fairchild Realty. People like you. You know that. You're a natural-born salesman."

Dick was beaming. He'd come up with a solution and all was well in the garden. He didn't notice the cyclone approaching from the south forty, though. Betsey had covered her mouth with her hand, but at any moment she'd drop it and suck the whole universe into her wrath.

"Dad, I agree with you that Craig is made for sales. I've been telling him that for years, but I'm not sure real estate is for him," said Robert, his voice calm and steady. Betsey's hand slowly dropped into her lap and joined the other, which was clutching her empty mug with almost enough force to shatter it.

"What are you proposing?" Dick asked.

Robert smiled at his brother. "What is the thing you've always been best at out of all of us—and loved the most?" He didn't wait for an answer. "Skiing, of course. The parent company of my company distributes ski equipment—downhill, boards, Nordic, and all the accessories. A salesman who knows the sport as well as you do would be invaluable to them. I've talked to him about this before," Robert said to the others.

"It's a possibility," Craig said slowly.

Not enough money, Faith thought. Not enough money for the Glendas he wanted. Not enough money to show the family he could make a killing. It wasn't just Roy, Faith realized, or Craig's investment woes, but the sight of Betsey's flashy ring that had hastened Glenda's decision. Craig would never be able to afford a bauble like that—at least not in the foreseeable future—and Glenda needed baubles. There had been little mention of the thefts. Faith wished she'd been able to search Glenda's bags, and person.

The phone rang, and Craig was up like a shot, grabbing the receiver before the second ring.

"What? Who do you want?"

It wasn't his wife.

"Faith, it's for you. I think it's one of the kitchen crew at Le Sapin."

He headed for the door. Marian made a little waving motion with her hand and Tom, Robert, and Dennis all got up and followed him out, pulling their jackets from the coat hooks that lined the entryway.

"Hello," Faith said.

It was Eduardo. He was talking rapidly.

"Señora, you have to come right away. We don't know what to do. People are very angry. They are leaving! The chef has drunk too much of his beer. He was yelling. Now he is sleeping on the floor."

"Did you call Mr. Tanner?"

"Yes, but he is not in his office or at the Sports Center. Vicente is looking for him. We called Mr. Freddy, but we can't find him too. We are trying to feed the people, but more are leaving."

"Okay, I'll be right there. Tell everyone there has been a delay and that their dinners are on the house."

" 'On the house'? But . . ."

"I'll explain later. Just tell the people at each table that. 'Your dinner and drinks are on the house.' "

The young Latin Americans were learning a number of unusual English expressions, Faith realized, as another popped into her mind: dead drunk.

NINE

Chef Wendell had collapsed in the corner next to one of the swinging doors that led into Le Sapin's dining room. Faith toyed briefly with the idea of dragging him to a more convenient spot, but the idea was repugnant. His mouth hung open and some kind of liquid—drool or beer—had collected in his jowls. His hair was plastered across his forehead in sweaty strands, and he was ripe. Ripe with alcohol, grease, and some indefinable smell all his own—something akin to wet dog.

"Should we try to move him?" Eduardo asked. He sounded no more enthusiastic than Faith was.

"No, we have better things to do." She wished she had a tarp to throw over him. She didn't want to waste a tablecloth on the mountainous mound. They'd never get the smell out. "You told everyone their meal and drinks were on the house, right?"

Eduardo nodded. "We've been pouring a lot of wine and serving soup and salads. But what does—"

"It means it's free; they don't have to pay. We're 'the house.' It's on us." Her hasty explanation wasn't altering the puzzled look on his face. "I'll tell you about it later. Now I want all the servers to go and take orders for entrées. I'll be out in a minute, so people will know that the chef has been replaced."

On the way over, she'd been thinking about what they could offer as fast as possible that didn't remotely resemble the evening's fast-food offerings. They'd go with steak, but offer it with béarnaise sauce or au poivre. There was still plenty of salmon. That would be tonight's special. She'd do it with a pecan crust and serve it with curried rice pilaf—quick dishes. And for pasta, they'd stick with good old Alfredo and primavera, plus the ravioli with sage and brown butter. She wrote it all out for the servers and sent them on their way.

Although it was obvious that the crew had been trying to clean up and get things organized, the kitchen was still a mess. Wendell had taken bags of frozen fries—his Continental touch—from the cafeteria's freezer, as well as hamburger patties. Faith could imagine the scene all too well. Le Sapin's freezers were well stocked. There wouldn't have been much room left to store the patties, so he left them to defrost on the counters. Plastic bags of buns were also strewn about. The crew must have been horrified, but given his treatment of them earlier, she was sure none of them had dared say a word. If he hadn't drunk himself into a stupor, Pine Slopes could well have been facing lawsuits due to food poisoning. There was no telling how long the meat had been sitting out. She told Vincente to shove it all into trash bags and get it out of the way, then scrub the counters.

Taking a clean apron from a drawer, Faith donned the toque she'd placed on a shelf when she'd left last night. Trying not to look at Wendell, who was now snoring heavily, she went out into the dining room, using the door Wendell wasn't blocking. Wendell! If he were a chef, she'd *eat* her toque. Short-order cook, possibly, but even that struck her as a stretch.

The bibulous offerings—or the prospect of a decent meal—had calmed the room, although there were more empty tables than she would have liked to see. People had fled in indignation before the crisis was resolved. Faith went from table to table, offering suggestions and apologizing for the contretemps. The French word was appropriate and infinitely more civilized than the English, *screwup,* which was what it was. A snafu. Outwardly smiling, greeting with special warmth the repeat customers she recognized from her previous stints, Faith was seething inside. What was the resort going to do now? She couldn't stay on, tempted as she was. There was only one solution, but she'd have to wait until all the diners were satisfied, leaving only with a lingering taste of dessert and words of praise on their lips.

They'd leave; then she'd call Niki.

Simon and Freddy were in the kitchen when she returned. Simon was slapping Wendell's face, a disgusted look on his own. He paused from his exertions to tell Faith that once again they were in her debt. Freddy was equally effusive, but it was clear that both men were more concerned with the matter literally at hand than Faith's presence, welcome as it was.

Simon nudged Wendell with the toe of his boot. Still cowboy boots, Faith noticed, but a snazzier pair than the ones he had been wearing the other day. She wondered if Simon drove a Subaru Outback, too.

"Come on, get up!"

"It's no use," Freddy said. "He's totally out of it. I thought you said he was one of the best new chefs in the Northeast? That his former employer was furious that he was leaving?"

"We've been had, Freddy boy. More like furiously happy. Let's get him out of the way. I don't fancy carrying him to his room, though."

Faith was busy preparing the fish, but she looked up.

"You can't leave him here; he's a health hazard! And we need both doors." She left the aesthetic considerations out, monumental though they were.

"You're right," Freddy said. "I'll get a stretcher from the ski patrol and another pair of hands. Maybe Josh can help. No, scratch that. Forget Josh. Where's Craig?"

"Try the pub," Faith replied. "Tom, Robert, and Dennis went out with him, so they'll all be together. More than enough hands."

Freddy left by the side door, skirting the restaurant. It would have been a good time to make an appearance. He couldn't have known that Faith already had. After all that had been happening at Pine Slopes, the more the clientele saw of the owners, the better, Faith thought. Either this hadn't occurred to Fred Stafford or he didn't want to deal with potential complaints.

The fish went into the oven and she started plating the steak orders with Juana, who was showing a real talent in this department.

Simon washed his hands at the sink and sat down. He was a fastidious man, and Faith imagined he'd also like to polish the toe of his snakeskin boot, which connected with the chef.

"Hungry?" Faith asked.

"I was—before I saw him," Simon said.

Her crew had had the presence of mind to serve one of their nightly first courses, French onion soup with plenty of melted Gruyère, and Faith placed a steaming bowl in front of Simon. It would go a long way toward reviving him. She wouldn't mind some herself when there was a lull. Betsey's lasagna had had far too much sticking power—and Faith had stuck as far away from it as she could. As she tossed asparagus spears with oil, salt, pepper, and minced garlic to pan-roast on high heat in the oven, she thought about what an international flavor this week had had—and all her weeks. So many of her staples for feeding large numbers of people had their roots elsewhere—chili, spanakopita, Swedish meatballs, and lasagna (Faith's recipe combined the essence of Italia with a soupçon of neighboring France in the form of the béchamel sauce she added to the layers. It bore as much resemblance to Betsey's as the wolf did to Little Red Riding Hood's grandmother).

"Phew! I think we've managed to stem the tide," Faith said as the last entrée went out the door. The wrong door. Which reminded her.

"What was Fred saying about Josh? Is he tied up at the Sports Center? He'd have Wendell out of here in no time."

Too late, she realized she had committed that cardinal female sin of comparing one's male's musculature to the detriment of the one present. But Simon didn't seem to be taking offense. He didn't seem to be taking anything—not the soup and not much notice. He did answer her, though.

"Josh has quit."

"What?" The edifice of Pine Slopes wasn't crumbling slowly brick by brick, but all at once, like something in a Looney Tunes cartoon.

"He's got his knickers in a twist about being told what to do. Doesn't want any changes made in *his* Sports Center. I tried to convince him to see the season out, thought he'd be loyal after all these years—he started here as a kid, working in maintenance for Pete—but he wants out now. Or better still, yesterday."

"Have you tried having Sally talk to him?"

"Sally?" Simon pulled the bowl of soup toward him. "Why Sally?"

"It's just a feeling I have. I think she may be able to convince him to stay, at least until the end of the season. He wasn't happy about giving more space to the Nordic program, but if Sally tells him those plans are on hold, as I'm assuming they are, what with everything else going on, then he might stay."

Simon was eating his soup now. He'd been deathly pale when Faith came in from the dining room. The hot soup was putting the roses back in his cheeks, and he actually grinned.

"Cherchez la femme, eh? Not a bad idea. I'll have a word with her. Josh would be as hard to replace as John—and now you." The roses wilted. "What am I going to do, wise Mrs. Fairchild? Where am I going to come up with a chef at such short notice?"

"I have a proposal. My assistant in the catering business, Niki Constantine, may agree to step in for a week or so. This is a slow time of year for us, and with my part-timers pitching in, I can handle what we have. Niki loves to ski and she loves to cook. You could also dangle in front of her the prospect of time away from her mother, who is micromanaging Niki's wedding plans. This will give you a chance to get the word out, and I can also help you there."

"It's too much. We can't ask this of you." Simon sounded very firm as he scraped the last bits of onion and cheese from the bottom of his bowl.

"What's your alternative?"

Simon spread his hands out. "Nada. At the moment, I have nada."

At the sound of a familiar word, Vincente looked up from the pot he was scrubbing.

You really will have nada if you don't accept my offer, Faith said to herself.

Then the troops arrived—Freddy, his father, Tom, Robert, Dennis, and Craig. With Simon, they loaded Wendell onto the stretcher and bore him aloft. They looked like pallbearers.

Would John Forest come back, unhappy at seeing the restaurant he had created go down the tubes? Come back, that is, if they could find him?

Thursday morning, they did.

Pete was the first to see it: a gruesome vista of white snow splattered with patches of red gore. And he was the first to know what had happened. Calling Simon and then Harold Stafford as he ran to the pump house, he relayed the news. His walkie-talkie always worked.

"Someone's fallen into the water reservoir in the pump house. You know we had the snowmaking guns on all night, and whoever it was got chewed up and sprayed out all over the mountain. I heard about something like this happening once at a resort out west. Some fool got drunk and dived in. I told you we shoulda kept the place locked! I'm headed there now."

Simon reacted tersely, saying he'd call the police and be there as soon as possible.

Pete repeated the grim news to Harold, who was having a harder time taking it in.

"What are you talking about, Pete? I can't believe it! You must be mistaken. No one would go near that pool of water, especially when the guns were going. And you know darn well that we've kept the pump house locked for years!"

"Alls I know is that the last few times I've been in to check the machinery, it's been open. I'm here now. You get ahold of Freddy and keep people away from the slopes. It's early, but some'll be up and looking out their windows soon. Post the ski patrol until the police get here. Call the Fairchild boys to help out."

Pete watched a lot of TV in the off-season, and he read a lot of mysteries. He knew he wasn't supposed to disturb anything. He'd already noted that there weren't any footprints either going into or coming out of the small structure. The light snow that had fallen in the early hours of the morning had obliterated them. His weren't going to mess up any investigation, he figured, and he had to get a look inside. He didn't know what he expected to see, but he knew he had to see it. Using the toe of his work boot to nudge the door open wider than the crack that had been left, Pete peered in. The lights were on, but other than that there was nothing out of the ordinary as far as he could tell. He was about to back off, when he noticed something sparkling in the sharp shaft of dawn the door was letting in, something gold. He squinted. It was a gold charm, but larger than the ones girls had on their bracelets. It was a frying pan. Last seen hanging from an ornate twenty-four-karat chain worn with a whole lot of others.

Pete felt his knees give way, and he toppled into the snowdrift the plow had made outside the pump house. His head fell back, and the sky seemed to be moving toward him. He let his face fall forward and caught it in his hands. The rough leather from his work gloves felt good. He was alive. But John Forest wasn't. John Forest was dead and would never be buried. John Forest was spread across Pine Slopes like some kind of hideous icing on a cake.

He'd worked with John a long time. Been surprised when he took off. It was out of character, and in Pete's experience, this didn't happen much with people. Whoever had done this was acting in character, only doing a good job of covering it up. Wasn't that what a murderer was? A damn good actor?

Pete turned around and sat with his back against the snow to wait for the police.

―――――

"Slow down, slow down! I can't understand what you're saying." Tom Fairchild had grabbed the phone next to his bed on the first ring, awakening from a deep slumber instantly. It went with his job.

"Who is it? What's wrong?" Faith looked at the clock. It was 6:36.

"My God! This is horrible! I'll get Dennis and we'll be right there. . . . Okay, that's better. We'll meet outside the lodge."

Faith grabbed Tom's arm. He'd hung up the phone and was flinging the covers off. She didn't let go. "What's happened? Where are you going?"

"That was Craig. There's been an accident. Somehow someone fell into the pool at the pump house. It supplies the water for the snowmaking guns. The guns were on all night and—"

Faith closed her eyes. She thought she might be sick. "There's blood on the snow, right?" she said quickly.

"Yes." Tom didn't go into detail, details that had spilled from Craig's mouth in a messy, almost incoherent, torrent. "I need to go help the staff and ski patrol keep people away until the police get here. Let the kids sleep in, and as soon as we can leave, we will. I have to tell Dennis and Betsey now. Dennis will probably want to go with me."

Faith got dressed, then almost collided with Betsey at the top of the stairs. Betsey'd pulled on jeans and a sweatshirt. She stared angrily at Faith; she didn't have to tell her to get out of the way. Her eyes were saying it for her. Craig must have called them too.

"I need to be next door with Daddy—and Mother!"

"Of course," Faith said. "I'll give the kids breakfast when they get up and keep them all here." But Betsey was already halfway out the door, not even stopping for a jacket.

Tom and Dennis were close behind her. Tom kissed Faith hard.

"Until we know what's going on, stay here by the phone. I'll call as soon as I can. Maybe you should start packing. No, that would upset the kids. Maybe—"

"Tom, go. It's all right. No, It's not all right. But we're all right. We'll figure out what to do later."

Dennis hugged her. "The boys may give you a hard time about staying here."

"Go!" Faith urged. "I'll take care of things."

They left, and she realized that she could count the number of times her brother-in-law had hugged her—her wedding, certain Christmases, when there had been the new babies—Scott, Andy, Ben, and Amy—and in the emergency room of the hospital, where Tom had been rushed for what turned out to be acute pancreatitis.

At loose ends—the kids wouldn't be up for some time yet—she made coffee. A lot of coffee. She took the last of the muffins she'd brought out of the freezer to defrost. It was all she could think of to do. Then she sat on the couch, her filled mug on the coffee table. She couldn't swallow any of it, not even one drop.

The window looked toward the slopes, but she couldn't see anything. The main lodge and the snowmaking guns were just out of sight. A figure came dashing by, heading away from the action—heading toward the woods. Faith jumped up and opened the back door. It could only be one person.

"Ophelia! Stop!" she called.

The girl seemed startled and froze for a moment. It was enough time for Faith to catch up to her.

"The boys are still asleep. Come in and let me give you something warm to drink."

The girl was obviously in shock. Wild-eyed, she remained poised for flight. Faith knew if she reached out and tried to hold on to her, Phelie would be gone in an instant.

"Please. Come in. You must have seen what happened. You need to sit down and get warm. I'll wake Scott up."

The suggestion seemed, if anything, to terrify Ophelia more. That was what she was seeing on the girl's face, Faith realized. Horror, yes, but also, more strongly, fear.

She reached her arm out tentatively. "Be with us. We all need to be together."

Ophelia looked at Faith as if taking in who she was for the first time.

"It wasn't supposed to be like this," she whispered. Her face was as blanched as the snow and her lips still bore traces of the dark red lipstick she used. Lipstick so dark, it was almost black. Lipstick the color of an ancient bloodstain.

It was freezing, and even though she was only a few feet from the door, Faith wanted to be back inside to listen for the phone, and for the kids. Ophelia wasn't wearing a hat of any sort, and Faith let her hand gently stroke the teenager's hair. It was as soft as a feather, the color of midnight, the color of a crow. Ophelia leaned into the caress, and then she was off, running for the woods as if pursued by demons—the ones she may have created and the ones created for her.

Wearily, Faith trudged back in, picked up her mug, and emptied it into the sink. The room felt colder after the door had been open. She needed to see her children. Look at them from the doorway. Look at them, but not wake them. Sleep, the sweet escape.

The bedroom door wasn't completely closed; she pushed at it and stepped in. Amy had thrown her covers off and was curled in a ball on the bottom bunk. Above her, Ben was sleeping the way he always did, taking up every available inch of space, with his covers, like Amy's, shoved to one side. Fairchild thermostats. Andy had inherited the warm-blooded gene, too, and lay deep in sleep, only a sheet pulled up over his shoulders. And Scott: Scott's bed had been slept in, but he wasn't in it. Quickly, Faith went to check the bathroom. The door was open, the night-light still on. No sign of her nephew. She ran upstairs. Maybe he had wanted to use one of the whirlpool baths. The silent rooms answered her before she checked them out.

Damn! He must have gotten up, seen her talking to Ophelia, and slipped out the front door. Maybe he's next door, she thought, immediately deciding against calling. If he weren't there, Betsey would go nuts.

No, he was with Ophelia at Gertrude's, and perhaps this was what both teenagers needed right now: each other—and a haven.

But she wished they had chosen her.

Ophelia must have heard the news when Freddy was called, Faith realized. Why else would she be up so early? And Scott? The adults had talked quietly, but even Betsey's whispers had a piercing volume, and he must have awakened. She'd try to reach him and tell him to come back, with or without Ophelia, before too long.

Gertrude Stafford's phone number was unlisted. Faith had done everything she could do until someone returned to take over for her. Then she would go to the Gingerbread House. For now, all she could do was wait.

She'd made their bed, thought about making the Parkers', then immediately decided that Betsey would take offense at having Faith anywhere near her turf. There was nothing to do except sit by the phone again. She tried to read, but even the latest Valerie Wolzien mystery she'd brought failed to take her to another world. This one was too much with her. She decided she could drink some orange juice and was pouring it when the phone finally ran. The sticky liquid splashed onto the countertop as she put the carton down and sprinted across the room.

"Honey, I'm afraid the news is bad," Tom said. "They're pretty certain it was John Forest."

"But how could they tell?" Wouldn't they have to check DNA? Faith thought. Dental records would be out, but maybe not. Maybe a tooth. Or maybe a scrap of clothing. She gagged.

"They found that frying pan charm he always wore around his neck with all those other chains. It must have come off in the . . . well, in the struggle. They'll have to confirm it, but they're proceeding on the assumption that the victim was John Forest."

John knew how the machinery at Pine Slopes worked. He wouldn't have taken a swim in that pool. It was murder. John had fought for his life, and the murderer hadn't noticed the small but distinctive piece of jewelry drop to the floor.

"Faith, say something. I wish I could have told you in person, but I knew you'd want to know. I'll get away as soon as I can. People are going crazy, and the police can't let anyone off the mountain yet. I'm still with the ski patrol, trying to keep everyone calm."

"I think I've known he was dead from the beginning," Faith said slowly, realizing that John's disappearance had never made any sense. He'd loved his job. Le Sapin had been his life. He'd been planning a feast for the Fairchild clan's last night. But where had he been all this time, and what had brought him back to Pine Slopes last night? Had he, in fact, heard about the Wendell fiasco? But how?

"I need to go, but tell me quickly: How are the kids?"

"Still sleeping, thank goodness. But you stay there. I'm fine. Really."

She heard voices in the background, people calling Tom.

"I've got to go," he said. "It's horrible, but we'll leave as soon as the police let us. We have to think of the kids."

"Okay, but take care of yourself." Although she hadn't really known John, that wasn't helping Faith. They'd been part of the same world, culinary soul mates.

"When the kids get up, go over to Mom and Dad's. I love you, Faith."

"I know. I love you, too. Now go. Don't think about us. Bye."

At 7:20, Amy came tiptoeing out of the bedroom. She was still wearing the footed fleece sleepers that Ben had rejected at her age, demanding "real" pajamas. Faith picked her daughter up and sat back down on the sofa, burrowing her face in Amy's sweet-smelling sleep-tangled hair.

"Should we make some buttermilk waffles for breakfast? There's Vermont maple syrup to go on top." Dick had included pints of grade-A amber in the adult goody bags.

Amy nodded. "When those sleepy boys smell the waffles, they'll jump right out of bed. But where's Scott, Mom? He's not in his bunk. He'll want some waffles. They're his favorite."

"Maybe he'll be back in time. He's with a friend. If he doesn't make it, we'll save him some. Now, why don't you run upstairs and get dressed while I get the ingredients ready?"

"Okay," Amy said.

As Faith reached for the flour and other things they'd need, she resolved to keep everyone here with her. If they went next door, they'd be bound to hear what had happened. Besides, she didn't want to intrude on Betsey's quality time with her parents. Although Dick would be with his boys, she assumed.

Amy appeared at the top of the stairs. "What should I wear? My ski clothes? I won't be going for a while."

How was she going to tell them? Faith hadn't been able to work anything out. Tell them nothing yet, she decided.

"Why don't you take a bath in our big tub? You can use some of the lavender bath stuff I brought. Those boys won't want to get up yet."

It would buy a little time.

Amy's face brightened. "I'll just use a tiny drop. Not like last time." That time, she'd produced enough bubbles for a truckload of pinup calendars.

"And for now, just put on some pants and a turtleneck."

Faced once more with nothing to do, Faith turned on the TV and switched to one of the local stations. *Wheel of Fortune* was on and judging from Vanna White's gown and hair, it was a vintage rerun.

"I'd like to buy a vowel," said a perky-looking older woman. "An *e*."

Vanna turned over the tiles, and the woman, who had obviously been well coached not to hide her excitement, screamed out, "I'd like to solve the puzzle!" Then, stolidly facing the impressive task before her, she said, "Still waters run deep," enunciating each word precisely.

Before Faith had time to reflect on the unhappy appropriateness of the phrase for more than a few seconds, the show was interrupted by a local news bulletin. She went close to the set and turned the volume way down.

"Skiers at the popular Pine Slopes Resort awoke to a grisly discovery this morning." Faith leaned her forehead against the screen, tempted to turn it off. She'd heard it all. But not quite all, she realized as the feed switched from the reporter live on the scene to another one standing in front of a motel complex. She sat back on her heels.

"Apparently, this is where John Forest, the man believed to be the victim of the tragedy at Pine Slopes, spent his last hours. Owners Marie and Joe Lafontaine say that Forest was a regular customer and often checked in late for what he called 'a little R and R.' They would leave a key in the door of the unit for him. They noted his car, a 2004 Jeep Grand Cherokee, this morning, but said it had not been there when they closed up at midnight. Hearing the news, they immediately contacted Williston police, who apparently are not revealing any further details. Back to you, Laura."

Apparently, thought Faith.

The camera panned the scene before switching back to the reporter at Pine Slopes. It was the same place where Faith had seen Dennis's car parked on Saturday. There was no question. She'd passed the motel again Tuesday night on the drive to and from Burlington. She tried to remember whether John's car had been there Saturday, as well. She knew there had been other cars parked near Dennis's, but had one of them been a brand-new Jeep? Faith had only noticed the Prius.

The Parkers had frequently spent weekends at Pine Slopes during ski season, even before the kids were born. Dennis certainly knew John. Another coincidence, another "Still waters run deep"?

Faith planned to talk to her brother-in-law as soon as possible.

"Mom, why are you watching TV? What's going on? Where is everybody? What's for breakfast?"

Faith was used to Ben's habitual Twenty Questions routine; he was the original "Why?" child. For the several hundredth time, she resolved to break him of it—or face the thought of him still at home at forty.

"Amy's taking a bath, and when she's finished, we're making waffles. Is Andy awake?" She could ask questions, too.

"Kind of. I mean, he said something when I asked him if he was getting up."

It was far easier to cope with the kids one at a time. "Let him sleep. You go get your stuff and change. Just jeans and a shirt for now."

"But aren't we going skiing? I told you I need to practice."

"Now, Benjamin."

Benjamin went to do as he was told. He didn't have to ask what *now* meant.

Making waffles filled the time. Andy had finally appeared, and the boys were now engaged in snowboard talk. Amy was happy pouring batter into the heart-shaped waffle maker Faith had brought along. Her kids were on seconds and Andy was on thirds when Marian arrived.

"Good morning, all," she said, and circled the table, giving each grandchild a kiss. "Faith, do you have a minute?"

They moved out of earshot by the back door.

"Has anyone told you that they're almost positive who the victim is?"

"Yes," Faith said. "Tom called me. And it's already been on the news."

"I can't believe it. All this time, we thought John had deserted us, and something else was going on."

"Something else"—such a Marian expression. Such innuendo, such tact. What "something else" could it have been that took John away on Sunday? A "something else" that had led to his death last night?

"We can't think about it now. Do the children know what's happened?"

Faith shook her head. "No, I couldn't think of any way to tell them. Especially with Amy around—and Ben."

"Betsey and I are going to take them to Waterbury, do the Ben & Jerry's factory tour, whatever anyone wants. The police have said we can. They're letting most people leave, people with no connection to John or the resort. Why don't you come with us? There's no reason for you to stay here."

Actually, there were a number of reasons for Faith to stay. Besides getting Scott away from the Hansel and Gretel cottage and talking to Dennis about the Williston motel's parking lot, she wanted to see how her staff was holding up. They had worked for John and liked him. This had to be a terrible shock—and they were young and far from home, which made it all much worse. The restaurant would, of course, be closed. The whole mountain was closed off, according to the news she'd heard earlier. It gave her an odd, almost claustrophobic, feeling. She knew the police were trying to keep ghoulish sightseers away, but did they also hope to trap someone inside?

Her thoughts returned to the young Latin American students. Where were they? Some of them worked in housekeeping as well as at Le Sapin. Vincente did some shifts in the cafeteria. That must be open to feed the guests still waiting for permission to leave, and the police, Faith thought. Wendell had taken supplies from the cafeteria last night. Did they have enough? There was plenty of food in Le Sapin's freezers. They could use it if need be. She'd have to check in with Simon.

Fleetingly, she thought about Wendell. He would have been her pick for prime suspect—except for his inability to move even one of his flabby muscles last night, let alone grapple with John, who, although short, had been in very good shape. And what would his motive have been? Professional jealousy? Highly unlikely. Faith doubted that Wendell cared enough about food, other than Tater Tots and McNuggets, to be envious of anyone's culinary prowess. Her mind continuing to whirl, she realized Marian was expecting an answer.

"I think I'll stick around here. I'm not sure what the food situation is," she said, "and they might need my help."

"All right. Perhaps they will. But, dear, go through the lodge. Don't go outside by the slopes."

Faith had no desire to view the hideous scene, and she hoped Marian had also stayed away. A hideous scene, a crime scene. She couldn't even begin to imagine how it could be cleaned up, what sorts of equipment and decontaminants they would have to use. Things beyond Pete's ken, things that required more than overalls as work clothes.

"I won't, and I'm sorry the rest of the family has had to be there. I also want to check on my staff. I'm sure they're terribly upset."

"Oh dear." Marian was looking terribly upset herself. "Didn't Tom tell you?"

"Tell me what?" Faith was close to panic. "Has something happened to one of them? Who is it?"

"I'm sorry, dear, I didn't mean to scare you like that. They're all safe and sound. It's just that the police have been questioning one of the boys in particular. He seems to have had a quarrel with John last Saturday night, and he's also the last person to have seen John—or at least the only person they have been able to find so far."

"Do you remember who it is?"

"I think his name is Eduardo. Now, help me get the children ready. Where's Scott? Still sleeping?"

Eduardo! Faith knew one thing for sure, and that was that Eduardo hadn't been the last person to see John Forest alive. That person had been John's murderer, and Eduardo was no murderer.

Anxious to find out what was happening, Faith had gotten the kids ready to go in record time. She'd told Marian that Scott was with Ophelia. Like Faith, Marian had felt that was the best place for him at the moment and would make the outing much easier.

"Betsey would resent anything I said, but Dick is going to have a word with her about what he calls 'loosening the reins' a little on Scott. After all, the boy will be a man before we know it, and he has to start practicing some independence. It's only normal. Poor Betsey. Dennis works so hard, and I'm sure when he is home, the last thing he wants to hear about is Betsey's master plan for each boy," Marian had said, revealing a full grasp of the situation, especially the influence "Daddy" had.

As soon as Marian and the kids were out the door, Faith left, too. Carefully avoiding any views of the slopes, she went to search for her staff.

The kitchen was empty and spotlessly clean. It should have been a hive of activity, the staff preparing tonight's menu. She pictured each of them at their stations, laughing and talking back and forth in a mixture of Spanish and English, the radio on, background music—the oldies station she'd found for them. John would never preside here again, a colorful presence and a truly gifted chef. Suddenly, the room was full of ghosts, and she turned the radio on. She needed to sit down for a moment. There were bottles of Pellegrino in the refrigerator. She opened one and poured herself a glass. "Time in a Bottle" was playing. Faith almost laughed and realized how close she was to hysteria. She wanted Tom— and she wanted to go home.

She went over to the phone and dialed the number for housekeeping. Maybe Candy knew where the students were.

"Housekeeping."

"Is this Candy? It's Faith Fairchild."

"Oh, hi, Faith. Isn't it awful about John? I told my Jessica that something must have happened to him, because he never would have left without a word to anyone like that. Even if just to me. I've known him forever, and he used to spend Thanksgiving with us."

Faith's attention was momentarily diverted. "He didn't have any family?"

"Not to speak of. Of course, there was Patty, his wife, but they'd split up years ago. I don't think they kept in touch, which is why this is all so weird."

"What are you talking about?"

"You haven't heard about the money?"

"No, what money?" Faith wished Candy would just spill it all out.

"Patty got a call from the police early this morning. Pete must have told them about her. They're trying to track John's movements since Saturday night. I would have told them not to bother. I mean, they weren't divorced, but they weren't on the best of terms, either. I never wanted to pry, but it had something to do with the way he was running the kitchen at her parents' inn—butter instead of margarine, he said, but that was just his side. I never met the woman or her mom and dad myself, but there're always two sides."

Faith was getting ready to scream, Get to the point! but settled for "Yes, that's certainly true. So the police called Patty Forest. . . ."

"And it seems John *had* been in touch with her recently. In fact, he went down there the Thursday before he died. The inn is near Quechee—it's closed, but Patty still lives in it. Anyway, he left a suitcase with her. It had one of those combination locks, so she couldn't get into it without wrecking it. Besides, John would have known. If he wasn't already dead, that is. He told her to keep it in a safe place and he'd be back for it."

Candy was a veritable gold mine of information. How does she know all this? Faith wondered.

"When she told the police about his coming and leaving the suitcase, they told her to stay put and they'd be there right away. Sure enough, the staties were pulling up almost as soon as she hung up. Her words exactly."

"You mean you've been talking to Patty Forest?"

"Called me as soon as they left. I guess I'm the only one she could think of, or maybe she wanted to talk to a woman."

Candy's voice trailed off as she pondered the possibilities. This is no time for the woman to become mute, Faith thought, and hastened to get her going again.

"Did she say why she was calling? I mean, I'm sure she was shocked and wanted to talk to one of John's friends, but did she give another reason?"

"She wanted to know what it looked like. Didn't want to come and see, but said she had to know. The police had only given her a general idea, and she wanted details."

Faith almost threw up. But Candy continued on in a matter-of-fact manner.

"You'd have to know if something like this happened to you. I went to see myself. Otherwise, you'd imagine worse."

Faith hadn't thought of it this way, but there was a certain logic to this line of reasoning. It was true that what you imagined was generally much worse than reality. Generally—not always. She had no desire to gaze on John's mortal remains and was trying hard not to imagine what they looked like.

"The police took the suitcase, then?"

"Patty wasn't about to let them have it without her knowing what was inside. 'It's my property, and you have to give me a list of the contents,' she told them. According to John, Patty was no shrinking violet. Too bad he didn't find that out before they got married, he said."

The tale was beginning to resemble one from *The Arabian Nights*.

"What was in the suitcase?" she asked, hoping this wasn't going to be another *Pulp Fiction*.

"Money! Fifty thousand dollars! Boy, was she glad she made them open it. After seeing it, she didn't even care that the suitcase probably can't be used again."

Fifty thousand dollars. Where would John have gotten his hands on that much cash? If he'd gambled, as Faith suspected from the kitchen staff's ready differentiation between *dice* and *dice,* he must have been playing with some pretty high rollers to accumulate that much. And the fact that he'd left it with Patty meant it was an unaccustomed sum—and a sum that he didn't want showing up in his bank account.

"You're probably thinking what I'm thinking: where did John come up with that much money? I mean, he made a good wage here—better than anybody, even Pete. The Staffords were always desperate to keep him from going someplace else, although in my opinion, they need Pete more, but that's neither here nor there."

Faith was beginning to feel dizzy.

"Do *you* have any idea where the money came from?"

There was a pause, a long pause, and just as Faith was going to ask the question again, Candy said, "No. Not a clue. But it's Patty's now."

Candy had told Faith that the Latin Americans were all working at the Sports Center. It was far enough away from the slopes to give the remaining guests the illusion that everything was all right. And the police had commandeered the indoor tennis courts, along with Josh's adjoining office, as their command post. Faith called both condos, and getting no answer at either, she headed down the drive to the Sports Center. Maybe Tom would be there—or one of the other Fairchilds, who might know where he was. She decided to walk by Simon's office on her way out. They could be meeting there.

Did this mean the end of Pine Slopes? Certainly for this season. Even if it could reopen in time, it was tainted, literally, and she was certain few skiers, especially families, would want to slalom down these slopes. It would take a marketing genius to figure out a way to lure vacationers back. Simon was smart, but was he that smart?

They had to be hoping that Gertrude would hold off on her demands, given the nature of this tragedy. But what if she didn't? The resort would be toxic *and* bankrupt. Faith didn't have the years of memories that had made this little piece of Vermont so special to Tom and his family, but in this short—very short—week, she had come to care about its future.

Simon's office had been empty, but the Sports Center was full of people, some of them in uniform. You could see into the tennis courts from the entryway, and there were more people there, most of them dressed in street clothes, more than ready to leave.

"Mrs. Fairchild." It was Josh. He looked terrible. "You know, right? I mean about John. Who could have anything against him?"

He looked as if he'd been crying.

Impulsively, Faith hugged him. It was like hugging a girder. The man seemed to be made of steel, but he was definitely soft inside. He hugged her back.

"I met him only briefly, but I liked him very much, and I am so sorry for all of you. It's hard to lose a friend, but to lose one this way is worse."

Josh snuffled a little and nodded.

"Your family was here for a while talking to the police: then some of them went back to help keep people away, and some of them are at Harold and Mary's." He nodded in the direction of the elder Stafford's A-frame.

"And how about the kids from South America? Candy said they were here."

"Juana and Vincente are over at the Sports Bar. I just sent Alessandro and Tomás back up to the cafeteria for more supplies. We're almost out of chili."

"Where's Eduardo?"

Josh looked upset. "He's in my office with someone from the state police's crime unit. I don't know what's going on. I've just heard rumors. Something about a fight he had with John."

Faith turned and headed straight for the tennis courts. Eduardo had the right to an attorney. He shouldn't be left to deal with all this by himself, and he didn't have anyone else to turn to except Señora Confianza.

The señora was wrong, as she soon discovered. The first officer she spoke to took her to the office as soon as she told him who she was. And there she found Eduardo, another officer—and her husband.

Reverend Fairchild was looking very, very tired. His morning had started at dawn and it had been difficult—first, confronting the sight on the snow-covered slopes, then keeping people away and dealing with the subsequent shock, which had spread through the resort like an avalanche.

"Are you telling them this is impossible? Eduardo can't have had anything to do with this! Does he need a lawyer? Has he spoken to—"

Tom put his arms around his wife and drew her to one side. "It's okay, honey. Eduardo's rights are being fully respected. No one knows what's going on yet. And a lawyer is on the way, although it's early days and he may not need one. I called Sharon for a name." Sharon McKay was a former parishioner, now teaching at UVM, someone both Fairchilds liked and respected. It wasn't Kevin Bacon, but the ecclesiastical net worked in much the same way.

Faith looked at Eduardo over Tom's shoulder. The boy seemed younger than his years and very frightened. She went over to him.

"My husband will take care of you. You mustn't worry. Do you want to call your parents or someone else at home?"

"Oh no, señora," Eduardo said softly, as if afraid to raise his voice and be noticed. "They would be very upset, and there is nothing they can do from so far away."

"But what's going on? Why are you keeping him here?" Faith addressed the lieutenant.

"We only want to ask the boy a few more questions, and it's in his best interest to stay where we can keep an eye on him."

"You mean you think he'll try to escape?" Faith was indignant.

"We're not thinking anything, ma'am," he replied patiently. "We just need him to stay put here, where we can find him."

"Tom!" Faith turned toward her husband, and they stepped over to a corner of the office.

"It's what's best for Eduardo right now—and I'll be here with him. Why don't you go back to the kids? I'm afraid we're not going to be able to leave today. Craig and my dad are with the Staffords. Robert and Dennis are helping out at the lodge."

Accounting for the rest of the family, Faith said, "The kids are with your mother and Betsey in Waterbury. They left after breakfast."

"Good. Now why don't you go back to the condo? I can reach you there if I need you or if Eduardo does. I promise. Get some rest, if you can. The police are doing a great job, Faith."

"Do they know about all the other things that have been happening this week?"

"Yes, and none of it makes any sense."

"Okay, I'll go as soon as I've talked to Juana, Vincente, and any of the others who are around," she said, then addressed the room. "Do you want some coffee, something to eat?"

"We're being well looked after," the lieutenant said. "I appreciate your concern for the young man here, and I'm sure he does, too. Thank you for coming in."

Faith had been with enough cops to recognize an exit line—her exit—and she left, but not without pulling Tom away to tell him what had just occurred to her.

"Eduardo wouldn't have known anything about how the snow guns work or even about the water source or where it is. You've got to let the police know that," she whispered quickly in his ear.

He whispered back, "Thought of that myself right away, but we have a little problem. Besides working in the kitchen, Eduardo's been on the maintenance crew. Turns out that he's some sort of mechanical genius."

Faith's sudden hopes crashed. "Call me when the lawyer comes. And don't leave him alone."

Tom nodded and ever so gently pushed his wife toward the door.

Alessandro had returned with the chili, which she was busy adding to what little remained. Juana and Sally were at the counter, serving.

"Would it be all right if I spoke with Juana for a minute? Can you spare her?" Faith asked Sally.

"Of course, Mrs. Fairchild," she said, then she beckoned Faith closer.

"It's like a nightmare, only I can't wake up. Josh says he feels the same way. I mean, on Saturday I thought I'd found a body, and now there *is* a body. Well not actually—"

"It *is* like a nightmare, but I'm sure the police will find whoever is responsible." Faith didn't mention the money. She didn't know whether it was common knowledge or not, although it was bound to be soon. She also didn't know whether the police would find out who was responsible. There was that Canadian border to think about, so conveniently close by.

"You don't think it's like a serial killer, some maniac, do you? That's what people are saying. One man was shouting at the police that he wasn't going to have his family spread out all over the mountain and that if they didn't let him leave, he was going to sue the whole state of Vermont."

"I'm sure it's not a serial killer." Faith wasn't going to weigh in on the maniac part. "It would be hard to repeat this kind of thing over and over."

Sally nodded, apparently reassured. "We're all set here. I know you're close to these kids and that they're really upset, so take your time."

Faith and Juana went into the ladies' locker room. It was deserted. They sat down on one of the benches.

"Señora, Eduardo would never kill anyone! What are they doing to him?"

"They are asking him some questions. My husband—you remember him; he was in the kitchen the other night with my children—is with Eduardo. He won't leave him alone."

"Yes, the priest, or whatever the word is. I can't remember my English good now."

"You're doing fine. Can you tell me why they are asking Eduardo questions? Why they think he may have had something to do with this?"

Juana burst into tears, grabbing a towel to mop her eyes.

"It's all because of me!"

"You? But how?" Faith asked.

"John was very friendly with all of us, but he was my special friend. Not like that," she said, looking a Faith's face. "Not a boyfriend. But he was teaching me some songs and also how to work in a restaurant. He said I was so good at plating that I could get a job here in the States. Saturday night, after the restaurant closed, we were in the kitchen alone together. Eduardo came in, and he thought . . . well, he thought something wrong was happening. He is very jealous."

Faith looked at Juana. Even with puffy red eyes, the girl was beautiful. Her cocoa-colored skin was smooth and unblemished. Unlike the other girls' long dark hair, which was straight, Juana's fell in waves. Her eyes were dark, too, but flecked with gold. She had reminded Faith of those very special French Bernachon chocolates called *palets d'or,* gold coins. The bonbons were round disks of bittersweet chocolate embedded with tiny pieces of gold leaf. It wouldn't be hard to be completely besotted with the young woman, whatever your age. Clearly, Eduardo was. Had John been, as well?

"Please, you must believe me. I didn't do anything wrong."

Faith put her arm around the Juana's shoulder. "I'm sure you didn't. But is this why the police are questioning Eduardo? He and John had a fight?"

Juana nodded, tears starting again. "Eduardo was shouting in Spanish. He was so angry. I was trying to tell him that nothing was wrong, but he wouldn't listen. John thought it was a joke, and then he thought it wasn't. He grabbed Eduardo by the arm to make him be quiet, but it made him worse. He was hitting John and John was hitting him back. I was screaming. People came and made them stop."

"Who came?"

"I don't remember everyone. Alessandro took me away. Tomás was there. Probably Vincente. The next day, when John wasn't there, Eduardo was telling everyone it was because John was afraid to face him. You know, machismo."

Faith did know. All too well.

"So all this week, you thought John had left to find another job because of you?"

Juana shrugged. "These things happen."

And for someone as beautiful as this Bolivian, these things must happen often, Faith thought.

"Will Eduardo be all right? Will they put him in prison?" Juana asked anxiously.

"He will be all right," Faith said, wishing she could state it with total confidence. Machismo engendered very powerful emotions.

Faith went back with Juana to the Sports Bar. Sally had left. Vincente, Tiny, and Alessandro were sitting on three bar stools. The crowd in the Sports Center had thinned considerably.

"You know the story from Juana now?" Vincente asked. "It is an unlucky thing for Eduardo that this happened."

Very, Faith said to herself. The timing was perfect—for someone.

She realized she was exhausted. After talking a little longer with the students, she gave them the phone number of the condo and wearily made her way back up the long drive.

No one was at either condo. She knew she should go get Scott from Gertrude's, but she had to lie down first. She wasn't sure she had the energy to walk all that way. She certainly didn't have the emotional energy for a scene if Scott refused to come back with her.

The sight of the kitchen triggered an onslaught of hunger pangs. She hadn't eaten anything all day. Hadn't had the stomach for anything. Now she was ravenous. She opened the fridge and, avoiding the sight of Betsey's leftover lasagna, took out some of the sliced smoked ham from Harrington's—a store in Richmond, just down the road—Havarti, honey mustard, and arugula for some crunch. There was still some rye left from the loaf she'd brought. Should I bother to do a kind of panini and fry it? she wondered. Yes, she decided. She needed the smell of food cooking, the sight of butter melting, bread turning a crispy brown, melted cheese oozing. The arugula could go on the side.

Mission accomplished, she was sitting at the counter, about to eat, when the back door opened and Dennis walked in.

Dennis.

She got another plate and put half the sandwich on it.

"Dennis," she said, "we have to talk."

TEN

G od, that looks good. I grabbed some doughnuts and coffee from the cafeteria I can't even remember when this morning. What a day." Dennis took off his jacket, sat down, and picked up the sandwich, seemingly oblivious to his understatement.

"I haven't really taken it all in," Faith said, realizing as she spoke how true her words were. She hadn't planned a way to start her conversation with Dennis, hadn't been sure she'd get a chance to have it, and this was the first thing that came to mind.

"I know. Horrible. You read about stuff like this in the paper, but you never think you'll be involved."

How involved, Dennis? Faith almost blurted out.

He kept talking. "And the kids. I want to get the hell out of here. I know Betsey and Marian took everybody off, which was a good idea, but now it's time to pack. I'm worried about how Scott and Andy are taking it. They knew John, hung around the kitchen a lot, especially when they were younger."

He'd devoured his half of the sandwich and was eying Faith's. She didn't slide it over.

"How well did *you* know John?" she asked, and took a bite.

Her brother-in-law stiffened. "What do you mean?"

She put the sandwich down. "Just that it must be hard on you. You've been coming here all these years, and you knew him, too."

"Yeah, well, we weren't buddies. I'd talk to him about the menu. Gave him a few ideas now and then."

Dennis, unlike his wife, was a foodie and occasionally knew about a new gem in Boston's increasingly dazzling restaurant scene before Faith herself. Could he have had a rendezvous with John at the motel café to discuss whether to offer skate wings, say, or Kobe beef? Faith doubted it, but it was the opening she needed.

"You didn't happen to get together at the motel café in Williston on Saturday to discuss haute cuisine, did you?"

Dennis stood up, knocking the stool over. He was flushed, and he angrily grabbed the counter with both hands. His hands were exquisitely cared for—no one wants a dentist with ragged cuticles. They were also large. Faith had the sense that he'd reached for the counter to keep from reaching for her. They were alone in the condo. No one could hear them. She'd have to watch her step. Dennis was a relative only by marriage, and in any case, Faith had never relied on blood being thicker than water.

"We saw your car, Dennis," she said softly, emphasizing the "we." "Tom and I were coming back from Burlington. It's where they found John's car today. I saw it on the news."

"And Tom knows that, too?" Dennis appeared to be considering some options. Faith was sure she wouldn't like some of them, and she answered firmly, "Tom knows." He would know soon, which was as good as knowing now. And there was this situation: She was alone with a man who had just learned that something he'd thought he'd hidden wasn't hidden at all.

Dennis picked the stool up and sat down. He didn't look at her. The minutes passed. Faith finished her sandwich.

"Have you told the police?"

"I haven't; I don't know whether—"

"Tom wouldn't. Not without talking to me first." Dennis sounded relieved.

"Why don't you just tell me what's going on? I'll make you another sandwich," Faith said.

He shook his head. She wasn't sure if it meant he didn't want anything to eat or he wasn't going to tell her anything. She waited some more. He looked miserable. Finally, he took a deep breath and said, "Come sit on the couch. These stools are damned uncomfortable."

They sat down, and Faith prepared herself for another long wait. Even at the best of times, Dennis wasn't much of a talker—at least not when the family was around—and this wasn't the best of times. But he started right in.

"Sometimes you get sucked into things and don't know how it happened. Like marrying Betsey." He shot a glance at Faith, whose face wasn't registering disapproval or much of anything else. It was his story.

"Don't get me wrong. I was all for it. She was beautiful, smart, and loaded with energy. Everything she said about the future came true. We'd have plenty of money. I'd be a big success. Great kids. But I remember standing at the altar and thinking, Jeezus, how did I get here so fast? That's the thing about Betsey. Everything has to happen right away and exactly the way she wants it. She's not easy to live with—and it's getting worse as the kids get older.

"Maybe she's worried about the empty-nest thing. Maybe she thinks she might have a completely empty house. And maybe she will. I can't see myself sticking with her once the kids are gone if things don't change."

Not a good week for the Fairchild family's marriages, Faith thought wryly. But then, Dennis and Betsey's problems went way back. As soon as Dennis had started talking, she'd realized where he was going.

He picked up one of the throw pillows and started fiddling with the fringe. "I did a very stupid thing. I've been having an affair with my secretary."

Faith was right. That old sweet song. That cliché come to life over and over and over again.

"That's what I meant about getting sucked in. I got sucked in, more like suckered in."

"So, you were meeting *her* at the motel, not John?"

"Yeah. I knew about it from John, though. He used to go there, knew the owners. Said they were discreet."

"But why did she come all the way up here?"

Maybe Dennis was hotter than he looked. Maybe his lover couldn't go a whole week without him.

"I didn't want her here. Didn't want her anywhere. It was a fling. I told her that at the beginning. I wasn't about to leave my wife."

Not yet, Faith amended silently.

"Sandy was okay with that at first, or at least that's what she said. Then she began to drop these hints. Said I should take her with me to one of my professional conventions, or Betsey might get a phone call. So, like a fool, I did. The meeting was in Saint Thomas. Nobody I knew was going to be there, but I was nervous as a cat the whole time. Then she wanted money for clothes, more to fix up her apartment. It was getting to be a nightmare, so I broke it off and told her she should start looking for another job. Major mistake."

How could the man have been so dense? Didn't he read the papers? Sexual harassment, duh! Faith thought.

"I told her I would straighten things out when I got back next week, but she wasn't having any of that. She was in the office when the ring was delivered, signed for it, and opened the package. Friday, as I was leaving to come here, she told me that if I gave her the ring, we'd be quits. If not, she'd make sure I lost my license and my wife. She promised she'd put her Joan Hancock on anything I wanted her to and disappear from my life forever, but she had to have the diamond. I told her it was impossible. Said I'd get her one exactly like it. But nooo, it had to be *that* one. It had to be the one I'd given my wife. If she'd taken a knife to my balls, it couldn't have been any worse. There was no way I was going to get the ring away from Betsey. The only time I ever saw her take it off was when she washed dishes, and she always put it right back on. I watched her like a hawk all weekend and Monday."

"But how would Sandy know it was the same ring? Couldn't you have gotten another one and told her it was Betsey's?" Faith was mentally adding up Dennis's assets. He was doing far better than she'd thought, by gum! Two rings that size could put a good dent in the national debt of some countries. And as for the lie, she didn't think an adulterer would have balked at a fib.

"I'd had something special engraved on the inside of the band. Sandy knew I wouldn't have time to get another engraved. She gave me a deadline—one week. I thought about driving back to Boston, getting a duplicate ring, and trying to get it engraved at one of those places that do it fast. But this was hand engraving, a tricky job. I called around, but I couldn't find any engraver who would guarantee it. Besides, Betsey had those damn walkie-talkies to keep track of everybody. I kept taking the batteries out and telling her they didn't work—I think the boys were do-ing it, too—but even so, she was keeping her usual eagle eye on us. It was hard enough to get to Williston and calm Sandy down. She was threaten-ing to come here."

"And then," Faith said, "on Tuesday, you came in from the slopes—to get something to eat, I guess—and there was the ring sitting in the saucer by the faucets."

Dennis nodded. Even now, relief flooded his face.

"It was a miracle. I grabbed it, and then I got Scott's laptop—to make it seem like a real burglary—and shoved that in my trunk. I knew Scotty backs everything up, and I guess I was pissed off at Betsey for making him work so hard. The kid barely has a life."

Faith wished that were so, thinking of Scott's recent activities, includ-ing today's trip to Gertrude's hideaway.

"I had to stick around to be here when someone found out the stuff was gone, but I called Sandy and arranged to meet her in Montpelier that night. The office is closed this week, and she's been staying in the area, skiing at Stowe mostly—or rather, mostly making me a nervous wreck. I gave her the ring. She signed the statement I'd prepared—she gets a good reference, plus severance."

Dennis sounded smug. He looked smug. Faith wished she could move farther away from him without making her growing distaste for the man obvious. As far as he was concerned, everything had been taken care of. He'd been used by a "ball-buster" and was married to another. Maybe he'd made it clear to Sandy that what they were embarking upon was a "fling," maybe not. Maybe Betsey had taken over his role as "man of the house," maybe not. At this point, Faith didn't care. What she did care about was all the harm he'd caused. Craig, the Staffords, Simon, and Ophelia but, most of all, to his sons, especially Scott. And what about the Fairchild family vacation? Dick's idyllic birthday?

"So what are you going to do, Faith?"

"I don't know," she said, "Except if you want another sandwich, you're going to have to make it yourself."

Dennis had started to argue with Faith—"Come on, you have to see it from my side!"—but she'd gone into the kitchen, put the food away, and made it clear that she wasn't going to discuss it any further. After a few sputtering tries, he went upstairs, presumably to pack. For Faith, his self-righteous indignation served to make the whole thing worse. She had no doubt now that Dennis considered himself the injured party in all this, ensnared by a devious woman and now minus a considerable sum of money. She wondered what he'd do about the laptop. Maybe he'd "miraculously" find it in a local pawnshop on the way home. She could hear him: Hey, let's check this place out; we're going right by. Maybe they have the ring or the computer.

She felt sick, and restless. The combination sent her scurrying for her parka, hat, and gloves. There was no way she could she stay under the same roof with Dennis until everyone else returned. Besides, she needed to talk to Scott and Ophelia.

It was one of those days that seemed endless, and when she looked at her watch and saw it was only one o'clock, she could scarcely believe it. The sky was overcast and it had started to snow, so she didn't have the sun to go by, and in any case, she had never been adept at things like this, unlike her friend Pix and her family. Every one of them could glance upward and give you the time to the minute; gaze at the moss growing on a tree and tell you your current longitude and latitude; sniff deeply and predict when the next rain or snow would fall.

She thought about Pix longingly as she entered the woods and set out on the path to Gertrude's cottage. Unlike Monday night, she didn't have Ophelia's path to follow, yet it was daylight—filtered daylight in these deep woods. She could find her way without using the moonlight to guide her as she had before. Again, it was a long trek, and if she hadn't been so concerned about the two teenagers, she would have turned back and gone to the Sports Center. She should have called there before she left and tried to talk to Tom, she realized. Not about Dennis, not over the phone, but to find out what was happening with Eduardo.

It was beautiful. So quiet. The woods reminded her of the Raymond Briggs classic, *The Snowman,* which had been made into a video. She could hear the music that accompanied the boy's journey into the forest with the kindly snowman. She wouldn't mind a kindly snowman or -woman herself right now. The farther in she walked, the farther away she was from the resort. And unlike the story, she wouldn't be emerging into a jolly celebration of dancing snowmen and a festive groaning board with Santa presiding.

She was cold and wished she could have taken the time to put her French long johns on, but that would have meant going upstairs and possibly seeing her brother-in-law. The thought made her shudder.

Then, just as the other night, the house suddenly popped up in front of her. It sat in a clearing, the white gingerbread trim gleaming, frosted by the falling snow. She noticed the front door was scarlet and besides the strings of tiny white lights, turned off now, the porch was festooned with brightly colored macramé hangings. Strings of faintly tinkling crystals sent rainbows dancing across the snow.

But that was the only motion, and sound. No smoke was coming from the chimney; no voices, no music.

Faith went up the steps, leaving faint prints in the new snow, and knocked on the door. There was no bell. And there was no answer. She walked across to one of the two large bay windows and peered in. She couldn't see a thing. Heavy drapes obscured her view. It was the same at the other one. Drawn to conserve heat? Or drawn because Gertrude was away? She went back down the stairs and circled the house. It appeared that all the windows were covered. She knocked on the back door. Silence.

The garage and a shed stood some way beyond the house, and she went over to them. The shed was locked, but the garage was open—and empty.

Gertrude wasn't home. So where on earth were Scott and Ophelia?

The shed had a stovepipe. A place for someone to live? To camp out in? Was that what they were doing? Faith walked back over to look in the windows. She wished it were open so she could get warm before starting back. The garage didn't offer much in the way of comfort. If she could only get into the shed, find a blanket and lie down for a little nap . . . Trying the doors of the house, looking for a key over the door was much too Goldilocks, aside from breaking and entering. A shed was different.

She trudged slowly back toward the small shelter, her head filled with thoughts of home. Her shadow was lengthening, she noticed. It must be getting later. Pix would be pleased at Faith's progress toward become one, truly attune to nature. Attune. A tune. Faith thought she heard someone whistling. Was Gertrude back? The kids? She whirled around and the sound stopped. I'm imagining things, she thought.

But she wasn't imagining the pain of the sharp blow she felt on the back of her head, nor the next, which shut out all thought and feeling.

———

S he's coming around!" Faith opened her eyes. She was in the ski patrol's hut. Tom was standing over her with several of the members and Simon. It was Simon who had cried out.

"How did I get here?" she whispered, then, realizing she was whispering, she raised her voice. "I was at Gertrude's cottage and someone hit me."

Tom looked worried. "The ski patrol found you in the woods, not that far from the condos. A branch broke off from a tree and knocked you out. It was on top of you."

"Lucky thing we found you. You could have gotten pretty cold," a young woman said.

"I *was* cold. That's why I was going to the shed—to warm up. It wasn't a branch. It was a person. There must be something in that shed. Tom, you have to get the police to go there and search it. I'm sure it has to do with John's murder. And Gertrude is gone. Scott and Ophelia, too."

"Honey, I'm sure you did go to the shed, or whatever it was, but you were on your way back here when you had the accident."

"Mrs. Fairchild. I'm Dr. Moses. You have probably suffered a very mild concussion. Fortunately, nothing worse, since they found you before dark, when the temperature drops. After something like what happened to you occurs, our memory often plays tricks on us, even blocks out whole segments of time. It's got a name: retrograde amnesia."

Faith closed her eyes. It was no use. She'd never get them to believe her. She'd have to wait to get Tom alone.

She started to sit up.

"Honey, are you sure you feel all right? The doctor thinks you should stay here for a while."

"I feel fine, except my head hurts, and I guess that must be because of the *branch*." Faith was sure her sarcasm was lost on everyone, but it felt good to express it. "Give me some Tylenol or something and I'll go back to the condo and lie down."

Simon seemed concerned. "Mrs. Fairchild, Faith, please don't be foolhardy. You don't want anything more to happen."

"Thanks, Simon, but I'm okay, and I promise to take it easy."

She had to get out of there and tell Tom what had happened—not just at Gertrude's but also about Dennis and the kids. Ophelia's face came back to her—the horror and fear writ large upon it this morning. Where was she? Where was Scott? And there were these other images nagging at her like certain dreams. The more you try to remember them, the harder it becomes, until they vanish completely. She was lying in the snow. Where? Someone was carrying her. Who? How long had she been unconscious? It was about one o'clock when she'd set out for Gertrude's place. About twenty minutes to get there, twenty minutes or maybe less poking around. She looked at her watch. Only a little after 2:00 P.M. She couldn't have been out long.

The ski patrol insisted on transporting her via snowmobile, strapped to a stretcher, which Faith had only agreed to when she realized they wouldn't release her otherwise. As soon as she was inside the condo, she asked Tom to make her a strong cup of coffee and take it upstairs. They were alone.

The Parkers' bedroom was in total disarray, half-packed bags strewn around. Dennis's work, calculated to drive his wife crazy, Faith was sure.

She went into her bathroom, washed her face, and tried to get a look at the back of her head with her makeup mirror. The skin hadn't been broken, but she had a lump the size of a Santa Rosa plum. Maybe I'd better lie down, she thought.

Tom appeared soon with two steaming mugs and a plate of cinnamon toast. He knew his wife's comfort food.

"Now look, Tom, it's just us. I know what happened to me, and it wasn't a branch, memory loss or no memory loss. You have to call down to the Sports Center and have the police look in that shed. Somebody didn't want me to see inside—so much so that the person knocked me out and arranged my 'accident.' It's probably too late, but at least tell them to try."

"Okay, sweetheart. I can't stand to think of your being attacked. I guess I want to believe it was the branch, but I'll call."

As Tom was talking to the police, Faith nibbled on the toast and sipped her coffee. Making a good cup of coffee was one of many talents Tom had brought to the marriage. He could also sew on buttons, which came in handy, as she couldn't.

"All right. They're sending someone out to check. The place is empty, though, they said. Gertrude Stafford left yesterday. You know the situation, right? Her brother and nephew are trying to get her to agree to holding off on her demand for the money they owe Boyd's estate. Simon has been trying to convince her, too. If Pine Slopes goes under, he's out of a job. But so far, it's no go, and she's taken off for parts unspecified."

"She's been known to do that before," Faith said. The image of Gertrude's smiling face as she left Simon's office surfaced in Faith's mind. Gloating? And where had she gone after that? "I thought for sure Scott and Ophelia were out at Gertrude's house. I followed Ophelia there the other night, and I'm positive that's where Scott's been going to get away from his mother. Ophelia was headed that way early this morning, and I assumed Scott had overheard me talking to her, because the back door was open. He probably left by the front. Could they be at the Staffords? Ordinarily, I'd say it was the last place Ophelia would go, but the house would be empty today, given what's been going on. Let's try calling there."

"I saw Ophelia at the Sports Center around noon, but I haven't seen Scott all day. I'll try the Staffords, senior and junior, but are you sure he didn't go with my mother?" Tom sounded worried.

"He wasn't with them. Remember, his mother is part of the outing—and in any case, he wasn't here when they left. Which reminds me. You don't know about Dennis. Oh Tom, when can we go home?"

Tom called both Stafford houses and left messages on their machines. He left one on Simon's, as well. Then Faith told him about Dennis, starting with seeing the Williston motel on the news.

"Poor Bets," Tom said softly when Faith had finished. "She and Dennis have been together so long. I never felt very close to him, and each time the family got together, I'd resolve to spend some time with him, but I didn't really try hard enough. Maybe he felt isolated and—"

"Just a minute," Faith said. "The man is a total sleaze, and you're beating up on yourself? Isolated in your family? You'd have to move to Mars to be isolated in the Fairchild clan." As she said it, she thought about Glenda's protest. Was the family a members-only club? Or was it the fault of those who felt excluded? But wherever the fault lay, it wasn't with Tom.

"You don't know what's going to happen, and we're certainly not going to tell Betsey what Dennis said, I hope."

Tom shook his head. "That's up to Dennis."

Faith lay back on the pillows Tom had arranged, then sat bolt upright as the phone rang. Tom picked it up on the first ring.

"Yes? . . . Oh, thank you for getting back to me . . . Nothing? . . . Yes, the snow is coming down pretty hard. . . . Okay, I'll let my wife know."

"The police?" Faith said.

"They didn't find anything out of the ordinary in the shed. It wasn't locked, by the way. And no one was at the house. The snow that's been falling all day would have obliterated any tracks, including yours. But they're sure no one's been there since Gertrude left."

"The shed was locked. I tried it before I went over to the garage. So someone *was* there after me. And it was that someone who hit me on the head when I went back to look in the windows. Whatever was out of the ordinary was removed."

Tom caressed the side of his wife's face and smoothed her hair back. "Darling, let's say it wasn't an old lock that stuck and it really was locked. What could have been in it that someone didn't want you to see?"

He had her there.

"Now, how about some soup? Or something else to eat? More toast?"

Faith looked at the empty plate in surprise. She hadn't realized she'd finished the toast. And Tom was right: She did want something more to eat. She wanted the half sandwich she'd so generously given to Dennis. But she'd settle for soup.

When Tom left, she tried to think what could have been in the shed? It was all getting to be a little like *Cold Comfort Farm,* that incomparable novel by Stella Gibbons with Ada Doom, who saw something "nasty in the woodshed."

But whatever it was, Faith was convinced it was tied to the chef's murder—and the rest of what had been going on this week at Pine Slopes. It wouldn't have been a murder weapon—that was all too present on location, so to speak. But what? She wondered if the police had found John's things in his car. Suitcases with what had been in his room. If not, maybe that was what had been hidden away. Which would mean Gertrude was involved—or Ophelia? When had Gertrude left yesterday? Another question for the police. Had anyone seen her drive away? She'd be hard to miss in her Flower Power VW bus. If she'd left in the afternoon, that would eliminate her as a suspect. John had to have been killed in the early-morning hours. But Ophelia had been around. Yet somehow Faith couldn't see the anorexic sixteen-year-old grappling with John by the pool at the pump house, forcing him into its lethal depths. And why? It was more likely she'd have tried to push her stepfather in—or her mother.

The bedroom door crashed open.

"Tom?" Faith was startled.

Betsey Parker came toward the bed so fast, she seemed jet-propelled. "What have you done with my child?" she screamed. Tom was close on her heels. He grabbed her from behind. Faith wasn't sure what Betsey had planned, but she was very glad Tom was stopping the escapee from the Furies in her tracks.

"I haven't done anything with Scott. I thought he was with Ophelia this morning. That's what I told Marian. Didn't she tell you?"

"She didn't say anything," Betsey said bitterly. "She knew what I'd think about that. If only she had. I would have made him come with us. I thought he was with his father."

Faith was feeling very guilty. But the boy was almost sixteen, and she had thought it would be better for him to be with a friend. She realized now that she should have left that up to his mother. "I went out to Gertrude Stafford's house, because I thought that's where he was, but no one was there, and—" Faith decided not to go into any more particulars. Betsey didn't need to hear about the attack on Faith, not when Scott was missing. But he wasn't missing. He was somewhere holed up with Phelie. If they could find her, they'd find him.

"Tom saw Ophelia down at the Sports Center. I'd try there." Faith was trying to keep her voice from shaking. Tom still had an arm around his sister's shoulders. He was looking warily from one woman to the other.

"That's a good idea, Bets. We'll go down there right now."

"Mom?" Andy was standing just outside the doorway. He didn't look like someone who had had a happy day. Maybe Ben & Jerry's had been out of his favorite flavor.

Betsey didn't turn around. "Not now, Andy. I'm busy. Go next door with your grandma and grandpa."

"*Mom,*" he said insistently. "I . . . well, there's something, um, something . . ."

Betsey turned around.

"What is it? Right now. Tell me. What is it?"

The boy put one hand on the door frame, as if to steady himself.

"Scott didn't come home last night."

"*What are you talking about?*"

Andy grabbed the frame so tightly, Faith could see his knuckles bulge out.

"I promised I wouldn't tell, because he was so mad, and you were, too, and anyway, I just promised. He's been going out at night, when everybody's asleep, and last night he didn't come back. Usually, he comes back."

The boy looked terrified. Betsey had stepped away from Tom and toward her son. She reversed herself and sat down on the bed. She looked at Andy again and seemed about to say something to him, then burst into sobs—heart wrenching sobs.

"It's okay, sis, we'll find him. He's with Ophelia someplace. You know that."

Betsey raised her tear-streaked face.

"A man has been killed by some maniac. My son has been missing for God knows how long. And you tell me everything is 'okay'!" She was speaking in leaden tones. It was better when she shrieked, Faith realized. The woman sitting so close to her was a very different woman from the one who had come raging in a few minutes ago. This woman was doing what every mother anywhere would do: assuming the worst.

"Call the police, Tom. Go down there. Take Andy with you." Faith reached her arm out toward her nephew, and he came close enough for her to hug him. "You did the right thing, telling us, even if it was a promise. Scott will understand. And everything will be all right." She waited for Betsey to echo her words, but she was in a far-off place, not taking in the scene at her side. Faith released Andy and said, "Betsey and I will stay here. When you leave, I'll call next door to tell them what's happening. Ben and Amy can stay there. The minute you hear—"

Tom was already dialing. "The minute I hear, you'll hear."

And suddenly, they were alone, the two sisters-in-law holding hands. Faith knew Betsey didn't want any coffee. Didn't want anything except her boy.

Dennis came in shortly after Tom and Andy had left. Without looking at Faith, who was still stretched out in bed, he went over to his wife, who was sitting on the end of it. She hadn't moved an inch since Andy had told her about Scott.

"They're bringing in the state Search and Rescue units. The ski patrol has already started covering the mountain. Everything's being done. They'll find him." He grabbed her hand. "Bets, they'll *find* him."

"What about Burlington?" Faith suggested. "Ophelia's friends there? Naomi must know who some of them are. They may have hitched a ride and be hanging out on the Church Street mall right now."

"The police have already thought of that," Dennis said. "They're checking in Burlington. We're pretty sure they're together. Nobody's seen Ophelia—damn stupid name!—since noon."

Betsey didn't say a word. Dennis had taken her hand, and Faith noticed it lay limp in his grasp.

"Robert and Craig are with the ski patrol. Tom is down at the Sports Center, and I'm going back there."

Faith got out of bed. She felt dizzy momentarily, but then the room stopped spinning. "I'm going downstairs to make some tea. When Dennis leaves, come down and we'll wait there." Betsey was obviously in shock, and Faith had to get her moving—and keep her warm. She'd light the fire. Maybe it would help to have Dick—Daddy—sit with them. But knowing him, he had probably joined the search.

"Is Dick next door?" she asked Dennis.

He shook his head. "He's with Robert and Craig."

"Do you want your mom to come over?" Faith asked. "I can trade places with her."

"No," Betsey said, her first word since the outburst. "Let her stay where she is."

Faith went downstairs and got busy. Doing something, anything, felt good. But lighting a fire and putting water on to boil didn't take a great deal of time, and all too soon she was sitting on the couch, looking at the waning light, wishing desperately she'd told someone that Scott wasn't around at breakfast. Maybe if she had, Andy would have cracked sooner. Gone since last night—had he seen something he wasn't supposed to? Seen the murderer? Was this why Ophelia had looked so terrified? Had she been with Scott? But that didn't make any sense. She would have raised an alarm.

Suddenly, Faith sat up straight. Maybe Ophelia hadn't known Scott was missing. Maybe they weren't together!

Dennis and Betsey were still upstairs. Events like this either brought couples closer together or split them apart. Which would it be for the Parkers?

The kettle was whistling. Faith got up to turn off the gas. That whistling at Gertrude's. It hadn't been a bird. It had been a human being.

What was the tune? No tune, just noise. Remember, try to remember, she told herself. She closed her eyes, but nothing came. Gertrude, and that house. Who had been standing behind her in the doorway, cloaked by shadows, the night Faith had followed Ophelia? One of the older woman's young frat-boy admirers? Who? Someone from Pine Slopes?

Faith hadn't asked Tom about Eduardo. The lawyer must have arrived if Tom had left the boy. Eduardo, a suspect! Insane, but not on the surface. He knew about the pump house. He'd fought with John. Jealousy is a strong passion, and maybe Juana was lying. Maybe there *had* been something between John and her. It was a motive for a crime. There didn't seem to be any others. Except the money. But John had safely stowed it away at Patty Forest's, and she hadn't killed her husband. Or had she? Faith assumed the police would have asked her to account for her whereabouts last night. Maybe she'd known what was in the suitcase all along. And what about an accomplice? A neat little crime. John is eliminated and his widow ends up with a giant nest egg. But where did John get the money in the first place? Sums like that meant drugs—and Vermont, "Green Mountain" in French, got pretty *vert* in some areas during the growing season. The marijuana planes patrolling the state couldn't keep pace with what some said was its major crop.

Drug money—or blackmail money. John hadn't seemed the type, or maybe Faith didn't want to believe that a fellow New Yorker *and* a chef would stoop so low. It was a distinct possibility, though. A sudden windfall and sudden demise. But where had he been all week? Why had he returned to Pine Slopes, only to meet his death in such a ghastly manner? Returned to meet his killer, who was also his victim?

And what about all the "pranks" that had been going on during the week, the vandalism? How were they tied to John's death? Was he responsible? Creeping back to set the dummy afloat, jamming the chairlift? A grudge?

Which led her to Josh. If anyone had a grudge against the resort, it was the Sports Center's director. What better way to pay back his longtime employers for letting him down? Perhaps John had found out and was blackmailing him? But the timing was wrong—and where would Josh get that kind of money?

Grudge. That applied to Ophelia, too. Her complete adoration of Gertrude was unhealthy, but how did it fit into the private war she was having with her mother, and, by extension, the whole Stafford family, except as a means of retreat? Scott was sure that Ophelia wasn't involved in any of what had been happening, but Faith wasn't so sure. The girl was involved in something. A mask of fear—that's how Ophelia had appeared in this morning's early light. Masks. So many masks.

Dennis and Betsey came downstairs. *His* face was a mask of concern. They'd been up there a long time. Had he been confessing? Now would certainly not have been the time, but he was calculating enough to have decided it *was* the time—Betsey would be so preoccupied with Scott that he could reveal all sorts of things with impunity.

Ready access to money. Dennis had no problem there. Had John found out about Dennis's affair, his unprofessional conduct, and blackmailed him? Was her brother-in-law a philanderer *and* a murderer?

Why hadn't Tom called? When, oh when, would they be able to go home? She'd spoken to Ben and Amy, explaining that Aunt Betsey wasn't feeling well and they needed to stay with their Grandma while Mom took care of her. Amy wanted to know if Aunt Betsey had a temperature, but Ben wasn't buying any of it. "As soon as she isn't sick, call me," he'd said in a "the world is too much with me" tone of voice.

"The water's just boiled and we have a good fire going. Sit down and I'll make us some tea," Faith said to Betsey. "I assume you're leaving now, Dennis." If she sounded inhospitable, it was because she was.

"Yes. I'll call as soon as we have news." He leaned down to kiss the top of his wife's head. Betsey had stationed herself in the chair closest to the phone. She didn't move, and Dennis left his pillar of salt without a backward glance. Faith felt absurdly better once he was gone. She brought Betsey a mug of sweet tea and a fleece throw.

Tucking the throw across Betsey's lap, Faith said, "Drink some tea.

Nothing I can say is going to help, but you have to keep going, Betsey. You are such a strong person. Hold on to that now."

Betsey took the mug and sipped slowly. Her eyes seemed to clear, and she focused on Faith, who was kneeling by her side.

"It's getting dark. They have to find him before dark."

"There's still plenty of daylight. And they have lights, strong floodlights. Did you hear the helicopters? They'll find him if he's on the mountain."

"And if he isn't?"

"They'll find him wherever he is."

"Dennis is upset. They're the only reason he sticks around, you know. The boys. It was around the time Scott turned eight. I remember thinking at his party that he wasn't a little boy anymore. That's when it started. The three of them. Worse when Andy got older. I stopped existing for them. Disappeared into thin air."

"Oh Bets, no! What are you saying? I've been there with you, remember. All these years. Your kids love you very much." And it was true, Faith realized. Whatever was going on now hadn't been going on long. In her mind she saw pictures of Betsey and the boys gleefully playing touch football or in the midst of snowball fights at Fairchild family gatherings. Saw the pictures clearly, because she hadn't been participating. The Sibleys were not a sports-minded family. As far as Faith's father was concerned, the Yankees originated in New England and the Knicks were a rather crude way of referring to his wife's ancestors.

When she thought about these pictures, Faith realized Dennis hadn't been around. Betsey had. She repeated what she'd said. "Your kids have always been crazy about you."

"Not now. Not for a long time. They have their club. It's what happens. I was born into an all-male enclave, and I've duplicated it. 'The Fairchild boys.' Did you ever hear anybody mention 'the Fairchild girl'?"

Faith hadn't.

"One of the boys. That's what I've tried to be my whole life. Maybe that's why Dennis is having an affair." She looked at her sister-in-law.

"Nobody knows. And he doesn't know I know, so I'd appreciate it if you kept this to yourself. And that means Tom. Especially Tom, my perfect big brother."

What would happen if I tried to hug Betsey? Faith wondered. She definitely needed a hug—and a whole lot more. She settled for a pat on the shoulder.

"Tom isn't perfect. Very, very far from it." How had they gotten into this conversation? Faith wished she believed in magic wands, as Amy did, and had one to wave over Betsey, instantly healing the old wounds and planting seeds of forget-and-forgive deep in her psyche. Not toward Dennis, though. Not unless Betsey really, really wanted to.

They sat for another forty minutes in the dusk before Faith gave in and turned on as many lights as she could find.

The phone still hadn't rung, and when she called down to Tom at the Sports Center, all he could tell her was that there was no news. No news at all.

It was a night of fervent activity, punctuated by long stretches of immobility, the two women sitting together mostly silent, not even trying to read. At dinnertime, the condo was crowded with hungry people. Betsey rallied, helping Faith prepare stacks of sandwiches and heat up soup. She put on a brave face, refusing the words of comfort and support offered, saying, "He's fine. We'll be hearing any moment." Betsey was the kind of woman you wanted during a national emergency—working the sandbag line or doling out sheets of plywood to nail over windows. And serving food. Tonight, everything went, even the leftover lasagna. Then they were all gone and Betsey lapsed into lethargy. Finally, Faith made her lie down on the couch, promising to wake her if there was news.

"Good or bad," Betsey said.

"Good or bad," Faith promised.

"I won't sleep," Betsey said. But she did. Slipping into a welcome oblivion.

Faith had gone next door during the feeding frenzy. Both children were in pajamas and Marian was reading to them from an ancient copy of *The House at Pooh Corner*. Ben had obviously forgotten he was not supposed to be interested in such childish reading matter and was so engrossed, he didn't notice his mother's entry until she greeted them. She sat down and he climbed onto her lap. That hadn't happened in a long time. Faith stayed until the end of the chapter, tucking Amy into bed, with Ben still clinging to her side.

"I'll hold the fort here," Marian said. "I wish Dick would stop for the night, but it's useless to suggest it."

"Scott is missing, isn't he, Mom?" Ben finally asked.

"Yes. We don't know where he is right now, but . . ." She struggled with what to say, wanting to reassure her son but fearing that whatever she told him might turn out to be false. She paused and then asked, "When did you see him last?"

"At the condo. Last night. We were watching videos, remember? Amy fell asleep and Phelie put her to bed; then I stayed up with them to watch *Inu Yasha*—you know, that cool Japanese *anime*. Then Dad came and made me go to bed. That's the last time I saw Scott or Phelie. Is she missing, too?"

"People saw her today, so she may be around, and Scott could be with her—maybe at a friend's house. Did they ever mention someplace like that?"

Ben shook his head. Faith had led him back to the living room and deposited him safely by his grandmother's side. She'd made cocoa, and the Hundred Acre Wood was waiting.

When Tom called, it was to tell his wife that he and Dennis were going to stay down at the Sports Center, sleeping on the pool chaises in shifts. His father had gone back to the condo. Robert and Craig were still out with the search parties. It was going to be a long night. He urged her to get some sleep.

After she hung up the phone, Faith stretched out on her bed again. She'd gone upstairs so that she could catch the phone as soon as it rang. There was no noise downstairs. Betsey was still sleeping deeply. With nothing to report, Faith decided to let her rest, and she turned off the light to try to get some sleep herself.

The phone jolted her from the light doze she'd fallen into. She grabbed the receiver.

"Yes?"

"Faith, it's Simon. I'm in my office. There is a message on the machine from Ophelia, and I'm very concerned. She sounds completely mad—said that everything was all her fault and she was going to be with John!"

"My God! I was afraid of this. She's seemed so angry, so depressed. Have you reached her parents?"

"I've been trying. They're not at Harold and Mary's or the Sports Center. Fred is out searching the mountain for Scott. I was, too. I just came in to grab some warmer clothes. You seem to have some sort of relationship with the girl through your nephews. What should I do? I've informed the police, but the officer I spoke to doesn't think it's serious. A bid for attention, he says. He's had some run-ins with the girl."

Faith was fuming. A plea for help, a possible suicide—not serious?

"Where do you think she was calling from?"

"I have no idea. Been meaning to get caller ID, but it's one of about a thousand things I haven't gotten to."

"She seemed to spend a lot of time at Gertrude's house. She might be there. But how would she get in?"

"Gertrude always keeps a key hidden alongside one of the front windows. Ophelia would know about it. So you think I should go check there? I've left messages for Naomi and Fred. I'll call back and add that."

"Good idea. Who knows, maybe Scott is with her, has been all along." Faith was happy that Simon was volunteering to trek out to the Gingerbread House. Aside from all its other associations, she didn't feel up to the long walk. "I'll check out the pump house, although that will surely be locked now."

"She could have taken a master key from Fred. That would open it."

Faith stood up. The snow guns were off, but she thought of that deep pool. The frigid waters closing over someone very determined to end her life.

"I'm leaving now. We don't have any time to spare. I hope it's not too late. Good-bye!"

Faith flew down the stairs, grabbed her parka, and went out the front door.

The pump house was on the other side of the employee parking lot, down a path, out of sight to the general public. The lot was filled with cars, and farther away, light was blazing from the Sports Center, the hub of operations. Would this dreadful night never end? She looked at her watch. It already had; it was almost 1:30 A.M. Now the dreadful day had begun.

The door to the pump house was open, and thin slivers of light shone on the new-fallen snow. A single pair of footprints led inside. She's here! Faith thought. She ran as fast as she could and, flinging open the door, called out, "Ophelia! Phelie! Stop!"

The room was empty. Faith put her head in her hands and sobbed. She'd been too late. The message on Simon's machine could have been there for hours. The girl was gone, and unless she'd left a note, it would never be clear why.

Suddenly, she was angry. Angry at Naomi and Fred, and at Ophelia's father and stepmother. Why hadn't they taken better care of this child? Why had they ignored all the obvious signs? And why had she? They were all to blame. She'd have to go find someone to tell. Simon was on a fruitless mission. Tom. Tom would know how to handle this. That's where she'd go.

First, she heard the whistling. Not a tune, just a sound. A meaningless sound. Someone was stepping from behind the door. She jerked her head up and turned around. "Ophel—"

But it wasn't the girl; it was Simon Tanner. Faith was confused. How had he gotten here so quickly? He said he was going to Gertrude's on his snowmobile. A quick trip, but this quick? And she hadn't heard the noise of the engine.

"Simon! I'm very much afraid that we're too late." Her voice caught. "There were footprints coming in, but none going out."

"Those were mine."

ELEVEN

Yours?" Faith said. Simon was smiling, but it wasn't the "How are you, mate?" grin she had seen before. It was a new smile. A smile she didn't like at all.

"Mine." He was still smiling.

"Ophelia didn't leave a message." Faith started to walk toward the door.

"Ophelia didn't leave a message. And please stay where you are. If you move, I'll have to kill you. Kill you sooner." His smile broadened. Simon Tanner was having fun.

Faith wasn't. "What on earth are you talking about?" She moved closer and faster.

He stopped smiling. "I mean it, Mrs. Fairchild." He raised his hand. He was holding a gun. He definitely meant it. "Gertrude found out about you from Ophelia. How you stick your nose in things, get involved in affairs that are none of your business."

Faith's heart rate increased. It was reassuring. She was still alive—and terrified. Scott must have told the girl about some of the crimes his aunt had solved, and Simon saw her as a threat. A threat to Gertrude *and* him. And she was. Sitting in the condo with Betsey all these hours, Faith had figured out that Gertrude had to be involved in John's death and in every-thing else that had happened during the week. It was Betsey's bitter words about her place in the family that had triggered Faith's thoughts. She'd gone over the scene outside Simon's office, witnessing again the hatred on Fred's face when he saw his aunt—his father's sister, who was destroying the whole family, an implacable foe on their very doorstep. But she couldn't have managed it all by herself. Apart from being stoned much of the time, she would have had to have an alibi for last night if she was go-ing to become the new owner of Pine Slopes. Which had to be her goal. Once Faith had gotten to this point, she'd started looking at the staff. Pete? Josh? Simon?

Yes, Simon was too right. Faith was a threat.

"I told her she was overreacting—Gert tends to get a little paranoid at times—then I began to see you popping up in all sorts of places you shouldn't have been. It would still have been okay—that is, if you hadn't followed Phelie to Gert's. She was positive you'd seen me, but I wasn't sure. We saw you, though. Then you followed Gert to Burlington. She spotted you one night when she was singing there. That's when I decided you were more than a nuisance."

Now Faith knew who the person standing behind Gertrude Stafford, in the shadows, had been Monday night. But it was too late. All she could do, she realized, looking at the dark water agonizingly close, was to keep him talking for as long as possible.

"Was John blackmailing you? Was that it?"

"I wouldn't have pegged him for a greedy man, and in a way, he wasn't." Simon seemed happy for a "chin-wag."

"All these years, the sap ran the restaurant on the up-and-up. Still not sure how he caught on to what I was doing. John knew a lot about cook-ing. Didn't know he knew about cooking the books though!" Simon laughed at his joke. It was like a hyena's cry. "He wanted to travel, he said. Was hot to see the world. More like hot to see it with one of those South American bimbos working for him this season. A break for me. Juana's boyfriend will never make it home again."

A circumstantial case, but with false testimony from Simon, workable. Simon, the real murderer, had carefully framed Eduardo for a crime of passion. Had he "just happened" to run into the young student and tell him that Juana was in the kitchen alone with John?

Simon leaned back against the wall. He isn't in a hurry, thank God, Faith thought, then wondered, What is he waiting for?

"I'm out a lot of money," he whined. "I was certain he'd have it in his room. There is no way I can get the suitcase from his wife without blowing the whole thing. I thought of sending Gertrude down there to try her hand at B and E, but Gert's not always reliable."

"Simon!" Faith yelled. "This is crazy. You can't possibly think you can do away"—a euphemism seemed infinitely preferable at the moment—"with me and get away with it. I called Tom before I left, and he knows where I am. Plus, I told my sister-in-law about your call. How will you explain yourself when they report me missing?"

He straightened up. "Oh, but I *will* get away with 'doing away' with you. Wish I could also do you," he added, leering at her, "but there isn't time. I was standing outside the window of the condo, talking to you on my satellite phone. Your sister-in-law was sound asleep on the sofa, and you came tearing out of the place as soon as you hung up. I had to run like the devil to get here ahead of you. You never called your husband, and she never budged."

Keep him talking. Faith scanned the small room for something to throw at him, something to catch him off guard, so she could get out the door and start screaming. She'd start screaming now, but he'd kill her at the first sound. No question.

"It's been all you," she said. "The dummy in the pool, the groomer, wedging the bull wheel, hiring Wendell. All to force the place to shut down. Why?"

"Don't like working for other people. Never have. Fancied running the place meself, and that's the plan. Gert calls in her markers. We buy it at the bankruptcy auction, and Bob's your uncle. She fancies me, you know. The old cow. But wicked moves in bed. You'd never suspect it."

Faith was shivering, both from cold and disgust.

"Now, Mrs. Fairchild, it's time for you to take a swim. You came here when you got a call from Ophelia threatening suicide, and like the good person you are, you rushed to save her, only you fell in instead of her during the struggle. So tragic."

"But you'll have to get Ophelia to corroborate your story. She won't."

Simon tucked his gun into his belt. It had a fancy silver and turquoise buckle. "Ophelia will do anything Gertrude tells her to—and has."

Faith backed toward the wall, eyeing the distance to the door. He couldn't shoot her first. That wasn't the plan. Ophelia wouldn't have had a gun, and when they recovered Faith's body, it couldn't have a bullet hole. But he could knock her out. She needed to stay as far away as possible. Make him come and get her.

Knock her out!

"You knocked me out when I was at Gertrude's this morning! What was it you didn't want me to see?"

If Faith was going to die, as was appearing more and more likely, she didn't want to die without all the answers.

"I've been so busy what with one thing and another that I haven't had a chance to get rid of a few things—like the container we used to keep John on ice this week. I had it banked in a snowdrift up at my place in the backcountry, but I took him down to Gert's on Thursday morning, and after his unfortunate end, I left everything in her shed. I knew if you saw the pine coffin, you'd figure out that John had been dead all week and that she had something to do with it. Too smart for your own good, Mrs. F."

Would I have? Faith wondered. Probably. The car at the motel, everything had been meticulously planned. Even the frying pan charm. Simon had wanted John identified immediately—all the worse for Pine Slopes.

"Now, be a good girl. I'll give you another tap on the head. Harder this time. You won't feel a thing. And no snow guns, I promise, although that was genius, wasn't it?"

"Ophelia! Scott! Thank God!"

Simon grinned. "Give me some credit, please. Do you think I'd fall for that old trick?"

Faith wished she had been able to suppress her outburst to ensure the element of surprise. Now there was the dread possibility that he might turn around or glance over his shoulder and see them. From the horror on the two teenagers' faces, it was apparent that they knew exactly what was happening—or about to happen. They couldn't see that Simon had a gun. How could she let them know? And fast! It had to be fast. She was terrified that Scott would tackle Simon and that the gun would go off in the struggle, with tragic results. If only she could get close enough to push Simon into the deadly waters! She shuddered, thinking of John's death. But he hadn't felt it. There was small mercy in that.

Starting to move toward her and away from them, he was grinning even more broadly now at what he assumed was a feeble last ploy by a desperate woman.

A few feet away, Scott motioned for Ophelia to get behind him, gesturing at the door. She shook her head, then leaned over, steadying herself on Scott while she removed one of her boots. Faith watched, almost gasping out loud, as Ophelia teetered on the absurdly high heel of the other boot and Scott reached out an arm to brace her. Faith began to talk loudly, insistently, hoping to cover any possible noise. If Ophelia dropped the boot, Simon would surely hear it.

"Why don't you throw your gun into the pool and take your chances with me? Not man enough," she taunted.

"You are one hell of a lady," he said, chuckling. "Want to make it one-on-one, do you? While I wouldn't mind getting my arms around you, I'm afraid I'll have to decline your very tempting offer. There's always that slight chance that I might fall—and I've come too far to take any more chances."

He started to move toward her again with lethal intent. His expression clearly revealed his patience was at an end. Cat and mouse had been fun while it lasted, but game time was over.

The room was hushed; Faith could hear cars on the mountain road.

Louder by far was the sound of her own blood pounding in her ears. Scott had Ophelia's boot in his hand and the girl, as still as one of Niobe's, not Naomi's, children seemed to be holding her breath. Her eyes were open so wide, Faith couldn't see the lids.

When Scott struck, it was like an adder, over before Faith could start talking again to mask his movements. With the agility of the athlete he was, he leaped for Simon and brought the stiletto heel of Phelie's boot crashing down on the man's skull. Simon screamed—and fell. Scott pinned him, grabbed the gun from his belt, and threw it into a corner. Ophelia, a whirlwind, rushed forward, kicking Simon with her booted foot over and over in a kind of delirium. Simon had been correct: Ophelia was mad.

Faith retrieved the gun and rushed over. "Phelie, stop! That's enough! Go get help. Run to the Sports Center. We can manage here."

Simon had gone limp, moaning. Scott was sitting on his chest, holding his arms to the ground. While she longed to embrace her saviors, Faith stood over the murderer instead, pointing his gun steadily at the spot where Tanner's heart would have been if he had had one. There would be time for embraces later. Time, she thought, as in life, her life.

Ophelia picked up her boot, put it on, and cleaned the blood from the heel on Simon's leather jacket. But before she could leave, Pete appeared at the door, took the scene in, and reached into his jacket pocket for the roll of duct tape no self-respecting Vermont handyman would ever be without. He bound Simon's feet and wrists tightly. The Australian had looked even more terrified when he saw Pete. He closed his eyes and was mumbling to himself.

"You go get the police, Mrs. Fairchild, and see to these children. I'll stay here. He's not going any place," Pete said, ripping off a piece of tape and covering Simon's mouth. "Language," he said reprovingly, then added, "Never did care much for you, Mr. Tanner."

It was pitch-dark outside, but Pete had handed them a flashlight. It would be dawn before too many more hours. The dreadful night *and* dreadful day were over. Scott held the flashlight and Faith grabbed one of

Ophelia's hands. The girl was stumbling on her high heels—those blessedly high heels.

"How did you know where I was? Where have you been? Do the police know you're here?" Faith's questions poured forth in a torrent of words.

"We were coming up the mountain road and saw you cross the parking lot, going in this direction. I wanted to go get Uncle Tom, but Phelie said we had to follow you right away."

Faith squeezed the girl's hand in gratitude.

"I drove Scott to the bus late Wednesday night," Ophelia said, her voice so soft that Faith had to bend close to hear.

Scott spoke over his shoulder. "I called my girlfriend—one of the things I've managed to keep from Mom. Phelie's been great to talk to, but I really needed to see Karen. Her parents are cool. They said I could stay there while I got things straightened out. I told them I'd called Mom. And I would have, except I kept hearing what I knew she'd say. Then Phelie called about John, and I had to be here, so she hitched into Burlington, borrowed a car, then drove down and picked me up. Everything has been so wrong this week. On the drive back, we kinda figured out it had to be Simon. I mean, well, Phelie has seen him and Gertrude—"

"She left without saying anything. She never said good-bye. The house was all shut. She said we'd be together forever." Tears were running down Ophelia's cheeks. The long magenta streak of hair glistened.

Feet of clay. Only worse in this case. Much worse.

"I'm sorry," Faith said, stopping to hold the girl tightly. "I'm so sorry. But you two saved my life. I owe you my life." Tears were streaming down her own face.

Ophelia shook her head slowly. "Scott saved you. I didn't. I'm a murderess. I killed Boyd Harrison."

TWELVE

Thanksgiving was Faith's favorite holiday. True, the menu didn't call for much ingenuity, but you could always fool around with the turkey stuffing and try something fun for a first course, like parsnip potage served in small scooped-out sugar pumpkins. What Thanksgiving meant was time to be together. Apart from an early-morning service, Tom was a free man. Unlike Christmas and Easter, Thanksgiving was short and sweet for the clergy.

Faith had put every leaf in the table, blessing the original occupants of the parsonage for demanding a decent-size dining room. Tom was carving, and steaming bowls of side dishes were being passed around. A few years earlier, Faith had finally convinced Dick to try her brussels sprouts. She'd tossed them with toasted walnuts and brown butter, hoping to entice him. Now they were his favorite vegetable. Marian had brought sweet potatoes, marshmallows on only one side, in deference to Faith. Hope, Quentin, and little Terry had come up with Faith's parents. Her father had handed his service off to the assistant minister, much to Faith's delight. It was their first Thanksgiving together in a long time. There was no children's table—at least not yet. Maybe when Terry and whoever might follow were older, she'd have to set up a card table for the cousins.

There were some empty chairs. Glenda's was one. She had stuck to her plan, and the divorce would be final soon. Faith was pretty sure she'd had someone waiting in the wings when she'd left Pine Slopes. Maybe the Norwegian, who turned out to be from a wealthy family, spending the winter in Vermont to—what else?—improve his English. And Dennis wasn't with them. He and Betsey had separated—at her request. Faith had been surprised to get a call from her sister-in-law last spring, asking if they could meet in town for lunch at Betsey's club. Knowing that this would mean creamed something on toast or possibly something in cream sauce, Faith had agreed, but suggested they meet at her "club" instead—Upstairs on the Square in Cambridge. They'd sat for several hours, Faith mostly listening as Betsey described the course of counseling she and Dennis had undertaken after their return from Pine Slopes.

"I realized in the middle of one of the sessions that I really didn't want to be with him anymore. That he'd been poisoning my relationship with the boys by making me take charge of everything, all the while complaining that I had. The therapist helped me see that all those years when I was feeling so isolated, it was because I *was*—but isolated from my husband, not my kids. When I began to confront everything, it came to me that Dennis was never around that much. He'd take the kids to a Celtics or Red Sox game—fun stuff. But everything else was up to me. So since he was acting like an irresponsible divorced man, I figured he might as well be," she'd told Faith. She'd also switched to another agency on the South Shore—no more working for "Daddy"—and was now, of course, their top salesperson. Craig had not stepped into her shoes. Dick had sold the business to Sheila Harding, a longtime associate and what he referred to as a "crackerjack agent." She was keeping the firm's name, though. Craig had moved to Vermont, living first at Pine Slopes, and now in Richmond, where he'd met a pretty lady who wove baskets for a living. He and Fred were running the resort, which, in the wake of its tragedy, had garnered so much goodwill that it was already booked for the season. But,

Tom had told her, Fred Stafford had insisted his parents take a nice long trip last February. They'd spent the rest of the winter in Tucson, which they liked so much, they were going back. It was Craig—not "Buddy"—and Fred—not "Freddy"—in charge now. Faith had smiled at the thought, praying for their sakes that Pete never followed the elder Staffords example.

Robert passed Faith her plate. Tom had given her a nice mix—mostly dark meat, her favorite, with a juicy slice of white. She smiled her thanks. Empty places, but one had already been filled by Robert's partner, Michael. As outgoing as Robert was taciturn, he kept them all laughing. Faith didn't know how long they'd been together—Robert had brought him to a family gathering for the first time last summer—but it was clear they would be together for a very long time. She pictured the two sportsaholics in their rockers before a large-screen TV, surfing from one game to the next on into the sunset.

Andy was sitting on one side of his mother, Scott on the other. Compromises had been made. Andy was playing the saxophone *and* the flute. Scott had attended a shorter academic program last summer, working in town the rest of the time. And Ophelia. Faith went back to that night. Heard the girl's words.

"I killed him. She told me he was using the pills as a crutch. That the doctor said he didn't need them and the only way for him to get off them was to stop taking them. One day, she got all the bottles together when he was off working. I dumped them out and put mints in instead while she sang. I was so stupid, believing her." Faith could still picture the scene in the cozy kitchen of the Gingerbread House. Ophelia at a table in front of the woodstove with its big black oven; Gertrude crooning "Me and Bobby McGee," making sure the only fingerprints on the vials were Ophelia's, just in case one was found. "Freedom's just another word for nothin' left to lose"—Gertrude Stafford didn't intend to lose anything. It would have been Ophelia's freedom lost, not hers. Faith looked down at her plate. The food was losing some of its appeal.

Ophelia had continued pouring her heart out, her voice barely above a whisper. "He didn't like me—Boyd. Didn't like having me out at the house so much. Maybe he was jealous. Maybe I was. She told me what we were doing was for his own good, but part of me wished he would die, and then I could live out there and have her all to myself. So I killed him."

Simon Tanner was doing life. His family—parents and siblings alive and well in Sydney—had assured the prosecutor that they had nothing to say on his behalf. They had moved on with their lives a long time ago, deciding to forget, although not forgive. And would someone please send his aunt's Aboriginal painting back? they asked. The one he'd stolen on his last visit.

The trial had been swift—and a terrible ordeal for everyone involved, especially John's wife, Patty, who'd ended up with an empty suitcase. And it had also been particularly difficult for Faith, who'd had to testify while looking at that face, empty of all expression except the smoldering hatred in his eyes. Ophelia had been kept out of it. At Faith's insistence, the Staffords had retained the lawyer Tom had found for Eduardo—now happily home and practicing his English via E-mail. The lawyer had brought in a family therapist after a briefing from Faith. What had happened to Ophelia—her manipulation by Simon and Gertrude, her parents' and stepparents' treatment—amounted to child abuse. Ophelia, now using her middle name, Christine, had ended up at a wonderful boarding school in western Massachusetts, where Scott and his girlfriend, Karen, visited regularly. Faith had invited Joanie/Ophelia/Christine for Thanksgiving, but she'd called and said she was going home to Vermont. "I miss the mountains" was how she put it, but Faith also had a feeling she missed her mother. Before hanging up, she'd fessed up to one last thing—taking down the notes Faith had left on the doors at the condo to say they'd gone to eat lunch at Gracie's in Stowe. "I wanted to piss Mrs. Parker off. She was, like, keeping such tabs on Scott and Andy." That wasn't the last piece of the puzzle, though.

Gertrude. She'd driven off in her VW bus on that winter Thursday, and so far the police hadn't had a single lead as to her whereabouts. Simon was evil, amoral, but Gertrude was worse. Gertrude, the free spirit, who considered herself above the law, filled the lives of those unfortunate enough to love her with poison. Faith wondered if Boyd had known during his last moments that the woman he had adored all his life had made the fatal substitution. Taking advantage of Ophelia's fragile psyche, her difficult relationship with her parents after the divorce, was another poisonous substitution. Gertrude had presented herself as the "good" mother, and the girl had become obsessed, literally bewitched. There was a lot of that going on last February, Faith thought, sighing.

The room came back into focus. Her plate smelled delicious again.

Everyone had been served. Tom asked that they bow their heads, and and then he made a mercifully brief blessing, mindful of the cooling food.

"Amen," said Faith.

EXCERPTS FROM
HAVE FAITH IN YOUR KITCHEN

By Faith Sibley Fairchild

A Work in Progress

APOLOGY MUSHROOM SOUP

½ *cup Madeira*
2¾ *cups unsalted chicken broth*
1 ounce dried morels or other dried mushrooms
3 leeks, white part only
1 medium yellow onion
4 tablespoons butter
3 tablespoons flour
2¾ *cups unsalted beef broth*
1 pound fresh mushrooms (stems removed), sliced
1 teaspoon salt
½ *teaspoon pepper*
sour cream or crème fraîche (optional)

Combine the Madeira, ½ cup of the chicken broth, and the dried mushrooms in a small saucepan. Cover and bring to a boil, then remove from the heat and set aside for 30 minutes.

While the mushrooms are soaking, clean and slice the leeks. Dice the onion. Melt the butter is a large soup pot and sauté the leeks and onions until they are soft, about 10 minutes. Stir in the flour and continue to cook for 5 more minutes.

Add the remaining chicken broth, the beef broth, the fresh mushrooms, the dried mushrooms and their soaking liquid, and the salt and pepper. Simmer covered for 10 minutes, then uncovered for 20 minutes more. Cool the soup slightly and then puree in batches in a blender, or in the pot with an immersion blender. Return the soup to the pot and heat it thoroughly over low heat.

Serve with a generous dollop of sour cream or crème fraîche.

This makes a hearty supper dish and will serve 6. As a first course or luncheon dish, it will serve 8.

Making the soup a day ahead improves the flavor.

I am indebted to my nephew, David Pologe, for this recipe and to his mother, Sheila, who first served it to me.

LLAPINGACHOS WITH SALSA DE MALI
POTATO CAKES WITH PEANUT SAUCE

CAKES

6 boiled potatoes, peeled and mashed

¼ cup unsalted butter

2 yellow onions, finely diced

3 cups shredded sharp cheddar cheese

salt

pepper

2–4 tablespoons canola or other vegetable oil

Put the potatoes in a large mixing bowl and set aside. Fry the onions in the butter until translucent. Add the onions and cheese to the potatoes.

Mix well and season to taste with salt and pepper. Form into 12 patties, packing the potato mixture firmly so that the cakes do not fall apart when fried. Fry them in the oil until golden brown on both sides, approximately 4 minutes per side. Set aside and keep warm.

SALSA

2 tablespoons canola or other vegetable oil

1 yellow onion, finely diced

1 clove of garlic, minced

*2 ripe tomatoes, peeled and chopped, or 1–1½ cups canned diced tomatoes
    with juice*

½ cup chunky peanut butter

salt

pepper

Fry the onions in the oil until they are translucent. Add the garlic, tomatoes, and peanut butter. Stirring constantly, simmer the mixture until all the ingredients are well blended and heated thoroughly. Add salt and pepper to taste.

Serve the warm salsa de Mali over the *llapingachos.*

This is a good buffet brunch dish, and you should figure on one potato (2 patties) per person. Faith likes to use Yukon Gold potatoes. Check ahead to make sure that none of your guests is allergic to nuts!

Incan and pre-Incan civilizations in Peru had more than two hundred varieties of potatoes, which were native to the country and were "discovered" by Europeans when the Spanish conquistadors arrived. Potatoes are still a staple in Peruvian cuisine. Many farms and markets selling organic produce offer a wide variety of potatoes, some of which are heirlooms— long-forgotten varieties. Experiment with these for fun.

Salsa de Mali is also good with rice. For a luncheon, it may be served in individual ramekins, accompanied by a salad.

SPANAKOPITA
GREEK SPINACH PIE

6 large eggs

2 packages of raw spinach

1¹/₁₂ pounds feta cheese, chopped fine

1 large yellow onion, diced

¹/₄ cup uncooked rice

salt

pepper

¹/₂ pound unsalted butter

12 sheets of phyllo dough (follow the package's instructions for handling)

Beat the eggs in a large bowl. Wash, dry, and chop the spinach. Add it to the eggs and mix well. Add the feta cheese, onion, and rice, then mix again. Add salt and pepper to taste, remembering that feta cheese is salty.

Preheat the oven to 350°F. Melt the butter in a small pan. Grease the bottom and sides of a 15"×10"×2" baking dish. Place 1 sheet of phyllo dough in the pan so that it covers the bottom and comes up the sides. Brush with melted butter and repeat this process with 4 more sheets. Pour the spinach, egg, cheese, and onion mixture into the pan and spread evenly. Then add the 7 remaining sheets of phyllo in the same manner. Be sure the top layer is well covered by melted butter. Pierce in several spots to allow steam to escape.

Bake for approximately 45 minutes. The top should be golden. Remove and let sit for 5 to 10 minutes, then cut into squares and serve. Serves 6 as a main course.

GLAD'S BROWNIES

4 squares unsweetened chocolate (Valrhona is a good choice)

1½ sticks unsalted butter

2 cups sugar

3 large eggs

1 teaspoon vanilla

1 cup sifted flour

1 cup dried cherries

1¼ cup chopped walnuts

1 cup chocolate chunks or chips (milk or semisweet)

Preheat the oven to 350°F. Grease and lightly flour a 13" × 9" pan. Melt the chocolate squares together with the butter. Cool it slightly and beat in the sugar, eggs, and vanilla. Stir in the flour. Mix well, then add the cherries, walnuts, and chocolate chunks or chips. Put the batter in the pan and bake for about 35 minutes. Be careful not to overbake. Cool in the pan and serve. Makes a very generous 1½ dozen.

You may vary this recipe by substituting dried cranberries, golden raisins, or dark raisins for the cherries and pecans for the walnuts. Attributed in the book to Faith as a child, this recipe is actually the creation of the author's dear friend Gladys Boalt, who lives in Stormville, New York.

AUNT SUSIE'S CAKE

Cake

1 box good-quality yellow cake mix

4 large eggs

¾ cup canola or other vegetable oil

1 11-ounce can Mandarin oranges packed in juice

Preheat oven to 350°F. Combine the cake mix, eggs, and oil in a bowl. Mix according to the directions on the box. Fold in the oranges, including juice, and mix well. Pour into 3 greased round cake pans. Be sure the orange pieces are evenly distributed. Bake for approximately 25 minutes. Remove cakes from the pans and cool on racks while you make the frosting.

FROSTING:

1 small package instant vanilla pudding
1 20-ounce can crushed pineapple packed in juice
1 large container Cool Whip or other whipped topping

Drain the pineapple, reserving the juice. Mix together the juice and the instant pudding. Add the Cool Whip and drained pineapple, then mix. Spread some of the frosting between the layers and use the rest on the top and sides of the cake.

This recipe comes from Linda Gronberg-Quinn. At the Malice Domestic Convention's auction for the benefit of Maryland's John L. Gildner Regional Institute for Children & Adolescents, she was the high bidder for a chance to put a favorite recipe in one of my books. Her husband's aunt Susie, Susan Houston, is a "prototypical southern lady" writes Linda, and "we are constantly amazed at how wonderful her cooking tastes, even though the recipes are seemingly simple ones." This is the dessert Aunt Susie takes to a pig pickin', where, after picking the succulent meat from the roast pig, people always save room for her cake. Whatever your main course, you'll save room for this layer cake, too. Thank you, Susie and Linda.

This particular group of recipes isn't as heart-healthy as some in Faith's collection. Perhaps this has something to do with the terribly cold winter so much of the country experienced in 2004 and the subsequent desire for hearty fare. Nonetheless, egg substitutes are excellent and may be used in place of eggs. Also, low-fat cheese works well in the spinach pie and for the Peruvian potato cakes. All the recipes can be made without salt.

AUTHOR'S NOTE

Growing up, my taste in literature was catholic—I read anything I could get my hands on—but looking back, I've noted that my favorites fell into two diametrically opposed categories: books about large families and books about orphans.

Cheaper by the Dozen and its sequel, *Belles on Their Toes,* recounted the authors' childhood with their parents, Frank and Lillian Gilbreth, the pioneers of time and motion study. The family lived not far from my own childhood home in New Jersey. The books are very, very funny, but it was the notion of being one of twelve that captivated me. The same was true with the lovely *All-of-a-Kind Family* books by Sydney Taylor, a fictional account of five sisters—and eventually a brother—growing up on New York's Lower East Side in 1912. With so many from whom to choose, there would always be a kindred sibling. Large families continue to fascinate me, although they are more rare these days, and it's easy to romanticize the pros and forget the cons (the Gilbreths shared a bathroom, for instance).

And then there were the orphan books: *The Little Princess*, by Frances Hodgson Burnett; Lucy Maud Montgomery's *Anne of Green Gables*; and the wonderful *Daddy Long-Legs,* by Jean Webster—an Electra fantasy come to life, and it doesn't hurt to imagine Fred Astaire in the title role, as he was in the movie. As it turns out, Sara Crewe, the heroine of Burnett's book, isn't the orphan she believes herself to be. Her father returns; Miss Minchin, the wicked headmistress, and the mean girls get their just deserts. I read and reread my Scribner's copy—illustrated by Ethel Betts—weeping each and every time I got to the part about Sara being forced into servitude. Montgomery's Anne Shirley and Webster's Judy Abbot are more feisty than Sara, but I realize now that what drew me to each heroine was her imagination. These characters are born storytellers and great believers in all kinds of magic. Frances Hodgson Burnett, best remembered for *The Secret Garden,* wrote a series that featured "The Story Girl" (another orphan), who entertains her cousins by telling them stories over the course of a summer—*The Arabian Nights* Prince Edward Island–style. Parents would have been in the way in these books—clipping wings that showed the readers how high they, too, might fly.

But back to families, which play such a central role in *The Body in the Snowdrift.* The idea for this book started with the notion of a family reunion. Tom's family was a natural—large enough and filled with people I'd thought about during the course of writing the series but had never presented. It was time.

In *Anna Karenina,* Tolstoy wrote, "Happy families are all alike; every unhappy family is unhappy in its own way." I've never agreed with this. For one thing, it makes the happy families sound so boring, and as the years pass, it seems to me that the reverse is true. Especially if you substitute the word *reunion* for that of *family* in the sentence. The Fairchilds gather for what Dick Fairchild fondly believes will be a happy family reunion, but Faith knows better. She's watched her husband's siblings repeat their time-honored familial roles over and over again, unable to get unstuck. It's a happy family, but an unhappy reunion—like so many that start out with good intentions and then run into obstacles. I like to think that in the ensuing years, the Fairchild family will get unstuck, although not unglued, and perhaps this is a good goal for every family, whatever size.

Food helps—family reunion, ritualistic food. Marian Fairchild's coleslaw and Aunt Susie's cake are just two examples. We spend Thanksgiving with my husband's family, and without Aunt Lil's cranberry mold, plus the little pigs in a blanket the children devour before the main event, the universe would wobble. For years, my family celebrated Christmas Eve in the traditional Scandinavian manner. My mother, one of seven children, and her sisters would start preparing weeks in advance. The night itself is preserved in memory as a joyous celebration of family— with so many cousins, I could imagine myself a Gilbreth. But time takes people away for various reasons—a long-distance move; holidays spent with a spouse's family; or permanent loss as one generation gives way to the next. We will never get used to those empty places at the table. New traditions spring up; new kinds of reunions.

We make our own families, perhaps from the family we're born into, perhaps from the friends we love, and, if we're lucky, from both.

Postscript: As I was looking up some of these books on the Internet to see whether they were still in print, I was interested to see that *Cheaper by the Dozen* was being paired with *All-of-a-Kind Family* as a special. I had expected to find Frank and Ernestine Gilbreth's book, because of the recent movie (which bears no resemblance to the 1950 film with Clifton Webb and Myrna Loy, and very little to the book), but finding Sydney Taylor so prominently featured was a joy. Family stories— sagas—will never go out of fashion.